GOOD TROUBLE

Alpine Valleys – Book 2

L. Simpson

www.BOROUGHSPUBLISHINGGROUP.com

GOOD TROUBLE
Copyright © 2019 L. Simpson

ISBN 978-1-948029-84-1

For my brothers and sisters. I'm a lucky little sister.

GOOD TROUBLE

Chapter 1

I told myself I was keeping my door open because I was trying to be friendly. But that was a lie. I left it open so I'd know when *he* arrived. He was due any minute. I was emotionally unprepared despite anticipating the appointment for days. He unnerved me. Too cocky by half, and too damn good-looking for his own good. Been there, done that. Gave the t-shirt to the charity shop.

Professionally, though, I was ready. No problem. I had reviewed my notes, restocked my tape draw, warmed the oil, changed the pillowcase, and had cleaned the bed. Twice. I'd even folded the towels. Colour-coded origami swans now sat on the shelf. I'd adjusted my computer, then I fiddled with my pens, making sure the blue ones were on the left, the red on the right, and the highlighters in the middle. I had repositioned the Oasis mug on my desk, taking a moment to marvel at how it had lasted twenty years after I'd purchased it at a concert. A small reminder of the home I'd fled.

My brain, acting like a cat in a bag, u-turned from thoughts of home to the rugged, chiselled, Thor-like, blond-haired, blue-eyed, fantasy Viking-lumberjack who was also the son of Satan. That I preferred to think about *him* and not my home in England was saying something.

Needing to move, I stood up, the nervous energy making my skin tingle and my limbs twitch. I rubbed my sweating palms on my jeans and walked to the back of my treatment room, quietly cursing a blue streak at my inability to get myself in order.

He was only a damned man.

"You know, I could listen to you swear like a truck driver all day with that pretty accent of yours."

My body froze, but my mouth didn't. I wished it had, but my mouth *never* cooperated.

"For fuck's sake," I muttered before taking a deep breath and turning around to see him lounging against the doorjamb. I scowled as I stalked to him, his compliment irritating, as all the others had before. Dressed in his usual work attire—boots, worn khaki cargo pants, a green button-down shirt with a plantation logo on it, and a thick green fleece jacket—Erik Strathmore wore a smug, shit-eating grin like it was part of the uniform. A person would have to be dead and buried not to notice his height and muscular build, and how he smelled like pure mountain man—rain and pine trees. His hair was equally as glorious, long and blond, tied back to expose his tanned movie-star-handsome face framed by a golden stubbly beard that ratcheted up his sex appeal from hot to incendiary.

"Annie, is this a double appointment?" Fleur's hesitant voice sounded from the reception area, getting closer as she headed to my office. Erik stood away from the door and entered the room, but turned his body toward me as he gave Fleur a friendly smile over his shoulder. Unfortunately, his profile was as good as the full frontal view. He was still smiling warmly as Fleur joined us. I didn't get those smiles from him. I got lascivious grins that promised orgasms and heartache.

"No, only a single today," I answered.

"That's a shame," he muttered.

"Um, well, do you mind if my son waits in reception until closing? I won't have time to take him home and get back again. I'm sorry, I wouldn't normally ask," she half stuttered, overly apologetic for something that was completely fine.

Fleur was the new receptionist who, for some unknown reason, seemed terrified that I was going to tell her off. I didn't think I came across that way, except for when I was with Erik or facing off with Geronimo, the self-indulgent naturopath who had a room in our clinic. Clearly, I needed to work on my friendliness.

"Yeah, of course. Any time, Fleur. No stress." She left, pulling the door closed behind her.

"Right, have a seat, take off your shoes and socks, and roll up your cuffs," I ordered, pointing to the bed, moving so I was facing where Erik sat. He really was massive, and not only because he was way more than a foot taller than me. Almost everyone was taller than me, except for young children. Quite literally, he took up all the space in the room with his personality and body size. After he'd stowed his shoes and socks under my chair, I put him through the motions, getting him to hop on his ankle, run on the spot, bend and flex his foot, then walk to the end of the room. After each "test" I asked him to report on his pain level. Thankful to have something constructive to do, I analysed his ankle and took notes.

"How is it looking?"

"Considering you damaged it a few weeks ago, it's looking pretty good, but get up on the bed and I'll take a closer look," I told him while giving the bed a pat.

"I love it when you ask me to bed," he crooned. "Face down or up?" He gave me a wicked grin that I ignored.

"On your stomach to start," I huffed.

"I like it when you take charge." His deep voice rumbled as he looked at me with twinkling blue eyes that were like the water on a Maldives holiday brochure: a blue that was fathomless and enticing. I sighed and gave him a bored smile.

I lowered the bed so I could reach his ankle. My hands were small, but they matched my size. It took a lot of work to move his large foot and muscular calf. As I rotated his ankle, he let out a hiss of pain that made his head snap up.

"I'm sorry. Did that hurt?" I asked, fighting the smile tugging at my lips.

"Woman, you know I like it rough, no need to play coy," he said, those wretched beautiful eyes flashing with all sorts of wicked promises.

"I like it rough too, but only with men who can handle it," I returned, probing the soft part of his ankle, causing him to hiss again. "I guess that rules you out. Flip over," I directed and he did as I asked, giving me another cheeky smile, which I worked hard to ignore.

I moved his good leg so it was bent, allowing me room on the bed so I could put a knee up and really test his ankle. We dropped the cat and mouse game while I asked him about his strength and how it felt when I moved his foot against my resistance.

"What's the verdict?" he asked as I kneeled on the bed between his legs that were bent and cocked to the side. It gave me a moment's pause. I was in a position one might be in if they were preparing to straddle him. Unable not to, I glanced down his body, taking him in.

Holy hell. What a body. I'd heard he could've played professional football. Looking at him now, I could see why. To my horror, I must've been ogling, or perving, as my Australian friends say, because when I glanced up, he was giving me a look that told me he knew what I was thinking. He linked his hands behind his head and raised his brows in invitation.

"Tape," I muttered, scurrying off the bed. He grunted in surprise. As I headed to my now colour- and size-coded tape collection, I was sure I heard him laughing. As I returned to the bed, he sat up and I pulled my stool close, placing his heel on my leg. I started taping his ankle and wondered if he would ask me out again. He had asked four times already in the month I had been treating him. If he thought I was going to gush over his prowess or fall prey to his bad-boy aura, he had another think coming. I wasn't stupid. I didn't do the same thing twice if it wasn't good for me.

"So, when are you going to let me take you out?" he asked as if it were a foregone conclusion. I wasn't going to dignify the question with a response. He didn't listen anyway.

"Okay, same exercises as before, but now, instead of doing them three times a day, I want you to do them six times a day, upping the reps each time." I didn't look at him, feeling exhausted by life and the mental effort required to not give in to his charms. It took effort to prepare for his visit and also to be on my game while he was here.

"When do I see you again?" he asked, moving close to me, too close, as I stood holding the door open.

"You can make an appointment with Fleur for Wednesday."

"I'll do that," he replied but didn't move away.

"Something else?" I asked, looking down the hall, but he hadn't moved. I was forced to look at him, needing to know why he was loitering. It was a mistake. With a smouldering gaze rooting me to the spot, it took everything in me not to brush back the stray lock of his hair that had fallen forward. I needed to look away. This man was no good for me, or any girl I supposed. But definitely not me.

I told myself not to gaze into his eyes like a pathetic doe in the headlights, but it didn't work. When he moved an arm to block the door, and leaned in toward me, my gaze dropped to his mouth. His wide, plush lips were surrounded by stubble and were hitched up at the side in an arresting half-grin. My brain chose that moment to completely fail in its duty to protect me. I licked my lips in anticipation.

"Erik. You're in *The Observer* today. Will you sign my copy?" a young boy called out from the reception area. I stepped back abruptly, the spell thankfully broken.

"Tate, I said wait until he gets out," Fleur admonished her son. My heart was beating rapidly and my stomach was somewhere around my knees. It took me a moment to refocus.

"It's fine, Fleur," Erik said. "I'll sign it for you, mate." As he began to walk away, he looked over his shoulder, letting me know he was aware of what had almost happened, and that he was planning on collecting what I had unconsciously offered.

I grit my teeth and scowled. He winked and sauntered down the hall to ruffle the hair of a young boy who was grinning at him. Still scowling, I stood there and watched him be friendly to the boy and kind to Fleur.

Which only served to irritate me further.

***

"You gonna get that?" Ben asked.

"No," I muttered, seeing it was an unknown number, again, and put the cell in my back pocket.

"Not another broken heart?" My best friend rolled his eyes as he took a swig of beer. Normally, I would have had a laugh and punched him in the arm. I was no stranger to the ladies. Only, the one calling me, with an unknown number, was a stranger to me. I knew it wasn't a drunken fling, I didn't booze like that because I knew better, and if I took a girl's number, I made sure I wanted it.

"I have no idea who she is," I said, finishing my beer and giving a heads-up to the bartender that we wanted two more.

"Is that why you're in such a shitty mood? You're acting like someone has pinched your favourite handbag."

"Piss off," I told him as I laughed. He was right, I was in a shitty mood, but not because of this person calling me. Though it was a woman making me want to hit something. A tiny, black-haired, tattooed pixie with deep blue-purple eyes, a pert arse, and a smart mouth.

"So tell me, what's going on around here?" For the past few years, Ben had been away as an aid worker overseas. He moved back to finish the house he'd started to build, get his farm up and running, and no doubt intended to settle down with a wife, kids, a house, and a damned dog. I didn't get why. What was the point? Who would willingly tie themselves to someone, leaving them open to hurt like that? This wasn't the commitment-phobe male arsehole point of view, women could feel the same way, and Ben knew that firsthand.

"Not much. I'm working hard, heading up four crews across the plantations, getting my ankle right so I can get back on the field, and trying to get up to the cabin whenever I can."

"Sounds like not much has changed."

"Not much," I replied, thinking it probably sounded dead boring and empty, given his work in South Africa feeding starving children. I got he needed to do that, but I loved it here in Bright. The town was changing, and for the better. Growing as more people decided to move away from the concrete mazes and traffic jams. I'd always lived here. It was where my dad was buried, and his dad before him. I loved the community, the alpine mountains, the clear rushing river, and the deep green forests. It was paradise, and I'd never had the urge to leave.

"So, is the new physio any good? Is he going to get you ready to play again soon?" Ben asked, dropping cash on the counter for our beers before I could.

"She's okay."

"She?"

"Yeah, she. Women can do all the things men can, you know." I nudged him. He knew full well they could, he adored his sisters.

"No shit. Now I'm wondering, have you tapped that yet?"

"Fuck no. I don't root every girl I meet," I answered, hating how defensive I sounded.

"No, every second girl," he ribbed.

"Piss off." I needed him to shut it.

"You're kidding," he scoffed, shaking his head in surprise.

"What?"

"Is this why you are acting like a grumpy old lady? Did she...? Wait. She did. She refused you." Ben threw his head back and laughed. I hated how well he knew me.

"Settle down, dickhead. She's not my type." I tried to play it off, focusing on my beer.

"I'm pretty sure she has a pussy and a heartbeat. That's your type."

"You kiss your mother and sisters with that mouth?" I asked and he rolled his eyes. "She isn't my type," I reaffirmed, needing him to get it.

"Maybe she wants a *life partner*, not a one-night stand," Ben stated. He and I didn't see eye to eye on long-term relationships.

"I am not going to be her life partner. It's not happening. I don't do relationships. Ever. Everybody knows that."

Chapter 2

I needed a second job. My primary occupation didn't keep me busy enough. Some people liked life laidback, so they had time to relax and partake in their hobbies. Me? I did not enjoy spare time. I needed to keep busy. I needed to keep my mind occupied to stay sane and to stay whole. Take Tuesdays for example. I had a shift at the hospital in the morning, then clients in the afternoon so I was busy for most of the day. I had run in the early morning, and I hit the gym after work, making it home late enough to shower, microwave my dinner, and binge watch Netflix before bed. Tuesdays were manageable, but Wednesdays were hard.

Today, I only had a half-day of client appointments. The town of Bright wasn't big enough to warrant me working all day every day. The money was good, and I was set financially, so I needed something else to do. This morning, after I'd cleaned the kitchen, swept leaves off my path and deck, and done my washing, I dressed in my running gear and headed out to the fire trails at the back of my house in Wandiligong.

When I'd done a hospital rotation as a physio here during my training years ago, it was the hills that had made me fall in love with the area. During my rotation, I'd met Hannah and Molly, and their friends Leslie and Carol, who made me feel like I belonged, trauma and all. So, when a job came open for a permanent physio at the local clinic, I'd jumped at it.

As I started my climb up my hills in the cold late autumn air, a low cloud settled in, fitting my melancholy perfectly. For the last few months, I'd started to feel more unsettled than usual, no matter how busy I was, or how many kilometres I ran. Perhaps it was because things were changing.

Molly was about to get married to her fiancé Dave, and Hannah was in love with Dave's best friend, Howard. I was going to be on my own. I knew I needed to be on my own. Relationships weren't for me. I didn't like who I became when I was into someone that deep. But listening to Molly and Hannah talk, hearing their excitement and knowing that weddings, kids, and minivans were on the way, I wondered what was next for me. Nothing came to mind— a dull and depressing reality to consider, but at that moment, the trail had become steep. I had to focus on my breathing and the energy required to propel myself forward.

This was why I loved running the hills—there came a point where my body took over, and my mind went blank.

Too soon, I was heading back down the mountain. Erik the Viking-lumberjack was coming in again today. Usually I had no problem fending off his and other men's advances. In fact, I took pleasure in not-so-politely declining. I looked at it like a test of my wit and cleverness, wanting to say no in a way that let them know never to try again.

But during Erik's last appointment, I'd almost succumbed. It wasn't as though he had been particularly persuasive. His method of approach was typically blunt and heavy handed, suiting his personality. But when he'd crowded me and had latched on with those bloody blue eyes glittering with challenge under his sexy dishevelled hair, well, I'd wanted to kiss him.

A terrifying development.

I hadn't kissed anyone, let alone thought of a man that way, since I'd fled England four years ago. I didn't want to start now.

After letting myself into my cottage, I decided my desire to kiss him was triggered in part by Hannah and Molly's state of loved-up-ness, which reminded my body it craved a lil' sumpin' sumpin'.

After showering and drinking as much coffee as I could in the hour I had to prepare for work, I went through my mail, flipping through the bills and opening up home renovation magazines. My miner's cottage was almost completely renovated. I had to work on the cover over the deck and I'd be done. I'd never had an inclination to renovate until I moved here. I needed to keep busy and the run-down, two-bedroom cottage I'd bought for a song had been in disrepair. I'd thought we both needed fixing up. While mending the breaks and rejuvenating rooms that time and neglect had decayed, I had done some healing of my own.

I'd kept the frame of the house with its high ceilings, and the floors were polished reclaimed boards I'd restored myself. Now they gleamed gold with flecks of paint and dark holes from nails, adding depth and character. I'd painted the walls and ceiling white, keeping the exposed Oregon beams natural to bring in the feel of the surrounding forest.

I'd commissioned a stone fireplace, and my soft tan leather sectional and armchairs were centred around it, sitting on a giant mottled green rug.

The bathroom was white with a wall of hexagonal tiles in blues and greens, concrete grey floor tiles, and a giant white tub I almost drowned in. The bath was heaven after a long hike, and I ordered Crabtree and Evelyn Pear and Magnolia bath products in bulk because I used the tub so much.

My bedroom broke the theme, with the walls painted sage green and all the furniture glossy timber, including my king-size bed that, yet again, I almost drowned in. My bed had too many pillows, including multiple Union Jack and Kath Kidson prints. Above the bed was a giant picture of a deer that Hannah and Molly had given me for my birthday.

The other room was a study, but I rarely went in there. It was decorated in the same motif as the rest of the house, with a foldout couch that was never used, a desk that collected dust, and all the parts of my old life, files and photos, that I couldn't look at, but couldn't bear to throw away either, shoved into a wall of shelving.

One picture in a frame sat on the desk collecting dust. It was of Theodore and me in front of his old car that was packed to the roof with my belongings the day I moved to London. We looked ready for the future, believing then that it was the start of something good. It was painful to look at, but a perfect reminder of what I'd done.

When I could take no more idleness, I headed into work, early needing the distraction. I found Fleur talking to Geronimo, the naturopath, at the reception desk and instantly, I felt sorry for her. He was a self-important arse and a wanker who was way too friendly with Fleur, and needed to shower more often.

"Hi, Annie, how are you?" Fleur greeted the moment the door opened, clearly happy to have something else to do other than be ear-bashed.

"Great. You?" I asked, smiling at her. She was so friendly and kind, I found myself smiling more than I had in a long time whenever she was around.

"Pretty good, thanks," she answered, looking around for something else to say.

"And you, Geronimo?" I asked, taking the mail Fleur handed over, my smile evaporating. "How's it going?"

"Really well. I was explaining to our Fleur here the importance of activated almonds for young people. The research is ground-breaking, and she has agreed to try it with Tate," he said with a smile directed at Fleur that actually came across as creepy and weird. She returned his smile with an awkward noise coming from the back of her throat. His phone buzzed in his pocket and he walked off toward his office to take the call.

"You should tell him to piss off," I said, but I knew she would never be so rude.

"I know, but I think he needs to feel important, and I'm a little flattered he wants to flirt with me. It's a nice change," she explained. I was surprised by her frankness.

"A change? I bet men flirt with you all the time. You're a knockout," I told her. She had this beautiful femininity to her, a soft womanly body, gentle golden waves that framed her face, and big brown eyes that were warm and kind.

We couldn't be more different. I had short dark hair that was long on top and shaved at one side, a pixie face, a muscular build, and boobs that barely filled a B-cup. Fleur was rocking some double-Ds for sure.

"Not really. I think I slip under the radar," she said as she returned her focus to the computer.

"I don't think so. Erik certainly notices you," I told her, sounding a little catty without meaning to.

"Not true. He's been a great help after everything that happened. I can assure you his feelings for me are purely platonic. I'm the sibling he never had," she said, and before I could ask her what had *happened*, the phone rang and our conversation was over. I wanted to know what she meant, but because I didn't know her well enough, I wasn't in any position to badger it out of her. I started to leave but Fleur reached out and grabbed my hand, giving me the *hang on a minute* finger, and I stopped.

"Annie, sorry. I've been meaning to ask, have you thought about filling in again at netball? We are getting desperate. And I could use a friend." Fleur squeezed my hand. One of our first conversations was about her playing netball again after twelve years. I'd told her it had been that long since I'd played in England. The local team, the Bright Belles, were short on numbers, and I'd filled in a few weeks ago, but after seeing Erik lingering around the grounds, I'd had no intention of returning. Until now. Clearly after this morning's acute case of loneliness, my desire to be busier, and irritation with wanting Erik while knowing he was no damn good for me, had me considering things I didn't want to. It seemed I was unhinged enough to reconsider her request.

"I guess so, but not this weekend. I have Molly's wedding." Why on earth had I said that? I'd gone straight form considering to committing. I wanted to take it back but seeing the relief on Fleur's face, I knew I couldn't.

"Next week is great." She beamed. I tried to smile. At least I still had a week to prepare myself for country netball and even more time with the Viking-lumberjack.

***

I didn't know why I was on edge and irritated. I didn't want to examine it too closely. I had a feeling my annoyance was related to the appointment I was about to have with a sexy, foul-mouthed pixie. As I jumped down from my truck, I winced. I'd forgotten the sore ankle that had me in here in the first place. Heading in, I saw Fleur looking bored as that dead-shit Geronimo leaned over the counter, talking and staring down her shirt. I shook the rain off my jacket as I scuffed my boots, announcing my presence.

"Hey, Erik," Fleur called in her soft, warm way. I didn't smile back. I was glaring at Geronimo.

"Hey, girl. Geronimo," I said, not taking my eyes off the motherfucker.

"Ah Erik, how's it going?" At least Geronimo had stopped looking at her chest, but he was now sizing me up. Idiot.

"Fan-fucking-tastic. What about you, Geronimo? What've you been up to lately?" I asked pointedly and he stupidly squared his shoulders.

"Life," he answered. "Spending time with Fleur is always a highlight." He tried to act like he was with Fleur, and I was a threat.

I was a threat, but only because he was a moron with wandering eyes.

"Highlight how?"

"Erik, I think…" Fleur started but Geronimo had already started putting his foot in it.

"Well, because she and I are so alike."

"You and Fleur? Alike?" I couldn't help but laugh.

"Yeah, we're both outcasts but have thrived despite what people think about us. Right, Fleur?" he said, and I couldn't believe he brought that shit up.

She didn't answer, but her eyes flashed with humiliation before her gaze dropped to the desk. This guy was an A-Grade, prime-cut, top-of-the-line dickhead.

"She is nothing like you, arsehole. You're lucky a beautiful, strong woman like her would even give you the time of day." I moved toward him, ready to teach him a lesson. He took a step back. At least he realised today was not the day to push me.

"Don't you have some kombucha to brew, Geronimo? Or maybe some crystals to worship?" Annie asked calmly as she moved between Geronimo and Fleur. I fought a smile when I saw her glaring at Geronimo, who was now pretending this was all a big joke.

"Now, Annie, you know that isn't what I do, but you're right, I am busy. I'll catch you later," he said as he moved backward down the hall, hands up in the universal sign of "don't shoot."

"You okay?" Annie and I asked Fleur in unison. She was blushing hard, embarrassed, and I didn't know what to do to put her at ease.

"I'm fine. I can handle his overtures. I don't need protection," she answered politely, but also with an edge, letting us know she could handle herself.

"I know you can. I wanted to make sure you were okay after what he said," I told her, putting an arm on her shoulder. She looked ready to cry. Clearly that was *not* the thing to do. Well shit.

"And as you know, I look for any excuse to give Geronimo a hard time. If I wasn't wary of a lawsuit, I would have let Thor here hammer him into next week," Annie said, pointing a thumb at me, giving Fleur a wicked grin. It worked and Fleur smiled despite the tears in her eyes.

"Kombucha?" she asked Annie wryly.

"Best I could do on short notice. At least I didn't swear a blue streak, be thankful for small mercies." She winked at Fleur before giving me a nod toward her office. Glancing at Fleur, I could see her still smiling as she sat down at her computer. Then my gaze returned to Annie and her fine arse filling her tight black jeans.

This appointment went like all the others before. The two of us in strained silence unless we were parrying back and forth with smart remarks. It was exciting *and* frustrating. The woman had an answer for everything, getting snappier the more I pushed her buttons. Which made me act more of an ass, because seeing her eyes flair in annoyance was my drug of choice. Why she was fighting our chemistry and what I knew to my bones would be great sex, I couldn't say. I saw how she looked at me, her eyes going a little hazy with lust when she lost some of the fight and was Annie minus the mile-high defences. And holy shit, last Monday she'd wanted me to kiss her.

"So what's the verdict? When can I play?" I asked as she stood watching me walk back and forth again. I tried to hide the wince but she caught it.

"A few weeks. You don't want to do more damage coming back too early and miss the entire season. Carry on with your exercises. We will have to see how it goes."

"Sounds good." I focused on doing my ankle raises as instructed, but when she spoke, I almost fell over and it wasn't because my ankle was aching.

"That was nice of you to step in with Geronimo like that," she said, giving me a tight smile. I looked into those almost purple eyes to see them warm and open, and my gut tightened in a way it never had before.

"He's a dick," I grunted. "Fleur is too good of a woman to have him bringing up shit he doesn't know anything about."

"I don't know what happened. That's her story to tell, but you're right. The past is the past and none of us need a reminder of shit we can't change," she said, focusing on her tablet. Well, that was a statement and a half, but by the set of her jaw I guessed she wasn't up for a chat.

"That's enough for today, you can put your shoes on." Her words confirmed that the door was firmly shut. I set about doing as I was told, trying to find a way to get that warm look back in her eyes. I felt like today was the day to push it. She had let down her defences, if only for a moment, and I'd had enough waiting.

"So," I said, moving in to stand close enough I could smell her. Shit. That sexy aroma would stay with me all day.

"The answer is no, again," she muttered, not looking up from her device.

"You don't know what I was going to ask."

"Yes I do. You are going to ask me out for a drink or dinner. Again. And I am going to blow you off. Again."

"And what if I have a different sort of proposal?"

"Will it end up with you asking me out?" she asked on a sigh but looked up at me with her big eyes partially hidden by her dark hair dancing across her brow and falling at her cheek. This look, the dancing spitfire eyes, a smirk on her mouth, head tilted to the side exposing her neck and shoulder as she waited to pounce on my next words, was one of my favourites. It's what I conjured when I took care of myself lying in bed, in the shower… Enough.

"Well, that would be up to you. If you want to go out after, then sure, but I don't do relationships," I told her, unable to hide my grin as her brows furrowed.

"After what?" she asked, trying to look bored and failing. I could see the heat in her cheeks as she figured it out. I stepped closer, forcing her back, and she ended up against the shelves.

"*After* I get you naked, give you an orgasm with my fingers, then my mouth, then fuck your brains out and you come again, but this time with me." I wanted to fist-pump as her eyes went unfocused and a soft breath escaped those pretty lips. "So, we *can* go out if you want to, but I'm likely to drag you back after one drink to bury myself between those pretty thighs again." I was being a shit. I knew it. But something had to give, and my crudeness was working. Her eyes dropped to my mouth, and her small white teeth came out to bite her bottom lip, giving my stiffening dick more incentive.

"Pardon?" she asked as though I'd asked a question but she hadn't been listening to what I'd said. Not wanting to let go of the advantage, I leaned in close and saw her chin tip up, her eyes drift shut, and her lips part. I brushed her lips with mine, barely touching them before I whispered in her ear, "We both know there is something between us. Personally, I think the sex would be mind-blowing. I don't want to marry you, but I do want you underneath me, naked and wet. Think about it." When I heard her suck in a breath, I stood back and took in her wide eyes and open mouth before heading out the door.

"See you on Monday," I called but heard no reply.

Feeling invigorated from my victory over the sexy, infuriating raven-haired pixie, I headed to the football club ready to lift weights and have dinner with my team. My optimism was short-lived when Daphne found me. Fuck. My. Life. She was part of the reason I didn't date. She was malicious, deluded, and I was done with her. Something about tonight had me taking on battles instead of brushing them off, so when she came up and put an arm around me as I entered the dining room, I couldn't help myself.

"Why are you doing that?" I asked, stopping dead in my tracks, forcing her to stop with me.

"Doing what?" She had a pretty voice, and when she used that innocent tone, any man who didn't know better would have been fooled.

"Touching me like that?" I asked, and she looked affronted and hurt, but after glancing around and noticing only a few old-timers looking at us, her eyes turned calculating.

"But I know how you like to be touched," she cooed.

"You think?" In reality, she did know how I liked it. I'd told her. I knew how she liked it too because she would make so much noise the neighbours had to have heard us.

"I don't think, I *know*. What I don't know is why you don't want to start up again. It was good for a while there, and it can be again," she purred.

"It was good, but that's because we were both clear that it was going to end."

"It didn't have to. We had good chemistry, and it was easy when we were together. Why not keep a good thing going? We *know* each other."

"Then you would *know* that I don't date."

"What do you call what we had then? It was four months."

"Yeah, two years ago."

"But it was still dating."

"Look, Daphne, I'm trying not to be a dick here. It was good while it lasted but I was never in it for anything more than sex. I told you that up front. I'm sorry if your feelings changed, I really am, but mine didn't and I'm not keen to go back there." I tried my best to sound reasonable, but it was a challenge; we'd been over this a few times.

"You're lying to yourself, Erik. We were amazing. Everyone knew it, saw how happy we were, that we had what it took to stay together," she said, glancing around, and I followed suit, seeing we now had an audience. I think this was her aim, to get me to concede because people were watching, or make me out to be an arsehole to the beautiful netball queen of Bright. Well, fuck that.

"Daphne, my position hasn't changed."

"No? Then how come you are seeing someone now? We all know you have a woman on the backburner," she taunted, going for betrayal. I had no idea what the fuck she was on about.

"What?" My confusion must have registered, and for a moment she looked perplexed. Then she smiled her crowd-pleasing smile, took advantage of my confusion, and leant in to whisper.

"Don't think we don't all know. But don't worry, I'll prove to you that I'm the one you belong with," she whispered before giving me a kiss on the cheek and sauntering off. What the fuck? Before I could figure it out, one of my dad's old mates, Churnsey, slapped me on the shoulder and said loudly so everyone could hear, "They all wear you down at some point, mate. Give in and let it happen." I knew he meant no harm and that he was trying to make a joke, but tonight wasn't the night for letting it go.

"There is no fucking way that is ever happening," I boomed before I stalked out. I went home to my depressing-as-shit unit, ate cereal for dinner, and slid into bed to think about Annie as I took care of business.

Chapter 3

I'd spent all night cursing Erik for his crudeness and unwelcomed perceptiveness. I cursed myself for letting my guard down. It had been scary not only because I'd been trapped by his sexy gaze, I'd loved it. I desired him as much as I despised him.

When my alarm finally went off, I got out of bed, put my running gear on, and headed outside into the woods to blank my mind. After my run I showered, dressed then went to see my friend Leslie for a coffee before going into the clinic. In Bright, when it came to coffee and delicious food, we were spoiled for choice. Despite being English and drinking tea like my life depended on it, I had cultivated a love of coffee. I considered this part of my assimilation activities, along with referring to football as soccer so people didn't get me confused with their national code, Australian Rules Football. They should put *that* on the Citizenship Test.

"Hey, love," Leslie called from her stool at the share table as I walked into Sixpence Coffee Roasters. The smell of fresh bread and coffee had my stomach rumbling as I kissed her on the cheek.

"What's news?" I asked, taking a seat.

"I'm getting excited for the wedding, you?" she asked, referring to our friend Molly's wedding set for that weekend. I was looking forward to it—it would be the event of the year.

However, weddings also made me think about my own situation. Not that there was much to ponder. In fact, there was nothing. Not. A. Bloody. Thing. Maybe that was the problem.

"I can't wait. I've made time to lend a hand," I said, smiling as I thought about Molly, who had become Bridezilla.

"I hope I don't cry." Leslie sighed. She was definitely going to cry.

"You'd better not, or else I won't sit with you," I teased as I stood and went to order my coffee and doughnut. As I waited for the machine to accept my payment, my mind happily on the custard and rhubarb goodness I'd ordered, the hairs on the back of my neck prickled and I froze solid. "Bloody hell," I muttered under my breath.

"Erik, how's it going?" the handsome, bearded barista asked the ass who was standing too close behind me. The Tap and Go machine was taking FOREVER and I wanted to be gone.

"Doin' okay, you?" Erik's deep voice sounded beside me as he found his way to the counter, our arms touching giving me an electrical buzz.

"I'm good, but tell me, when are you back on the field?" The barista was looking at Erik with that bro-mantic anticipation shared between men who love sport. It was cute. And annoying. Because it involved Erik.

"A few weeks, right, doc?" Erik asked, nudging me, forcing me to join the conversation, which only made my irritation with him and technology increase.

I tried to glare at Erik, but even taking the smug, half grin he was giving me out of the equation, he was too beautiful to look at. His hair was wet and pulled back, emphasising his square jaw, his needing-a-trim beard, and massive shoulders.

"Pixie, take a picture if you want." When I heard the barista laugh, my blood pressure skyrocketed.

"No need, I'm merely concerned by the white viscous substance in your hair. *There's Something About Mary* style. It's a little worrisome," I said calmly before turning to the barista. "He might be good at football, but his hygiene leaves a lot to be desired." I sighed as if there was nothing that could help poor Erik. "And it will be at *least* a few weeks before he's back." The barista's jaw dropped before he bent over laughing. Thankfully the card machine beeped and I left Erik brushing his hair then looking at his hands.

"Who was that?" Leslie asked as I took my seat.

"A client checking in."

"Bullshit."

"Huh?" I tried to play dumb.

"You know exactly what I'm talking about. That big ol' hunk of mountain man who you were making eyes at."

"Are you crazy?" I rolled my eyes.

"There's nothing wrong with it—I'm a lesbian and even I can tell he's a panty-dropper. You could do with a bit of happy," Leslie said, her tone low, her seriousness catching me off guard.

Usually my friends didn't push me into my discomfort zone. They knew why I left England and how I felt about love. But her intention was to tell me I deserved to be happy so I couldn't be angry.

"Not with trouble like that. Not again," I told her. She assessed me for a long moment before she turned the discussion to her crazy job setting up community services hubs with the love of her life, Carol.

Erik left the coffee shop without any further drama, and I finally started to relax.

At work, Geronimo was studiously avoiding me after the uncomfortable situation with Fleur yesterday, and I was thankful. Fleur seemed happy enough until a scary woman who I could only assume was her mother came in, bringing Fleur new torment when we were sitting at reception going over appointment schedules

"Mum, I'm at work." Fleur tried to smile and tilted her head to indicate her mother should leave.

"I don't see any clients," the woman huffed, looking around the empty waiting room.

"We are looking at the clients for next week," I explained, summoning as much politeness as I could.

The woman turned her narrowed gaze on me for the first time, then proceeded to inspect me, head to toe. I didn't care what she thought, but the look on her face suggested she wasn't thinking anything good. I wanted to laugh. I knew I absolutely would not be her cup of tea. I had short hair with one side shaved, and people either loved or hated it. I was wearing my usual attire for work: faded black jeans, motorcycle boots, and a black Ramones shirt, none of which earned Fleur's mother's approval. All that was missing were some piercings and she would completely flip her lid.

"They let the receptionists dress like that and have tattoos here, do they?" she asked disdainfully. I heard Fleur suck in a breath.

"Yep. They also let the physios dress like that too," I replied, smiling, and she reared back slightly.

"You look too little to be manipulating body parts." She didn't apologise for her rudeness. Instead she looked like she'd been sucking on a sour lemon.

"Mum," Fleur tried to conciliate, but I cut her off.

"I'm only too little to reach the top shelf in the supermarket," I said, holding her glare. "Do you need any body parts manipulated?" I asked, standing up and she stared at me.

"Of course not. I use natural medicine when things aren't right," she scoffed.

I grinned. "I'm sorry. If you decide to use a professional then let Fleur know,"

"But I use Geronimo," she stuttered, clearly confused by my statement.

"I guessed as much," I said, and her mouth dropped open.

"Mum, please, I'm at work, I'll call you later," Fleur half begged while standing. Her mother looked her over, then returned her gaze to me, unsure what to say. She huffed exaggeratedly then walked out, waving over her shoulder at us.

"I am so sorry," Fleur said once the door had closed with a heavy *thunk*.

"For what?"

"For my mum. She's a bit of a...difficult woman," Fleur muttered.

"I can see that, but I don't care. She's not my friend, you are," I told Fleur, giving her a smile.

"Thanks," she said, relieved but still humiliated. I hated this look on her, and I wanted to make it disappear, so I uncharacteristically opened up to put her at ease.

"My mother is a difficult woman too," I said, shrugging my shoulders, unsure how to go about sharing like this. I was sober for a start.

"Really?" she asked, concern etching her kind face.

"Really. I've always been a disappointment to her, and she wasn't afraid of letting it show."

"How on earth are you a disappointment? You're a physio, fit and healthy, successful and have the sharpest mind I have ever seen." Fleur said, looking genuinely perplexed, and I wanted to laugh.

"My mother doesn't rate any of those attributes. She wanted a conservative replica of herself, but instead she got a girl who loves rock'n'roll, laughing too loudly, and going out on the town. But part of me thinks that even if I hadn't been so wild, I would never have been as good as my brother." It still hurt to talk about Ted. I missed him so much, but he was never far from my thoughts.

"You have a brother?" Fleur asked, surprised I hadn't mentioned my sibling.

"Yeah, Ted. He's older by two years."

"I wish I had a brother, it would have diverted some attention off me growing up. Is he fun like you?" she asked.

I drew in a deep breath, preparing to talk about my best friend. "Yeah, but not un-controlled like me. He was responsible, wise, and so good to people. He was smart, funny, and generous too. He always made sure everyone was safe and having a great time. Ted was also a great soccer player, studied engineering, and was going to be an aid worker," I told her.

"You're lucky," she said.

"I was," I replied and realised my slip-up when Fleur's face drained of colour. "I am, I meant I am." She must have thought he was dead, and as far as I knew he was alive and well. It was me who was dead to him. Fleur visibly relaxed.

"Do you think he'll come to visit?"

"No, we don't talk anymore." I tried not to sound cold, but it didn't work.

"Oh no. Why?" Fleur's reaction was so open and honest I ended up feeling bad for her feeling bad about me.

"We didn't leave on the best of terms, and I haven't heard from him since I left London four years ago."

"I'm sorry to hear that," Fleur said, giving me a sad, understanding smile. She didn't push for information, and that made me like her even more. She needed to meet Hannah, Molly, Leslie, and Carol. She needed us at her back. I knew they would love her no matter what her past entailed.

I worked back-to-back appointments for the rest of the day, finishing with enough time to get a quick haircut before heading to Molly's to help with the wedding setup. This was the only problem with having short hair. It had to be cut *all* the time. Knowing I needed to hurry, I rushed into the salon to find Erik sitting in a chair, having his beard trimmed while a young woman chatted away, trying hard not to flirt but not managing it.

"Hey, Annie," my stylist called as I waited at the reception desk, eyes squinted with irritation. Hearing my name, Erik turned his head, his gaze snapping to mine as a slow, smug smile spread across his face.

I greeted my stylist as I scowled at Erik before taking my seat. There had to be fifty hairdressers in Bright. How was it possible we used the same one? Before he proposed we become bed partners, I'd rarely seen him around town. But since yesterday, I'd seen him twice, and each time I had been struck dumb by desire and how I hated desiring him.

It was a small mercy that my head needed a shave, so for a small amount of time, I didn't have to listen to the young girl natter as she trimmed his blond Viking locks. Sadly, when the shaver stopped, I heard his deep, musical baritone carrying across the salon. I tried to block him out, but other customers and my stylist joined in a whole-of-salon conversation with him and his sodding football career. I could see him looking at me in our respective mirrors, grinning because clearly he knew how irritated I was. Not missing a chance to really piss me off, he started talking about me being a physio, trying to draw me into the conversation in a way that I would look like a bitch if I didn't participate. Well, so be it.

"You know I don't mix business and pleasure, Erik," I said in warning, and the young girl trimming his locks gasped as if I'd lost my mind for not drooling over his attention.

"That's a shame, my business is giving pleasure," he said ridiculously, and all the women tittered. I rolled my eyes at him in the mirrors.

"I doubt handling wood all the time is pleasurable for anyone other than yourself." At my comment, there was silence in the room as my stylist blushed, fighting back a chuckle. Erik boomed with laughter, breaking the tense moment, and the women joined in. My plan had backfired. And he was a prick.

"Handling wood is pleasurable. I'll give you a go anytime you want." He gave a smug look, but I wasn't having it.

"I prefer to watch it catch fire."

"There is nothing making my wood catch fire," he said grinning.

"That's not what the chemist said," I muttered, and at this my stylist spat out a cough-laugh that had Erik's eyes narrowing, and his stylist's young innocent ones going wide.

Thankfully he was finished having his hair cut and stood to leave. On his way out, he came up behind me and whispered in my ear, "Don't forget to think about my proposal. It would be fun." And curse me, but I shivered as his voice licked over my skin. He laughed softly, the puff of hot air at my neck eliciting another tremble. I wanted to come back with some witty retort, but my brain had melted right along with my underwear.

**

"Winner, winner, chicken dinner," I said as my chicken parmie was set down in front of me. Ben and I had returned to our usual Friday night beers now he was back in the country. Tonight, we were trying the pub in Porepunkah. Not our usual haunt, but the vibe was good and the evening was shaping up nicely.

"What has you so happy?" Ben asked, and I gave him a knowing look. "A woman then. The physio who was playing hard to get?" Ben laughed as he finished his beer and gave a nod to the bartender for two more.

"Something like that."

"So, she's decided to give up her dreams of a wedding, kids, and dog for one night in the sack with you?" Ben asked, ribbing me.

"Not exactly, but let's just say her body isn't opposed to the idea," I replied, not liking the idea Annie was giving up anything, but not sure why I even gave a shit.

"Well, as long as *you* don't fall in love with her." Ben pointed a chip at me.

"Why would you say that?" It was no secret I wasn't into that sort of thing.

"Because you haven't had a woman under your skin since Daphne was trying to trap you, but this time around the woman is putting a smile on your face, not making you fucking furious."

"Don't talk to me about Daphne. She bailed me up at training this week. Reckons she knows about a woman I'm seeing or some shit, and wants to get back together. I thought she was cool and that we were good. At least she had left me alone for the last year, but this week she was up in my face and letting everyone see. Sure as shit she's up to something."

"Fucking games," Ben said, grimacing, clearly remembering the bullshit he was put through by his ex-fiancée. She was in the same category as Daphne—a knob rotter. Once you took your knob there, bad shit followed.

"I know. All I want to do is chill, get some side action, and live my damned life. So what if marriage is not for everyone? I've seen firsthand when it goes to shit and I am not signing up for that." I looked at Ben, both of us too serious and grim.

"Well, that is deep and meaningful. Thanks for sharing your feelings," he deadpanned and I burst out laughing.

"Piss off, you idiot."

"This woman *has* changed you. Look at you opening up." He grinned and I threw a chip at him.

"No woman can change me," I assured him.

"What about the one who keeps on calling you?"

"Yeah, well I confirmed it's a she. She called again, leaving a voicemail this time, but it was really hard to hear. I could tell it was a female voice." It was strange and seemed off. Not like a scam, but something close.

"Fuck. What if she's a fling who found out she is pregnant?" Ben asked, looking worried. His worry was unwarranted.

"No way. I always cover up. And besides, I haven't slept with anyone in months, and I never do it drunk." I enjoyed a few beers, sure, but I never got lit up. Being that inebriated was something my dad taught me not to do, and I wasn't about to go down that road.

"Sorry, I know that," he said, looking apologetic for even thinking it.

"It's cool. Let's talk about something else, anything else," I muttered before shoving food into my mouth. We were so absorbed in our catch-up that I almost missed it when flashing eyes and a pert arse entered my line of sight.

"What?" Ben asked when I couldn't stop the smile that spread across my face.

"Nothin'." It was a lie.

"Clearly it's not," he said, swivelling his head to follow my gaze. "Fuck me. That's her, the physio?" he guessed. I didn't answer him. I didn't need to.

Annie was at the bar with another woman. As ever, she was in black, but tonight she wore tight leather pants, high-heeled black suede boots, and a slinky black top that exposed her back and had a deep v at the front. I was surprised to see a tattoo peeking out on her shoulder blade, and decided when I got her naked, I was going to explore her body to see what was pictured on her smooth creamy skin.

"Wow, man, she is all that and then some." Ben smirked as Annie turned to scowl at me. She was wearing sexy, heavy dark makeup and blood-red lipstick that was so hot, my dick twitched.

"Yup," I replied and Ben chuckled.

If Annie thought glaring at me was going to push me away, she couldn't have been more wrong. When her eyes flashed in irritation, it only made my dick harder.

"What are you going to do about that?" Ben asked, clearly amused.

"Win."

Chapter 4

I'd loved every second of Molly's wedding. It was as it should be, full of love, laughter, friends, inappropriate relatives, and Bruce Springsteen. Seeing Molly and Dave together reminded me that love was possible. Molly and Dave were carefree and it showed. It was also heartening to see Hannah and Howard all loved up. Hannah deserved every drop of happiness after she'd pulled herself out of a hole with her ex who had cheated on her and drained her bank account. It seemed that she had found her happy ever after in the handsome, quiet Howard, who was happy to let her shine.

So, given all this, I should've been in a better mood. I was truly happy for my friends, but the guilt-ridden, selfish sickness that riddled my body was bubbling under the surface of my skin, looking for a fight. It was a not-so-gentle reminder that I couldn't have what Molly and Hannah had. I was not to be trusted with love. This feeling of yearning and fear was at its worst after the wedding on Sunday afternoon. I roamed my house with a mild hangover, looking for a distraction to avoid going into my spare room to punish myself. Eventually, I'd settled on cleaning my house again, chopping firewood, and watching *The Handmaid's Tale*. Given my melancholy, it was a particularly poor choice but periodically, visions of Erik and his warm, cocky grin invaded my gloom. I considered seeking him out and taking him up on his offer as a reprieve from my sadness. I found myself craving the warmth his embrace would offer, wondering if a few hours of mindless pleasure was what I needed.

Somehow, I managed to refrain.

Monday morning I woke with an emotional hangover—that deep heaviness that settles in your chest, reminding you life was shit, and there was no chance of improvement. As usual, I went for a run in my woods, ready to be mindless and free in the cold mountain air. The icy drizzle didn't bother me in the slightest. In fact, I loved the additional numbness it brought. I made it to the top of the Mystic Hill launch area, but no views were to be had today. It was all grey and miserable. You would think coming from England this weather wouldn't bother me, but today it mimicked my mood too closely.

I headed back down the path in thick fog, knowing I needed to head into the clinic at some point. I was halfway down when I was partially blinded by flashing orange lights cutting the grey. As I got closer, I could hear men's voices and as I ran a little farther, work vehicles came into focus with signage emblazoned across them reading Alpine Valleys Plantations. The Plantations were a major employer in the area, and the surrounding hills often resembled patchwork quilts of dark green, brown, and a motley mixed colour as old wood was harvested, the ground was rejuvenated and then replanted, and new trees grew.

Not wanting to engage in small talk, I passed a group of lumberjacks as quickly as possible.

"Pixie." Shit. Was this some sort of sick joke? I stopped and turned to face Erik, who was staring at me, as were his fellow lumberjacks.

"Are you following me?" I asked furiously as I took him in. He was wearing his typical uniform: cargo pants, boots, green fleece, and today he had on a black waterproof jacket. He also wore a charcoal woollen beanie and I hated to admit it, but it made him look even hotter with his hair poking out and framing his handsome face.

"Ah, no, I'm not following you. The road is public, but these plantations belong to the company, you know, where I work." He was being a smart-arse and I probably deserved the chuckles from his comrades, but I wasn't in the mood to be laughed at.

"Whatever. Have a nice day, guys," I said, nodding at him, then the other men hanging about before turning to leave.

"Wait, Annie," he called, and I could hear him getting closer to me. He needed to keep his distance. I couldn't handle him whispering in my ear or letting me smell his manly goodness. My defences were in disrepair.

"I don't have time for this, I have somewhere to be," I told him, throwing as much attitude as I could. He stopped a few feet away from me, eyeing me suspiciously. I knew I sounded off, but that didn't mean I wanted him to notice.

"Okay, pixie, I won't hold you up. But you need to be careful running up here dressed like that." His hands were out as if he were worried I might bite or hiss at him like a wild animal.

"Like what?" I snapped, making his cautious approach warranted. He was up to something because I wasn't showing any skin at all.

"All in black. I meant dressed all in black. I know it's your signature colour, but there's going to be logging trucks and equipment coming up and down this road. You want to be visible, trust me." Huh. Well. I had no answer to his thoughtfulness, which threatened to take the wind out of my sails.

"Trust him, love, the trucks can't stop that easily," an older lumberjack chimed in.

"Well, I don't usually trust men who have hair longer than I do, but if you say so, I'll get some fluoro," I replied with my hands on my hips as if I had a real reason to be snappy. At my comment, a few of the men stifled a laugh, but Erik grinned at me.

"I wondered where my girl went," he whispered.

"I'm not your girl," I reminded him while giving him my flintiest gaze. It was my own attempt to cover up the tightness in my chest. My glare had no effect though. He looked at me with a small smile and heated eyes.

"Not yet," he said, giving me a wink. A bloody wink.

I huffed, turned, and continued to head down the mountain toward home.

If I was tired before my run, I was exhausted when I was done. I'd sprinted home at breakneck speed, almost giving myself a heart attack.

***

Annie had looked hot as hell in her running gear. All that tight spandex and sweat-strewn hair was sexy. It was lucky for her I was talking to one of my crews, or else she might have found herself horizontal in the back of my truck. It was going to happen soon enough, and I could hardly wait. She'd given me grief as always, but there was something else in those big, expressive eyes, a vulnerability and a defensiveness that I hadn't seen before. I didn't like it one bit. Her confidence and sass were a beautiful thing. They turned me on. But that brittleness today made me feel worried, and I needed to know what was up with her.

She'd been on my mind more than I'd like to admit. Heading in for my appointment, I decided that now was the time to do something about it and press my advantage. She was driving me crazy and we both needed to scratch our itches so we could get on with life.

"Hey, Fleur," I called.

"Hey, Erik, how's it going?" She gave me an easy smile.

"Good, and you?"

"All good, thanks."

"And Tate?" I always asked after him. Tate's father, Reece, was a former friend but complete deadbeat and since he'd left her pregnant, and her family had left her all alone, I always checked in with her about her not-so-little boy.

"He's great. thanks. And thanks for dropping the football around. He loves it. You didn't need to, but it's really appreciated."

"No worries. Tell him I'll come around for a kick again sometime soon."

"He would love that," she said.

I headed to Annie's room, knocking on the open door before entering. Now dressed in faded black jeans and a black shirt that was skin-tight, she was facing her shelves, moving towels around.

"Pixie," I said in greeting.

"Viking-lumberjack," she replied flatly without looking at me.

"Shall I assume the position?" I asked, and she finally glanced my way, her eyes wary.

"Take off your shoes and socks, and walk back and forth for me," she instructed as if by rote; she planted her arse on her stool. She acted like she would rather be cleaning her eyes out with vinegar than communicate with me, but I didn't buy it. Our appointment continued as per usual. Her trying to do her job, me trying to throw her off her game. It wasn't until she had me on my back on the bed, my knee bent, my ankle in her hands as she kneeled between my legs that I made my move. Locking my hands behind my head, I looked her dead in the eye and put my best *let's fuck* face on.

"So, have you thought about my proposal?" I asked, surprised at how raspy my voice sounded. It caught her attention and her gaze flew to mine. I saw heat and indecision. She *had* been thinking about it.

"No, I've been busy," she lied as she forced her focus back to manipulating my ankle.

"Bullshit," I grumbled, trying not to get frustrated. "Your eyes say you have been thinking about it, and enjoying yourself. The pink in your cheeks backs that up, and the rapid breathing confirms it."

"Now that *is* bullshit." She snorted, returning her focus to my ankle.

"It's not, and you know it. Why do you fight it?" I asked, surprising her as I sat up so we were nose to nose, as she was forced to release my ankle. She was kneeling between my splayed legs and I liked her there a whole fucking lot.

"I…ah…what?" she stammered as we locked stares and I could feel her soft breath on my face. My gaze roamed her face, noting she was even more beautiful this close up. Her skin was soft and pale, making her dark lashes and pink lips stand out. Her face was delicate, in contradiction to her personality. When my eyes dropped to her lips, they parted and she licked her lower lip in an unconscious invitation.

"You know it will be good." My voice had dropped even lower; the need to touch her was almost more than I could bear.

"You could be a dud," she murmured as she looked at my mouth and I fought a smile.

"Let's find out," I said, dropping back and taking her with me. The movement caught her off guard and she let out an "oomph" as she fell forward, landing on my chest as I trapped her in place with my hands on her hips, my knees caging her. I dragged her farther up so we were face-to-face, her body resting fully on mine. She used her elbows to push herself off my chest, allowing her to look me in the face. She was so small against me, sexy and gorgeous.

Her hips were flush against mine and no doubt she could feel how aroused I was. She didn't pull away. She pressed in ever so slightly, and I sucked in a breath as her breasts pushed against my chest and she applied pressure to my hard cock.

I ran my hands down her sides, moving up to right under her breasts, my thumbs grazing the underside. Now it was her turn to suck in a breath, and when I moved them back down to palm her perfect arse, finding it as round and tight as I'd imagined, she rocked her hips into me, letting out a soft mewl as her eyes became unfocused with desire and pleasure. It was a look that would forever be etched in my memory.

"I'll make it good for you," I murmured roughly, on the edge of losing it. I wasn't going to kiss her. I'd stated my intentions and proved my point. Now it was her turn to come to me. Her gaze held mine again, and amidst the lust I saw something else. She looked lost, and almost afraid of what might happen.

She blinked slowly and looked back at my lips as she lowered her head slightly, then she froze and jumped off the bed like I was on fire. She was quick, using my stomach to vault onto the floor, and I grunted as the air whooshed out of my lungs.

"Why did you do that?" she hissed, sounding furious. I sat up and turned, seeing her facing me, back against the wall, breathing heavy, eyes looking wild.

"You know why. You were right there with me." I tried to stay calm, but my words sounded more like an accusation than I wanted them to.

"No I wasn't. I don't want that," she stammered her lie.

"Yes, you do. But you're too afraid to admit it," I said, running a hand through my hair in frustration. She had some serious self-control, and it was fucking irritating.

"I'm not. You're too afraid to consider that maybe I don't want what you're offering." This was another lie. I knew she wanted me, and I'd be damned if she told me otherwise.

"You're full of shit, you know that? I felt you on me, I saw it in your eyes and I heard it when you moaned for me." I stood up, feeling ready to explode. I was turned on like I'd never been before, but listening to this woman talk shit and play games? Well fuck that.

"No, I'm not," she said, squaring her shoulders. "Your problem is you don't know when to quit."

"Well, I do now. You want to play games, fine. But I don't. I want to fuck you. You want to fuck me. That is all I'm offering. That is all I'm up for and you know what, Annie? You want it. Your body is screaming it. Whatever is going on in that pretty head of yours is fighting it and to be honest, I do not have time for bitches who play games," I growled as I grabbed my boots and put them on.

"You're a real arsehole, you know that? I am not some conquest. Don't get your knickers in a twist because you're not getting your way. Other women might fall prey to your charm and good looks, but I see through all that. I know you're trouble and I am not having any of it."

I'd had a gutful of this rubbish and I let out a humourless laugh. How had we gone from being on the verge of orgasming with our clothes on to this? Her denial was a fucking joke, as was her judgment. I didn't even look at her as I walked out, telling Fleur to cancel my next appointment before the door closed behind me.

Chapter 5

I found myself replaying the almost kiss with Erik. The feel of his big, hard, warm body beneath me, the look of promise in his gorgeous eyes, and that excited nervous feeling I got right before I kissed someone for the first time. It was a heady feeling, until I remembered that it was something I had almost done. After swearing off men, especially ones like him—the charming troublemakers—I'd almost given in. Almost. So close, it was scary.

Added to that heap of steaming emotionally challenging shite in my head, I'd also seen Hannah, who had come up for air after a hot weekend with her man. They were cute together, deliciously cute, and her guy was handsome, smart, and thought the world of her. But being selfish, her happiness was weighing me down and it highlighted that I was miserable.

Taking up Fleur's request to help the netball team was a good option. With Erik injured for another few weeks, I was in the clear to be competitive to let out some frustration.

I arrived at the netball courts to find the younger girls finishing up their training session. Fleur waved me over and I noticed Tate sitting on the benches with his nose in a Harry Potter book. As I made it to Fleur, I surveyed the team, most of whom I had met before when I filled in.

"Ah everyone, this is Annie. Annie, this is everyone," Fleur told them.

A woman I didn't know introduced herself. "I'm Daphne," she said, holding out a manicured hand. She had long nails and I hoped she taped them. I had no desire to bleed before the game. She also wore a matching lycra outfit the same colour as her nails. Her assessing gaze remained on me and I got the feeling she didn't like me. Whatever.

The coach came over and directed us through our warm-up. After, positions were assigned, and I was handed the Centre bib.

I stood holding the ball, ready to start when the coach snapped, "Daphne, are you ready or do you need more time to get Erik's attention?"

Before I could stop myself, my gaze snapped to where Daphne had been looking. Erik, in skins and a grey t-shirt, hair in a higher pony, dripping with sweat, was watching us from near the clubhouse. His lumberjack attire was hot, but his sweaty gym gear was a close second. Men in lycra were usually a turn-off, but his compression tights did nothing to compress the beauty that was between his legs. As my gaze drifted up to meet his, I was surprised that he was glaring at Daphne.

"I'm pretty sure he's here to talk me," Daphne said smugly, and we all turned to look at her. "We're getting back together," she told the coach, pretending to whisper. When she said the word *together*, she flicked her gaze at me and I looked at her like she was talking gibberish. Princess Daphne was unhinged if she thought Erik was giving her *come hither* eyes.

"I don't care why he's here. We are training, and you need to focus."

Wisely, Daphne didn't say anything else although she cast a murderous glance toward the coach who scoffed at her, then blew the whistle and it was game on. Erik mustn't have watched for long; by the next centre pass, he was gone. As training wrapped up, I packed up my things ready to leave and avoid more visions of him in Lycra.

"You coming for dinner in the club rooms, aren't you?" Fleur asked, grabbing her bag. "We always grab a bite after training, you should come."

Sitting having drinks with some of the team, listening to them gossip, one of the women leaned in and said, "Daphne isn't that bad, she only goes a bit crazy when Erik is around."

"Why is that?" I asked, hoping I didn't sound too eager for information.

"They were together for a few months, years ago now. She wishes it lasted, but Erik isn't the relationship type. She knew that, but then I guess you can't help what your heart wants." Something about knowing they were together bothered me and it shouldn't.

"We were surprised they lasted that long, but I knew it was destined to fail when she was bragging about him being the one, and that he was finally settling down," another teammate added. "I didn't get that impression but then again, I didn't pay them too much attention at the time."

"He's never had a relationship before?"

"Not that I know of. He's a great guy really. Helpful, fun, a bit too charming, but then I was never in his sights. He doesn't want to settle down and I think that's *all* Daphne wants." Fleur sighed. "Unfortunately for her, she wants Erik to give it to her."

"Sounds like he's not the type," I muttered.

From the table across from us, Daphne asked, "So Annie, what do you do again?" She wore a friendly smile that didn't reach her eyes.

"I'm a physio."

"I see. I've never needed one of those," she said as if she was relieved she didn't have to lower herself.

"Good for you," I said, giving her a bland smile, returning my focus to the group at my table. They had stopped talking and Fleur was looking from the bar, to Daphne, to me, eyes wide. I turned to find Erik watching me with an unhappy look on his face. I picked up my drink and saw Fleur giving me a knowing look.

"What?" I asked and she grinned at me.

"Yeah, what?" Daphne called out, and we all looked at her. She was glaring at Fleur now, her dark eyes squinty and her gloss-covered lips pursed.

"I beg your pardon?" I asked.

"Do you know Erik?" Princess Daphne asked as if that was impossible.

"Yes. Do you?"

"Of course. We're sort of together."

"Really? That's great. He's a real catch," I said, giving her a fake smile.

"He is," she said, clutching her hand to her breast.

"Strange. He hasn't mentioned you. I see him a few times a week, but then, he's pretty focused on me." I'd decided to rile her up. I didn't want to battle her for Erik's attention, but girls like this were so selfish and rude, they needed a reminder every now and then.

After making fish mouth Os, she sputtered, "He's only seeing you so he can get back on the field." Her voice verged on shrill, causing a few looks from other tables.

"Of course. Why else would he be seeing me?" I asked, giving her a smile and a look of confusion. This seemed to perplex her; she eyed me for a moment longer before returning to her posse, talking in hushed tones.

When I left the club rooms for the muddy parking lot, it had turned cold and dark outside. The lighting was so poor that when Erik came out of nowhere to my left, I yelped before spinning to face him, keys ready to scratch his eyes out, my feet in a defensive stance.

"Whoa. Relax. Shit, Annie, I'm not going to mug you." Erik's eyes were wide, and his hands were up in front of him.

It took a moment to slow my thundering heart. "Sorry, you can take a girl out of London," I said while straightening.

"Look, I wanted to make sure you're all right," he said, running a hand through his hair in seeming frustration.

"Why wouldn't I be?" Did he think I'd shed tears after our argument?

"I saw Daphne talking to you, and I, ah, have a history with her." He sounded awkward and apologetic.

"So I've heard."

"Well, I wanted to make sure you knew that it ended a long time ago. She can twist facts sometimes and I, ah, didn't want you to think I was…" He ran another hand through his hair, clearly uncomfortable.

"You didn't want me to think you were trying to get me into the sack while you were with her."

"Something like that," he said on a shaky, self-deprecating laugh, and I felt myself wanting to laugh with him, but fought it. He may be a dick who couldn't take no for an answer, but I was starting to learn that he wasn't evil, and clearly he wasn't completely daft. He'd dodged a bullet with Princess Daphne.

"Ahhh, you worried about me."

"And what would be wrong with that?" he asked.

"Nothing, but you don't need to be. I can handle myself," I stated.

"I'm sure you can, but she knows a lot of people," he told me.

"I don't need you to watch out for me. I'm your physio. That's it," I snapped, not liking the warmth creeping into my chest.

"Woman, you know there's more to it than that, but for some stupid fucking reason you're fighting it," he growled.

"Fighting what? A quick fuck with the town's most eligible bachelor? I've already told you I'm not going to join that *exclusive* club."

"Don't be like that."

"Like what?" I asked.

"Like everyone else. You don't know me. So I like to have sex. So what if I don't want to get married? It doesn't make me a bad person." He sounded wounded and I felt a pang of guilt. He was right, and my reasons for not taking him up on his proposal was because I'd lived this before and didn't want a repeat performance.

"You're right. I don't know you, and you don't know me either." I sighed, feeling exhausted. I wanted to tell him that I was not the woman he thought I was, but I couldn't.

"I'm trying to get to know you," he said quietly, and my heart hurt a little. I knew he was trying, but it was in everyone's best interest that he didn't.

"As I've told you, it's not going to happen."

"You've yet to tell me a good reason why." He put his hands on his hips, pinning me with a look that said he was calling my bluff.

"Well, that's not going to happen either. I have to go. If you want to keep me as your physio, book in with Fleur. Otherwise, I'll see you around." I walked away before he could answer, needing to get away and hide.

***

I prowled back into the club rooms, more frustrated than ever. The more I spoke to the woman, the more I wanted her despite the fact she was fighting our attraction. Walking through the dining room to get my bag, I kept my head down, not wanting to deal with any more bullshit. Wishful thinking.

"You need a new physio," Daphne called out, and I stopped, drew in a deep breath, and turned to face her. Taking her in, I noticed she was looking ready to party, not like she had just finished training. I never understood why she put makeup on to exercise. She stood looking at me expectantly, and while I wanted to blow her off, I knew it would be a total dick move with the people around us watching, so I responded.

"Yeah? Why's that?"

"She wants to sleep with you. It's totally unprofessional," Daphne advised, taking the concerned friend approach. It was funny really, hilarious even. For once Daphne was right, Annie did want to sleep with me, but not as much as I wanted to sleep with her. Daphne's concern was complete bullshit and that was *not* funny.

"What makes you think that?" I asked.

"The way she looks at you, talks about you. She inferred you have alone time together, as in *alone time*." Well that *was* interesting. I was going to have to ask Fleur what Annie actually said.

"Why were you talking about me?"

"She was looking at you and I called her on it," Daphne huffed.

"She's allowed to look," I reminded her and this made her drop the friend act. She went straight to pissed.

"Is she?"

"Uh, yeah. It's a free country and as we discussed last time, I'm unattached. Remember?"

"You are such an arsehole."

"Why am I an arsehole? Because I don't want sleep with you?"

Daphne went from pissed to furious as she looked around to see who was listening. The fact I was using Annie's argument on her wasn't lost on me, and it made me want to hit something. Fuck. I needed to get out of here now.

"You lead women on, and it's sick," she hissed.

"I'm not leading you on. You're misreading the situation. Again."

"I wasn't talking about me and you. You have Annie and *Freya* both on a string." I froze at her words. Who the fuck was Freya?

"What the fuck are you talking about?" I growled, stepping into her, letting her know exactly how I felt about this game she was playing. At least she had the sense to step back.

"The girl who is calling you," she replied, her confidence faltering.

"How do you know someone is calling me?" I asked, and more of her bravado left.

"Everyone knows," she hedged, trying to brush it off.

"Everyone? How?"

She licked her lips nervously, clearly trying to come up with a new lie. I didn't know why I was bothering, I couldn't trust a word out of her mouth.

"It's the word around town. I haven't gone through your phone or anything."

"You sure about that?" I pushed, but I didn't think she had. I wouldn't put it past her, but I haven't been around her enough for her to have access.

"I'm looking out for you." She returned to the concerned friend act, after not getting her way with being rude, manipulative, or pushy. Then she put a hand on my chest in a gesture that was too intimate and completely insincere.

"Well, Daphne, let me make it clear. You're off duty."

"What do you mean?"

"You don't need to look out for me, and you're sure as shit not my friend. You got that?"

She nodded as tears filled her eyes, and I blew out a breath in frustration. This woman brought out the worst in me, and I didn't need this shit tonight.

"Fuck me," I muttered as I turned and grabbed my bag before storming out, knowing everyone was watching.

I drove to my piece-of-shit apartment, hating it more than usual. I had a cabin in the the mountain up near Dinner Plain. I'd inherited the shack from my dad when he'd died, and spent my money and spare time fixing it up. It was still rustic, but it was what I considered home, my place away from the world. But when I was working during the week, it took too long to drive down the mountain every morning, so I had a one-bedroom unit in town. It really was a shoebox, with a bedroom, tiny bathroom, and a kitchen/living/dining space the size of a postage stamp. I wasn't there much, and that was a godsend. Too long in that place did my head in.

I pulled up to see my neighbours outside smoking and drinking. No women lived here—mostly older bachelors who didn't care about much in life, except drinking, gambling, and smoking. It was safe, but it was also a stark reminder of what happened to men when they spent their life alone. I'd seen it with my father, and despite the life he'd lived and how much I hated it, I found myself surrounded by men exactly like him.

After I got inside my apartment, I dumped my bag and turned on the TV, needing the background noise as I got myself sorted for work the next day. When a show I didn't absolutely hate came on, I sat on the tartan two-seater couch, which, along with the TV, a table, and two chairs, was the only furniture in the room.

I needed to get away, up to the cabin and get my head straight. I thought I'd had life under control until I walked into Annie's physio room weeks ago. Now, she was on my mind and invading my dreams. She was saying no, but everything else—her reaction to me, her words, her glances—were saying yes. Maybe this was what my dad was talking about, that women can't be trusted because they didn't know their own feelings. I didn't think Annie was lying necessarily, but she wasn't being honest with herself or me and that was driving me crazy.

Chapter 6

I'd stooped to new lows in order to avoid Erik. I'd changed coffee shops, run different tracks, and taken Jason Bourne-worthy circuitous routes to work, keeping my eyes peeled for the big truck I'd seen him in last week. But all that effort was in vain: this morning he was there in his man-bun Viking-lumberjack glory at Wills Street, with a colleague drinking a coffee when I snuck in before work. When our gazes met, I could see heat and frustration in his eyes, and I understood that to some extent. He wanted me but was frustrated I wouldn't give in. I wanted him but was frustrated that I couldn't rein in my raging hormones.

As the day wore on, I was convinced that the world was conspiring against me. At lunchtime, I saw him at the petrol station filling up, and again in the supermarket an hour later. Each time he smirked at me, seeming to see through my brittle defences. In reality it didn't matter whether he smiled or glared, seeing him kept reminding me of what he'd offered and how I badly wanted it. I needed to bolster my resolve, and there was only one way I knew would work. It was going to be terrible, but I needed to remember why guys like him, the charming, fun, popular types, need to be avoided.

"Hey, Annie, are you okay?" Fleur asked as I headed past her reception desk on my way out in the afternoon.

"Yep, all good. I need to check on something at home. I'll be back before my next appointment."

She'd known things were off with me, caught on to the *something* between Erik and me, and today she'd been watching me like a hawk. I was not up for divulging this ugly part of me. I needed to get home, give myself a stark reminder what happens when you were consumed by someone who was larger than life, then head back to work to help Erik with his bloody ankle. End. Of. Story.

I unlocked the door to my cottage and went straight to the spare room, turning the lights on even though the blinds were up. It was a cold, dreary day outside, and the soft light from the lamp by the couch only made it marginally less depressing. I knelt at the shelves and moved books around until I found what I was looking for. Pulling out a shoebox, I took it to the couch and sat, drumming my fingers on the top of it. The thrum, thrum, thrum filled the silence of my empty place until I took the lid off, and my thundering heart took over as lead percussionist.

I didn't have to sort through too many keepsakes and photos from England to find what I was looking for. I pulled out the folded newspaper article, put the lid back on the box, and unfolded it, pressing it flat on the box. It had yellowed a little, but not enough for it to be illegible.

"*Man left in coma, paralysed after ride with drug addict,*" the headline read. It was directly above the sub heading reading: "*Drugs have become as prevalent in driving-related deaths and accidents as alcohol.*"

Then there was the full article about how Theodore Clarke, a twenty-six-year-old engineer and Manchester native, had been injured in a car collision with a tree that involved his friend and sister. I didn't need to read any further to remember. I was there and recalled each moment vividly. Instead, I focused on the images. The first was a wrecked car and the second was my brother, looking handsome in his cap and gown the day he graduated as an engineer. Ted was handsome, always had been, and he was also so full of life, generous and responsible. Ted was athletic. He'd been into cycling and soccer at the time, and had the physique to show for it. But this wasn't how I remembered him anymore. I remembered him lying in a hospital bed, looking at me like I was a stranger, unable to move his legs beneath the white sheet and cotton blanket covering them, his jaw held in place by pins and metal.

This was what I had needed to remember. That because of my stupidity, and my inability to see through charm and my own heady, romantic feelings, my brother had to give up on his dreams. He didn't get to travel overseas for work or join the army. He didn't get to keep cycling. He couldn't even walk up stairs.

My eyes pricked before the tears rolled out as I sat for a moment longer, taking it in, feeling the familiar heaviness invade my heart and gut. This time, the memory felt worse. Aside from the crushing guilt, I remembered that I needed to keep away from men who so completely consumed me, who charmed me, to make sure I had my wits about me and prevent anything like this happening again. It was harder to accept this today, because I'd met a man who made me want for more. Erik had reignited a part of me I'd tried to extinguish, and it was going to take more effort to put that fire out for good. Erik was a repeat of Paddy, and I couldn't go there.

Glancing at my watch, I packed the article and box away, then got in my car to return to work, feeling more morose and despondent, if that was possible. On the drive back, I decided that I needed to give up my frustration with Erik. It wasn't his fault. He was who he was. I simply couldn't. It was almost a relief to replace my irritation and indecision with melancholy and resignation. It felt more definite, so I didn't fight it. I knew why I needed to stay away from him, and while the sadness was almost suffocating, it took my feelings out of the equation. It just plain was.

Fleur eyed me suspiciously as I walked in but was wise enough to let me be. As I waited for Erik to arrive for his appointment, I didn't restack my towels or organise my pens as I usually did in an effort to keep busy. This time, I sat on the bed waiting for him to come, forcing my mind to go blank. I was so focused on this task that the knock at the door had me jumping off the bed, hands to my throat as a startled scream escaped. I stood staring at Erik wide-eyed and frozen in place, his hand still on the door handle, looking at me warily.

"We have an appointment, right?" he asked cautiously as he stepped into the room, seeming afraid I was going to bolt or lose my schnitzel.

"Yes, right. We do. Sorry, I was lost in my thoughts," I explained, trying to slow my heart rate and keep my voice calm. I glimpsed at him, to see his beautiful eyes filled with concern, but I looked away quickly. I did not need to see that.

"Must've been some deep thoughts, if the look on your face is anything to go by," he murmured gently. I didn't answer him. I smiled vaguely at his shoulder.

"Close the door and take off your shoes and socks."

He did as he was told, and I used all my strength to focus on his ankle, not the fact his presence made me want to stand close enough to take comfort in the warmth his big body produced.

I managed to get through the appointment, noting that his ankle was improving and he was almost ready to run on it. He did not make any lewd comments or ask me out, and in a strange, my-future-is-so-bleak kind of way, I missed it. It was a stark reminder that something good that could have been was over before it started and I was in mourning, heading toward acceptance.

As he sat on the bed putting his shoes and socks on, I added notes to my tablet and emailed him a list of new exercises to try. The silence was strained and I knew I was putting out strange vibes, but we were about done. A few more minutes and it would be over until next time.

"Annie." His voice sounded different than usual. His baritone was smooth and deeply masculine, as always, but now it held an edge of authority, like a command for my attention.

"Hmm?" I asked, still typing notes, feigning being engrossed in my work to avoid looking at him.

"Can you come here for a minute?" he asked, still demanding but softer, almost coaxing. It was this change that compelled me to look at him.

"What do you need?" I asked while staying rooted to the spot a few feet away. I was too much of a coward to go any closer.

"I need you to come here," he said, putting one foot on the floor then reaching out with one hand to snag mine and pull me between his legs. My gaze flew to him as panic took over. If he kissed me, I wouldn't be able to hold back. I wasn't strong enough and anything that happened between us would spell *disaster*.

But he didn't kiss me. What he did was much worse. He pulled me into a hug, his huge arms surrounding me, one around my waist with his forearm snaking up my back, the other around my shoulders, with a big hand holding my head to his shoulder, my face in his neck. I tried to struggle out of his hold, not able to cope with this kindness, but my struggles were short-lived as I breathed him in, feeling him strong against me.

"I don't know what has dimmed the light in your eyes, pixie, but you need to get rid of it. You can give it to me if you want, but it needs to go. I don't care if you're pissed at me. In fact I like it when you are. But this look? This empty, desolate look? It has to go."

I held my breath as his words sunk in. If I let the air out of my lungs, tears were sure to follow. Instead, I pushed closer for a moment, relishing in his heat before I spoke. "I'm fine, really." My voice was muffled as my lips moved against his exposed neck.

"That's bullshit," he said, and I loved how his chest vibrated against mine.

"I know." There was no point in lying. The gig was up. He would get this, but no more.

"Is it me? Have I done this to you? If I have, you have to know that it was never my intention." Shit. His honest, regret-filled words made me fight off a second assault of tears. Why did he have to be like this? Show me this? I wanted to dislike him, but my shitty attitude was not on him. It was all on me. And he had to know it.

"It's not you, it's me," I said, voice tight with leashed emotion.

"That's normally my line." He chuckled and I appreciated his attempt at levity. I took a deep, steadying breath, then pushed to get up and this time he let me.

"Thanks."

"For what?"

"For the, ah, hug." I sounded awkward, and I didn't know where to look. I couldn't handle that intense gaze that was looking past my outer shell into the real Anne Elizabeth Clarke.

"I thought it was more like a cuddle." His grin was cute and unhelpful.

"Whatever. It was a nice gesture, but truly I'm fine. I had a rough day."

"It was nice. We could do it more, you know?" he said, giving me a cheeky grin, returning the ballsy, flirty Erik. It was a relief.

"You're incorrigible," I sassed, and he flat out smiled.

"Thanks."

"It's not necessarily a compliment."

"Whatever," he muttered, and I smiled, unable to help but enjoy our banter. Then I realised where I was—between his legs, my hands on his shoulders, his on my hips. It was too intimate and too close to being exactly what I wanted. What I needed. I jumped back, desperate to have space between us.

"Don't do that," he said, shaking his head but keeping his tone gentle.

"Do what?" I asked as I leaned against the wall, the farthest away I could get without running out the door.

"Pull away."

"I'm not. It was a nice hug, er …cuddle, and now it's over."

"You're still fighting it. Haven't I proven I'm not an arsehole?"

"Because you hugged me when you thought I was sad, instead of trying to get in my pants. You think that makes you a hero?" I asked, desperate to put distance between us.

"I never said I was a hero. I have no idea why you are hell-bent on denying yourself. But you know what? Fuck that," he said, standing up, and I pushed into the wall, giving him as much room as possible to walk out. But he didn't leave. He crowded me, so we were inches apart, and I held my breath. Then he moved even closer, our hips touching, and grabbed my face in his big hands and kissed me. I froze, but only for a moment before his tongue licked at my lips and my traitorous body let him in. My mind was trying to stop this madness, but the pressure of his lips against mine and the feel of his tongue—my body was completely in charge.

Hell, the way he kissed—well practiced and talented—I felt rusty as memories of intimacy and touch returned slowly. I felt off balance as his tongue delved inside my mouth, exploring me with a hunger that I returned, but was too afraid to unleash. He held me in place and made love to my mouth with such skilled fervour that I hung on to his shirt and let him take me where he wanted to go. I heard myself moan, which only served to increase his intensity, and he let out a low, deep growl that had damp gathering between my legs. Sensing this, he pushed his hard length into me and I let out another moan. I had to grip tighter as the kiss went on; I was at risk of sliding down the wall. Sensing I could take no more, he eased the pressure and slowed the kiss, ending with gentle, almost reverent lip touches.

When he pulled back and looked down at me, his eyes were glittering with desire and triumph. I have no idea what I looked like. No doubt a lust-filled woman who'd had the life kissed out of her and didn't know what her name was. I expected him to say something, an *I told you so,* but nothing came. He simply held my gaze as the sounds of our heavy breathing filled the space and reality sunk back in.

Then I felt sick. I could not believe I'd given in, let this happen. I'd even made a point to revisit that horrible article and all that had happened, torturing myself, forcing myself to remember why I couldn't fall prey to Erik's charisma. But it hadn't worked. All he'd had to do was be kind, and then assertive, and I'd gone willingly. I hadn't even put up a fight. Instead, I'd held him to me and moaned as he kissed me, my first kiss in more than four years. Weak and pathetic. Realising my mood was plummeting, and tears were threatening, Erik surprised me yet again.

"Pixie, that was nothing but goodness. Don't twist it in that brilliant, insane, sexy head of yours," he whispered before pressing his lips to mine briefly, then he moved away and out the door, leaving me against the wall.

***

Fucking hell, that kiss was even better than I'd thought it would be, and she was into it too, had been right there with me. What was not good was the darkness haunting her beautiful eyes when I'd found her lost in her thoughts. She didn't know I was there so I'd been able to observe her for a full minute, and what I'd seen concerned me. She looked lost and almost ready to break. Clearly she was hurting, suffering alone, and was too stubborn to talk about it. I knew I should be patient and wait for her to come to me about whatever was holding her back, but it was going to be difficult because after today, things had changed.

The next day it was all I could think about, and when I arrived at the sports grounds to see the netballers warming up, I looked for Annie straight away, wondering how she was going to react. I'd thought she was going to ignore me or give me shit but she did neither. When she looked at me, she gave a quiet, shaky smile before returning her attention to the coach. It was a surprise, but then she never did what I expected.

Of course damned Daphne was there, glaring at me, but honestly I could not give a shit. I headed straight for the weight room to get a workout in, then I thought I'd catch up with Annie to check in with her, to make sure she was okay. I wouldn't push her. She had to come to me now. I'd laid it out there. She needed to meet me halfway. The only good thing about being injured was having the weight room to myself.

I got through my workout easily and even squeezed in a quick shower before heading to the club rooms to eat. I wish I'd gone to the pub instead. I entered the side door by the bar to come in on the back of a conversation between Annie, Daphne, and Fleur. It was clear from the look Daphne gave me that she was up to something. She was the only one who could see me and before I could announce myself, she jumped in.

"So, Erik told me all about you," she said to Annie.

"Did he?" She did a good job of hiding her panic, but I caught a little of it. I stayed put, interested where this was going to go.

"Yep, said you're not too bad for a physio, but that he's looking forward to being back on the field."

"Of course he is," Fleur said, but Daphne didn't look at her.

"That's right, but he is a regular client. Do you have any others to fill his spot?" Daphne asked.

"Of course. I'm not exclusively his," Annie replied, realising how it sounded.

"Oh I know that," Daphne said smugly, thinking she had caught Annie out.

"I'm sure you do. He isn't exclusively anyone's," Annie said conversationally, taking a sip of what looked like red wine.

"What does that mean?" Daphne asked. She was out of her league and didn't even know it.

"It means, Daphne, that whatever bullshit you're trying with me here isn't going to work. I actually don't think you and Erik are together and that's not because he told me so. It's because you and him are at opposite ends of the spectrum."

"And what spectrum is that?" Daphne asked, trying to hide her fury and failing as she flicked her eyes to me.

"The reality spectrum," Annie answered, and I wanted to laugh. Fleur looked at the ground. I wondered what trash would come out of Daphne's mouth next but thankfully, nothing came. Instead she looked at Annie with calculating eyes, gave her a small smile then turned her gaze to me with a look that communicated she was making a strategic retreat, then walked off.

Fleur grabbed Annie's arm. "I can't believe you said that."

"She had it coming," Annie said.

"But be careful, she doesn't take losing badly," Fleur warned.

"But she isn't going to lose," Annie said and my gut tightened.

"But you laid it out that Erik doesn't want her," Fleur stated.

"She isn't going to lose because it's a one-horse race. It's not like that between Erik and me," Annie stated, and my heart sank.

"Of course it isn't," Fleur replied with a rare show of sarcasm, but Annie ignored her and took a big sip of wine. Needing to get out of the doorway, eat, then get home, I walked past them as though I hadn't heard a thing, but I could feel their eyes on me.

After another fitful night of dreaming about Annie's sad eyes and warm mouth, I woke up exhausted and there was no reprieve at work. I had to complete four site visits but at least my teams kept their heads down to survive my foul mood. My thoughts oscillated between the high of our kiss, and the irritation and disappointment of her continued attempts to convince herself there was nothing between us. I needed to stick to my guns. She needed to take the next step.

But my resolve didn't stop my mind from wandering to that brittle look on her face before the kiss, and the vulnerable, needy one after. Something was up with her. Something serious. It wasn't my business and I knew I shouldn't care, but I couldn't shake the feeling that she needed help.

After knocking off work, I headed back to my apartment to pack my bag for the cabin. I wanted to get away early in the morning and spend quality time on the mountain—to clear my head and get a grip on my overly emotional state. Given the football team was travelling and I still couldn't play, I'd decided not to get on the bus. It was too good an opportunity to get away. Once I'd packed, I got extra supplies from the supermarket to stock up the pantry and freezer, fuelled up then headed to Tomahawk to meet Ben for what his sisters were calling our *date night*. He was waiting at the bar for me with a cold beer when I walked in. He greeted me in his usual fashion.

"How's it going, dickhead?" He grinned at me.

"Fine, thanks, cocksucker, and you?" I threw back, wanting to return his good humour, but I couldn't make it genuine.

"Come on now, rainy face, dry your eyes. What's got you blue? It's got to be a woman to have you looking this shitty," he teased as I sat next to him.

"Something like that," I muttered, taking a pull of the beer he had ready for me.

"Let me guess, is it *Delusional Daphne* hoping to rekindle what you had?"

"Fuck off." I sighed.

"Or is it the mysterious *lady caller,* calling to confess her undying love for you based on your Instagram account?" Ben grinned stupidly. I mustered a small smile at this. He hung shit on me for my Instagram account, but he was probably jealous at how many followers I had.

"You're an idiot." I chuckled, shaking my head.

"That leaves box number three. The sexy physio who is resisting your golden penis." When I said nothing, Ben's laughter died. "What the fuck is going on?" he asked, giving me a suspicious, assessing look. Fucking great. He was like an old woman wheedling secrets out of people.

"Are you trying to get me to talk about my feelings again?" I asked in a lame effort to get him to lay off.

"Yep. Tell Benny-boy your problems. I've had shit luck with relationships but I'll give advice for free."

"Like I said, you're an idiot."

"True, but something has to give, man. You're not okay," he said, dropping the humour.

"We kissed," I huffed.

"That's good, right?" he asked.

"It was fucking great. We have burn-the-sheets-to-ash chemistry but she's holding back, saying she doesn't want it, but acting like she does. Her body certainly did." I ran a hand through my hair. This shit made my head hurt.

"Why?"

"Something is up with her. Something is playing on her mind, worrying her, and I have no clue what it is," I told him, and instantly Ben dropped the friendly banter.

"Is she okay?" he asked, his concern making me smile. He was the best big brother.

"No. Whatever it is, it's serious. Maybe she needs to talk to you, Dr Phil, and open up about her feelings." It was a joke, but it would probably work.

"I do have a way with the ladies," Ben said ruefully, and I laughed. He had a good way of being friend-zoned.

"Not with this one." Annie would eat him for breakfast.

"Maybe it's you. I hate to scare the shit out of you, but it's possible that you want more than sex from her," he said, and my immediate reaction was to deny it. But as my words came out, they felt uncomfortable.

"I was clear with her. I'm not up for that," I muttered.

"Then give her time," Ben suggested.

"I'm going to have to. My cards are on the table. It's up to her now." We placed our orders, then talked about my nearly healed ankle, his sister's new deadbeat boyfriend, and the cabin at Dinner Plain. My uneasiness about Annie had settled some when Ben's brows furrowed low.

"What?"

"Ah, well, your girl walked in."

Like a fifteen-year-old with a crush I snapped my head around to see Annie at the bar, looking over the takeaway menu. She hadn't seen us, but I knew from one look at her that the brittleness was back.

"Hey, Annie," I called before I could stop myself, and her gaze met mine, a mixture of panic and tears filling her beautiful amethyst eyes.

"Erik," she replied, her eyes moving to look at my shoulder, giving me a tight smile.

"You getting takeaway?" I asked as she held a menu that said TAKEAWAY. Ugh.

"Yep," she answered, going back to studying the menu.

"Come and join us for a drink while you wait," I invited, completely ignoring my edict to let her come to me. She looked up at me again, and for a brief moment I saw a painful something contort her face.

"I'm not good company at the moment. I'm going to grab my food and run. I have dogs in the car."

"Dogs?"

"Yeah, I'm minding them," she explained, then placed her order. Ben kneed me and when I looked at him, he had raised brows going between the two of us.

"Hi, I'm Ben," he said, standing and walking around, holding out his hand.

"Hi, I'm Annie, Erik's physio."

I bit back a growl at her physio comment. Clearly that wasn't the state of our relationship.

"I know. He's almost on the field again, the town owes you a debt," he said easily, and so it began, Ben employing his friendly charm and Annie being polite with her smile never reaching her eyes.

"I'll leave you to it," she said when our food arrived and finally looked at me.

"Nice to meet you," Ben said while Annie looked around, desperately wanting to be anywhere but here. I stood and moved close to her, needing to make sure she was okay.

"You all right, pixie?" I asked, bending to whisper in her ear to give us privacy.

"Please, don't." At her plea, I froze.

"Don't what?" I softened my voice, letting her hear my concern.

"Don't do that here," she said, drawing in a deep breath trying to control her breathing.

"What? Give a shit?" I asked.

"Yes."

"Okay, I'll give you that, pixie."

"Thanks," she said, squeezing my forearm almost absently.

"Will you do something for me?" I asked and she looked at me in panic.

"Take care of yourself," I requested, and the tears threatened again.

"Sure." Her voice cracked as she spoke her lie.

When they called out her order, she practically ran out the door as I returned to my seat to see Ben looking at me.

"You're right."

"About what?"

"She isn't okay. But it has nothing to do with you."

Chapter 7

Hannah's dogs Patsy and Eddie were good company even though all they did was sleep and eat. It was me who was dead boring. After seeing Erik and his friend Ben, and knowing that I wanted to join them but couldn't, I'd gone home, sat on the couch, and wallowed in this new, uncontrolled misery I'd created for myself. Kissing Erik had given me a taste of what life was like with someone again. This, coupled with my forced trip down memory lane, was not a recipe for happiness and rainbows.

Saturday morning, I woke up with lead in my stomach and the low hum of an overburdened mind. I knew I needed my hills, my escape into the numbness brought on by physical exhaustion even though I had a netball game that afternoon, but I didn't have the dog leads to take them. So, I headed to Hannah's house to collect them, only to find her car parked awkwardly in the middle of the driveway. Worried, I raced to the door to start knocking loudly. I could see a light on in the kitchen from the window and her handbag on the floor. Panicking, I banged on the door, the dogs barking in my car, moving about and rocking my Mini. Eventually, she stumbled to the door and gave me a confused look, not expecting me.

She had red, puffy eyes surrounded by smudged mascara, blotchy skin, and hair that resembled a rat's nest. She told me to come inside and headed toward the kitchen to put the kettle on. With a heavy heart that was now breaking for my friend, I got the dogs out of the car, called Fleur to tell her I couldn't play netball, and headed inside. Hannah moved about her beloved kitchen, and I let her be. I wanted to push her, get her to tell me what had happened, but I couldn't. She was too fragile. I knew the space she was in. I'd been there before, knowing that nothing was going to ever be as good again.

I waited, and when she was ready, she unleashed her heartache. She'd met Howard, the man of her dreams, who was as clever as she was, who adored her, respected her for all she was but who wasn't without challenges. Hannah wasn't like me; she was brave, she attacked challenges head on. I, on the other hand, was a coward. Since leaving England, I avoided challenges, finding reasons to say no, not to say yes.

When she told me that Howard had cheated on her, I was floored. I'd honestly, deep down to my bones, believed it was true love between them. The way they looked at each other, like each was the most precious person in the world, had me believing that they were the rarity—two people who loved each other and could manage being in love. But my emotionally ravaged friend told me he'd been seeing his ex and had lied to Hannah. This was her deal breaker, her kryptonite. She'd been betrayed before with devastating circumstances, and my heart broke for her. My fears were different than Hannah's. I was the one who did the betraying. I'd lost myself so deeply in love that I hadn't wanted to see the truth and as a result, my brother was in a wheelchair.

I sat and listened, hating seeing my friend like this; her usually optimistic and vivacious approach to life had been dimmed, and that was the true tragedy. She needed my help and I was here to give it to her. I laid out the plan to get her through the worst of it. I was going to physically exhaust her. I knew from experience that it would help. I would also make sure she ate, and had time on her own to wallow, but not too much. It was hard to heal on your own. You needed people, distractions, and life to bring you back from the brink.

As I spent the weekend managing her, I realised that while it was a terrible time for Hannah, it gave me purpose and human connection that I hadn't realised I'd been shying away from. Over the weekend, when Hannah had been lost in her thoughts, I'd found myself talking about my situation. I wasn't keen on sharing my past, but Hannah knew my story and hadn't judged me so I talked about that and the other oppressive weight on my mind.

Erik's name came out of my mouth regularly in conversation. It was as though I couldn't keep it in. I told her the sordid details, and while she didn't agree that I was better off alone, she understood.

By Sunday night Hannah was still in bad shape, but I could see she was coping, and I was astonished yet again at her inner strength. When I returned to work on Monday, I tried to keep my seesawing emotions in check. My poor acting skills gave me away—Fleur kept looking at me with the type of concern reserved for the pathetic. At least Geronimo was oblivious, reminding me it was my turn to bring in reading material for the waiting room and telling me I wasn't pulling my weight.

As Erik's appointment drew closer, I knew I had to bolster my resolve. Bodily responses be damned, I was not ready to be a head case for him to scrape off when he realised I wasn't what he thought I was.

He arrived on time, and my defences were tested in a different way. There was no innuendo, no frustration, and no attempts at intimacy. Worse, he was kind and gave me space. My disappointment was ridiculous. Hadn't I been pushing him away from day one? What did I expect?

This was to be the new world order.

I'd done what I'd set out to do.

Instead of being happy, I was miserable.

***

Ben understood women. Having grown up with sisters and a loving mother, he'd also had experience actually *dating* women. I hadn't. The connections that involved sex *and* friendship were not in my wheelhouse. But Annie was making me question my lifestyle, and it didn't make me happy.

Ben's most irritating nugget was that I wanted more than sex from Annie. The more I thought about it, the more I realised he was right. I did want Annie. I wanted to spend time with her. I wanted to know about her life, and I needed to know what gave her that haunted look. Clearly, she had something significant holding her back. I'd asked myself too many times to count: did I care enough to wait for her to figure it out? Between our obvious explosive chemistry, and wading into unfamiliar waters, I was off kilter.

I'd spent the weekend at the cabin chopping wood, hiking, finishing up the deck, and installing more storage space in one of the bedrooms. Growing up, we'd rented in Bright but spent most weekends up at the cabin until I started playing football. When Mum was around things were great, but after she was gone, Dad wallowed, holed up watching TV and drinking. While he was drowning his sorrows, I explored the countryside, hiking, mountain biking, and snowboarding. Him leaving me the cabin was the best gift he'd given me.

Fixing up the small home was cathartic. I loved being on the mountain. It cleared my head and gave me a sense of purpose. So far, I'd repolished the wood floors, restored the panelling, redone the kitchen and bathroom, and finished the deck. Ben was the only person who'd ever seen my sanctuary. I'd been content making it somewhere I wanted to spend time instead of the place where my father had drunk himself to death.

I'd returned to Bright as late as I could on Sunday night, not ready for the workweek to start, but clear-headed enough to know I needed to give Annie space and decide if I wanted to pursue an "us." I had an appointment Monday and I hoped seeing her would help me make up my mind.

When I entered her office, my stomach tightened. Normally, I felt excited. She was sexy, beautiful, and I wanted her. But when I saw her trying desperately to keep me and the world at bay, something snapped inside me. This was no friendly desire to help. I felt a visceral desire to make her happy—which, of course, scared the shit out of me. But I let her be. She gave me a strange look at the end of the appointment, and I thought it may have been disappointment. Maybe I'd hoped that was what she felt.

For the rest of the week, whenever I saw her around town or at training, she put on a show of being okay, but I could see her desolation. I had to fight not to hold her and make her tell me what the fuck was going on. I needed her to return to the sexy, sassy firecracker who didn't take shit from anyone. It wasn't only about my desire to get into her pants—I needed the old Annie back.

On Friday night, Ben and I had our usual man date, continuing our bromance, as his sisters teased.

"So, what's the go with the sexy physio? Has she opened up about whatever is fucking with her head?" he asked as we sat in front of beer and menus.

"No, she's putting on a brave face, but I think she knows I'm not buying it."

"Did you ask her?"

"No. I don't know why I even give a shit."

"As if you don't know," he answered smugly. It was great having friends who really knew you, but it was also fucking annoying.

"I don't, shithead. I'm not looking for long term." I may have wanted more than a fling, but that didn't mean marriage.

"Just because you're not looking doesn't mean it won't find you." Ben looked down at the menu.

"Did you turn into a psychologist when you were away?"

"No. I had time away from this pressure cooker of a small town to really think about what happened with Sheridan. You go to the cabin, I went to another country for a decade."

"Smart," I muttered.

"It was, but I missed home." I understood that and I wondered what on earth brought Annie here to Bright, all the way from England. My gut said it had something to do with whatever was fucking with her.

On Saturday morning, I'd considered telling my coach that I wasn't going to make the big road trip to Bonnie Doon with the team since it was a long weekend where I'd have an extra day at the cabin. But I'd bailed last weekend and if I didn't go, I wouldn't get to check in on Annie. Ben's words buzzed in my brain. He was turning into a real smart motherfucker. So, at eight thirty in the morning, with a huge coffee in hand, I boarded the team bus.

It was a cold and grey day in Bonnie Doon, that typical weather right as winter starts where everything is dead and miserable. But despite the chill factor, watching Annie in her netball dress was hot. She had defined, muscular legs, soft, creamy white skin, and when her dress flew up as she jumped, I got a few glimpses of her perfect, firm arse in her bike shorts. There was no doubt about it: she did it for me. Every. Damned. Time.

Finally, with all the games done, and enough hot dogs, meat pies, and soggy chips eaten by both sides, we boarded the bus to start the two-hour drive home. I was glad that the day had been relatively drama-free. Daphne had kept her claws retracted and I enjoyed continued radio silence from the woman who had been calling me for weeks. I was considering heading straight up to the cabin when we made it back into town.

When I heard Fleur, my head snapped around. "Annie. Are you all right? You look like you've seen a ghost." Fleur was right; Annie looked pale and ready to pass out.

"I need to check my messages," she replied, her voice eerily calm as she stood and walked to the back of the bus. Fleur started to follow, but I shot her a look that let her know that I had this. I followed Annie to the back where there were a few empty seats.

Annie didn't know I was standing by her seat as she sat in the back corner and listened to her voice mail. I watched her closely as I stood there, seeing the panic, worry, and fear written all over her face. Eventually she looked up as I leaned into the seat, surprised, then a heated flush of embarrassment covered her face.

"Are you okay?"

"No. I'm really fucking not."

Chapter 8

I watched the countryside fly by, unable to comprehend what was happening. I knew Erik was beside me, looking concerned as he sat partially forward, protecting me from any prying eyes. No tears were coming, not yet at least. I felt sick and numb, buzzing panic sounding in my ears. I needed to get home, drink a bottle of wine, and try to wrap my head around the voice mail I'd replayed three times.

I didn't know for how long I was staring out the window, but when Erik placed a big, warm hand on my thigh, reality finally penetrated and after blinking a few times, I took in my surroundings. It was almost dark, and we were close to home. I looked around the bus, hoping I wasn't drawing attention.

"You're fine, pixie," Erik murmured, and I glanced at him, feeling like I was looking at him for the first time. I craved his strength and warmth. He was crowding me protectively, giving me his soft blue eyes that held only worry, not judgment. He gave me a small encouraging smile and squeezed my thigh in support. The heat from his hand penetrated my pants and I found myself relaxing as I grabbed his hand, hoping he felt my appreciation.

"Ah…" I started, but I had no idea what to say.

"You don't have to say anything. We're good." He flipped my hand to link our fingers.

"I think I want to."

"I'll listen to whatever you have to say, but not here."

I nodded and leaned into him.

"Let's get off this bus, okay?"

"I'm getting dropped off at the Wandi Pub. I can walk home from there. Come with me?" My voice sounded small and desperate, and suddenly I was anxious he wouldn't help me.

"Sure thing. I'll organise takeaway and eat at your place, where it's private." He gave me a warm look that made my heart thud, before pulling out his phone. I sat back as I heard him order enough food for a small village. He never let go of my hand, and I didn't loosen my grip.

Most people exited the bus in town, with only a few exiting at the Wandi Pub. When the bus was empty, Erik stood, pulling me with him. We didn't speak, and I was glad for it. I didn't know where to start, what to say, and how he would take it. Outside in the cool air, I stood looking at the pub, wondering if we should go inside and get rip-roaring drunk. I'd spill my truth easier and the drink would take me to a happy place of oblivion.

Erik took charge. "Let me go get the food, then we can go to your place and you can tell me what has you breaking inside." He looked down and gave my shoulder a squeeze. The prospect of telling him what I'd done would probably mean there would be no mind-blowing sex in my future. Ever.

I heard myself say "sure," and he left me to think about what I wanted more, to tell him or to have him lie beside me. Desperately, I needed both. He returned minutes later with a big bag of amazing-smelling food, slung my bag over his shoulder then grabbed my hand.

"I can carry my bag. I may be an emotional train wreck but I can assure you, my limbs are fine," I told him as I led the way down the road toward my house.

"Pixie, I'm being chivalrous. Get with the program," he teased, and I felt a smile ghost across my lips. The moment our eyes had met on the back of that bus, everything had changed, and I couldn't say I wasn't relieved. We were quiet as we walked in the freezing night air, and I was thankful Erik knew I needed to be in a safe place before I could talk.

We headed up the small lane to my cottage, and the floodlights came on to light up the stone path and front porch. I peeked at Erik, wondering what he thought, to find him looking around with interest. I unlocked the front door and as we headed inside, I turned on the lights, leading him to the back of the house where the kitchen and living space were. I went straight to the fireplace to load and light it as Erik put the food on the counter then stood taking in my house.

"Let's drink," I said, sounding breathy and nervous. "Wine, beer, or something stronger?" I asked, finally able to function like a human being.

"What are you having?"

"I think it's a red wine kind of night."

"Perfect." Erik pulled the food out of the bags while I got wine, glasses, plates, and cutlery, and set them on the bench.

"I got a few things." He pointed to the containers. "I didn't know what you liked to eat."

"A few?" I asked, taking in the two chicken parms, steak, chips, and sticky chicken. I moved my hand to indicate my body. "I don't have room for that much."

"I've got it covered," he said, patting his stomach, and I felt my eyes drop to his torso, noticing his Henley clinging to his rock-hard abs. I moved my gaze back up his chest, and the pull of desire had me questioning my decision to tell him my story. When I made it back to his face, he was busy putting food on his plate, but I didn't miss the sexy half grin curving his full lips. Bloody hell.

"Let's eat in front of the fire," I said, desperate to move on from my ogling as I grabbed our wineglasses and the bottle, putting them on the coffee table, then returning for my meal. Erik sat at one end of the couch and I was up the other, both of us angled to face the other.

"You have a great place," he said, taking in the exposed beams.

"Thanks, I've been restoring it since I moved here."

"You did all this?"

"I had help. It seemed sad and neglected when I bought it, and I wanted to give her a new lease on life. It's cathartic work, restoring a place to its former glory." I took a big sip of wine, loving the burn. Erik smiled before digging in.

We ate in silence, and I tried to organise my thoughts but eventually the dread, confusion, and panic inspired by my brother's voice mail could not be kept at bay, and I could feel myself start to buckle under its weight.

"Annie." Erik gave a softly delivered command to look at him. I didn't want to, but there was no escaping it. So, I filled my glass with wine and then his, before nestling back in the couch.

"Here." He tapped the cushion directly beside him.

"It's fine," I said, not sure how I would cope being close to him.

"Pixie, *I* need you close," he insisted. I huffed then shuffled closer. Once I was within reaching distance, he yanked me against his body. Yelping, I didn't resist; I was too busy trying not to spill my wine. I did *not* waste wine. Even when I was having an emotional breakdown. A girl has her limits.

I settled into the couch and he put his arm around me, squeezing my shoulder. It took a moment for me to relax into him despite his warmth.

"Talk to me, Annie. Who left you a message?"

I drew in a deep breath and held it for a moment, feeling sick at the thought of sharing this, but Erik was right. It was time.

"My brother, Theodore."

"Is that unusual?"

"I haven't spoken to him in more than four years. Last time, he was in hospital unable to move." My voice cracked as I remembered my best friend and brother lying in bed with a brace holding his jaw in place, pins all down his legs, and his arms black and blue, giving me a look that let me know his injuries were all my fault.

Erik didn't say a word. He took my wine and put it on the table with his, then pulled me in even closer and his big calloused hand closed around mine. His show of comfort and support broke something in me, and the tears welled then ran down my cheeks as I moved to sit in his lap, resting my head in his neck, needing him all around me so I didn't break apart.

When his arms wrapped around me, securing me in place, I drew in a deep breath and started. "I grew up in Manchester with my parents and big brother Theodore. My parents thought Ted was perfect. He actually is and they wanted me to be exactly like him, but I wasn't made that way. I wanted to sneak out at night and see bands play at the pub.

"Ted understood me and would come with to make sure I was okay. He knew our parents were unfair to me. When he turned eighteen, he moved to London to go to university and I had to wait two long years before I could join him. Those two years were horrendous, and despite doing well at school and keeping out of trouble, I was never good enough. The day after I finished my A levels he took me to London to live with him.

"I'd been accepted to study physio and was going to work at his best mates' pub to pay my way. I was finally free and when I left my parents' home, it was the best day of my life."

I paused as Erik handed me my wine, and I took a long sip before continuing.

"When we arrived at my brother's tiny two-bedroom flat, I met his friend Paddy and fell in love on the spot. Paddy was larger than life. He was charming, funny, and made me feel like I was someone. It took only a few weeks before we had hooked up and I believed that I'd hit the jackpot. I'd fallen in love, stayed close to my brother, and was able to party and let loose.

"For a few years we all lived together and worked at the pub. Ted and I studied and Paddy worked full time. We would go out around London or hang at Paddy's pub, drinking too much beer into the wee hours of the morning. I don't know if I was too young to see it or perhaps I didn't want to, but Paddy started to drink less but seemed more excited. I had suspected he was doing drugs, but he acted like the same person most of the time.

"One day, Ted had gone home early and found Paddy with some guys snorting coke at our apartment. He was pissed, and told me what had happened. I defended Paddy because I loved and trusted him. I convinced Ted to let it go, then I talked to Paddy, and told him he needed to stop. He said he would and I believed him."

Erik sensed my growing agitation and reached for my glass again, then his. We both sipped silently before he took my glass and put it on the table next to his. I sighed and shook my head.

"Paddy and I carried on for a few more months as we had been. He decided to do a stint in Australia and I registered for the exchange program with the University of Melbourne. I was looking forward to us travelling together. I was sure we were heading in the right direction. Then the accident happened."

I stopped and sobbed. Erik held me close while rubbing my back in big, slow circles, telling me it was okay. When I reined in my emotions enough to speak, I began again.

"We were going to a party out of town and Paddy, who had been at the bar all day, was driving. Ted and I had a few drinks at home as we got ready and waited. When he came home to get us, he was more hyped up than usual and Ted accused him of being high. Paddy denied it and blindly, I believed him. I remember thinking that he *wouldn't* lie and figured Ted was being overly sensible. Ted ordered me to stay home, but I was too in love with Paddy and I got in the car."

I looked up to see if Erik was disgusted but found a mask of neutral calm staring back at me. In for a penny, in for a pound.

"Ted wouldn't let me go without him. He sat up front to keep an eye on Paddy. Ted was fuming and Paddy was equally pissed and drove like a madman. I sat in the back, not sure what to do. We were almost there when Paddy took a corner too fast and lost control. The car hit a tree on Ted's side. Glass shattered and the car caved in around him."

I said, letting a sob escaped from my soul, "Everything moved in slow motion. All I could do was sit there and watch metal and glass break my brother." I stopped, my heart shredding in my chest.

"Shhh, baby, it's okay," Erik murmured, kissing the top of my head. But it wasn't okay. I needed to finish.

"The ambulances came and took us all to hospital. Paddy and I were fine. A few cuts and bruises. Paddy was charged with driving under the influence. He admitted that he'd been snorting coke all afternoon at work. Poor Ted had a broken jaw, dislocated shoulder, damaged spine, and shattered femur.

"I waited with him in hospital, and when my parents arrived, I withstood their censure and accusations. Ted was in and out of consciousness, but when he was fully awake, he told me that I was blinded by Paddy's charm, and I needed to remember what that cost. My mother had pulled me out of the room and reinforced everything I knew was true. I had ruined my brother's life.

"I left the hospital and went home. My life was in shambles. Ted was in hospital and might never walk again. Paddy had big legal problems, and my parents hated me. I had already lined up my study in Melbourne so I sold everything I had and paid for a full year of rent for Ted, and told Paddy money was on deposit with a rehab facility for him to utilise when he was ready. I also told my parents I was leaving England, and they transferred what would have been my inheritance to my bank account and cut me out of their lives." I crumbled against him, and he stroked my back for what might have been minutes or years.

"Pixie, that was rough." Erik's voice brought me out of the vortex of pain and guilt.

"And avoidable."

"The accident wasn't your fault," he stated.

"I knew you were going to say that and I appreciate it, I really do. But Ted was right. I was caught up in the charm and the fun and didn't see the obvious. Thinking back now, I knew Paddy wasn't fit to drive. I also knew Ted would get in the car with me to keep me safe. But I did it anyway. I chose Paddy over my brother and look what happened. I ruined his life." I turned into Erik's neck, wanting to disappear beneath his skin. Eventually my tears slowed and my sobs abated. I pushed against him, letting him know I was ready to sit up, and he let me.

"So, that's my little story. Tragic, huh?"

"It is tragic, but it's not little, it's immense. How long have you been torturing yourself with this?"

"More than four years."

"And today?"

"Ted left me a voice mail. He said he'd been trying to find me, and that he wanted to speak to me. He didn't say anything else, only that he hoped I was okay." My chest ached at the thought of Ted, even now, giving me love I didn't deserve.

"Are you going to call him back?"

"I don't know. I want to. I'm afraid of how I will feel when I find out how hard his life has been because of me. Erik, he had to give up on his dreams, and is probably in a wheelchair for life. Because of me. I don't know how I can cope with that, and I hate myself for being a selfish coward."

"I get it, but you owe it to him to call back."

Erik was right. I didn't want him to be, but damn it, he was.

"I need to get my head clear before I talk to him."

"Annie, you can do anything if you put your mind to it." He brushed the hair out of my face with gentle tenderness that had the tears threatening again. It felt good to be touched this way.

"I'm such a coward. I've been hiding from this for years."

"No, you haven't been hiding." Erik's beautiful eyes filled with a quiet fierceness and held mine as he spoke. "You've been grieving. Consider what happened to you. Your brother was injured and you were too. Your boyfriend ended up being a drug addict and your parents disowned you. That is a lot to deal with. Paddy and your parents are responsible for their actions. You need to cut yourself some slack."

"Not so easy."

"The important things never are."

I returned to my position of my face planted in his neck, wanting a bit more of his strength and support. We sat for a long while, him holding me, letting me find my way out of the hurricane. When I could trust myself not to break apart again, I sat up.

"Go put the kettle on, and I'll stoke the fire," Erik said, gently pushing me off his lap. He had to steady me as I regained my balance after having my legs tucked up for too long. I looked down at him as he did this, his strong palms on my hips, looking at me with a warmth I hadn't expected. He didn't think I was a terrible person, and I still couldn't believe it.

"Thank you." I put my hands on his shoulders, leaned forward, and placed a soft kiss on his mouth.

I'd intended it to be quick, but once my lips hit his, I couldn't break the connection. He felt warm, strong, and steady, and I needed more. I licked his bottom lip, wanting to take the kiss further, to move away from where we had been and head toward something that felt good and right.

"Hey," he murmured. "You've had a rough couple of hours. You're too raw."

I shook my head. "I need this." I put my hand on his cheek. "I need you."

He stared at me for a long moment, then nodded and gave me what I wanted. He pulled my hips forward, forcing me to straddle his lap, and his tongue delved into my mouth, hot, wet, and deep.

He kept my hips grounded with one steely arm around my waist while the other snaked up my back to palm my nape. My hands were in his hair, holding him to me as I ground my hips down. I let out a frustrated moan when he pulled me back, breaking the kiss. Looking down at him, I could see his chest rising and falling as if he'd run a marathon.

"Annie, do you know what you're doing? Do you really want this?"

"I want to feel alive. To feel like something in life is good. I need everything you can give me."

Chapter 9

I knew what she wanted. What she needed. Fuck, I needed it too. But…she was reeling from her brother's call, and I was concerned that I was taking advantage of her. If she regretted this…us tomorrow, I wouldn't get over it. Which was fucked up. I wasn't looking for more. Was I?

When she told me she needed everything I could give her, seeing her pixie face full of vulnerability and desire flicked a switch in my soul. I wanted to…had to give her whatever she needed. Leaning in, I kissed her, fusing our lips as I thrust my tongue inside, demanding she tangle hers with mine. She responded instantly, letting out a little moan that went straight to my cock, which pushed painfully against my jeans. I adjusted her body so her core was over my hardness. She rotated her hips, and she used me to get off. Her greediness pushed the detonation button and after a few grinds and rotations my balls drew up. Christ, I hadn't come in my jeans since I was a kid.

Desperate to feel her skin against mine, I edged her back, pulled up her shirt, and she went straight for mine to return the favour. She wore a silky black bra that pushed her pert, perfect tits up and out. I leant forward to plant kisses on all that creamy goodness and took small bites along the edge of her bra, eliciting another breathy moan as she arched her back, offering me better access.

I caught a glimpse of a purple stone in her belly button and a tattoo of a bird's wing wrapped around her side. The dark ink was made more vivid by the paleness of her skin, and if all that wasn't enough to spike my need for her, the defined muscles of her stomach did me in. My firecracker pixie was hot as hell.

"You like what you see?"

"Fuck yeah," I murmured before kissing her neck and chest as I ran my hands up her sides to grip her and rub my thumbs over her hard nipples. Her hips jerked against my erection in a way that had me sucking in a breath.

After reaching back and removing her bra, I sucked one little pink nipple into my mouth. Annie's hands were in my hair, gripping tight as she held me to her breasts. The noises coming out of her were needy and raw.

"Fuck, Erik. Please," she moaned when my teeth pulled on her nipple.

"We'll get there." I wanted to last, but my dick needed freedom and I let her undo my jeans and yank down my underwear.

She went up on her knees to give her space to free me. The feel of her small, hot hand wrapped around my length was almost too much. I threw my head against the couch, sucking in a breath. When she rubbed her thumb around the head, spreading the precum, I almost lost it.

"Slow down, pixie," I managed to get out before she did another sweep over the sensitive tip.

"I don't want to." She dropped her head into my neck and murmured, "We'll go slower on the second round." In the midst of this blinding desire, I had the presence of mind to remember, my girl needed care.

"Sounds like a plan," I said, lifting her off me. She seemed unsure of my intentions until I undid her jeans and pulled them down her legs to expose a silky black scrap of material covering her sex. She gasped as I rubbed my thumb against her folds while I held her gaze, giving her a hum of approval. Without breaking eye contact, I lowered her jeans to the floor and she stepped out of them. Then I kissed her hipbones and the soft skin below her belly button. Then I kissed lower, directly over her clit. I grinned at the wetness I felt there, and her head fell back as her hips rolled into my mouth.

I loved her greediness. It was honest, and it felt like she was letting her guard down. Her enthusiasm and sweet-tasting pussy were doing nothing for my self-control. I agreed with her—we needed to take the edge off, and I didn't think we'd make it to the bedroom.

Reluctantly, I pulled back then fished around in my pocket for my wallet and pulled out a condom. She moved away from the couch and waited for me as I stood, my undone jeans riding low. I toed out of my shoes and pushed my jeans all the way down. I wanted to laugh when her eyes dropped to my cock that was stiff as a board and pointing straight at her, saying loud and proud, "I pick you."

"Do you think it will fit?"

I laughed, and her eyes followed my bobbing dick. I was going to have fun remembering this moment when I wasn't desperate to be inside her. Eventually, her gaze moved slowly up my body and when it met mine, I could see hers was hazy with desire. It was a fucking sexy look, and when she bit her lip, I was done for.

I tore open the condom and rolled it on before grabbing her around the waist and lifting her up. She let out a cute squeak as I moved a hand under her fine arse and the other into her short-cropped hair. She wrapped her legs tight around my hips and her arms went around my shoulders.

"I'm heavier than I look," she murmured.

"Nah, pixie. I have you." I moved us to the nearest wall. "I can't wait," I muttered as I shifted her underwear to the side and positioned myself at her entrance.

"Me neither," she said, pushing her hips down, sucking in a breath as she took me all the way in.

"Faaark," I groaned as her hot, wet, tight-as-all-fuck pussy clenched around me. I took a moment to enjoy the feel of her, and to be honest if I started moving without collecting myself it would be a short show. She didn't give me long; she started rotating her hips, letting me know to get a move on.

"Okay, pixie, I hear you." I kissed behind her ear and shifted a hand between her legs to play with her clit as I started to thrust inside.

"Erik. Fuck. So. Good." Her words were punctuated with each drive inside her and it didn't take long of rubbing circles at her sensitised flesh to feel the ripples of her orgasm start.

"I'm. Fuck. Come. Ing," she panted as I drove her against the wall, her core clenching my dick like a fist.

My body was straining, holding back as she came so I could enjoy every moment. When she stopped shuddering from her orgasm, I moved away from the wall, placed both hands under her arse, and drove into her. She gripped my neck tightly, moving with me, a small puff of breath leaving her each time she took me to the hilt. She weighed practically nothing and I wasn't gentle about it as I drove her down onto me. She hung on tight as I picked up speed, bouncing her on my dick. I was close to coming and when a second orgasm hit her and she screamed, her tits pushing into my face, I lost it and thrust inside her as deep as I could as I emptied into the condom.

"How many condoms do you have?" she asked, still breathing heavily. I squeezed her tight and shook with laughter, feeling sated and light after what we had shared. She was even sexier like this, swollen lips, hair askew and sweaty, and her eyes were completely unguarded. My dick twitched and her eyes went huge. "Bloody hell, you do have that pillaging Viking blood in you," she teased, giving me a mischievous smile.

I grinned. "You bet. Now, where's the bed?"

"Down the hall on the left."

I walked with us still connected while she gave me big eyes and an astonished smile until I found her bedroom. This was her private space, and I felt privileged to be in there. Gently I laid her down and pulled out.

"Bathroom?" I needed to get the used condom off my cock.

"Next door," she said, lying back on the bed, moving some of the cushions onto the floor.

I needed to take care of business and get another condom, but the sight of her sprawled like that had my mouth watering.

"You okay?" she asked as I stood there perving on her.

"You're beautiful, you know that?" By the blush on her face, I guessed she didn't know.

"You are too," she replied shyly, and I waggled my brows, causing her to grin and roll her eyes. I liked her sass as much as I liked the rare soft looks she gave me.

"I'll be back, and those panties better be gone by the time I am."

I headed to the bathroom and was yet again impressed by her design although the tub was a little concerning. If she sat in it, she'd drown. After cleaning up, I headed back to the living room to grab our wines and my other condom before heading back to her. She wasn't sprawled on the covers any longer. She lay with the sheets turned down on her side with her head in her hand, completely naked. She gave me a smile when she saw the wine and patted the bed, giving me a sultry look.

"It's my last one," I told her as I threw the packet on the bedside table then handed over her wine.

"Let's make it count then." She moved into me as I lay down.

I rolled her to her back and kissed her hot, slow, and deep. I wanted to savour her this time, taste her, touch her, and feel her skin under my fingers. She shifted beneath me so I was cradled between her legs. It felt good to have her hands roaming the skin on my back, her warmth all around me, the smell of her lightly fragranced hair intoxicating me.

Our kiss started slowly, but before long we were at each other, our bodings shifting and rubbing, building the pleasure once more. I broke the kiss to start my journey down her body. I wanted to taste more of her. I lavished attention on her perfect tits, and her moans let me know that she liked what I was doing.

I moved to her flat stomach, and when I made it to her navel, I kissed her small hollow before sucking the purple stone into my mouth. It was my turn to moan low, letting her know what I liked. Her hips started to buck up as her need built and I teased her a moment longer before I moved, my shoulders spreading her legs wide, revealing her pretty pink pussy.

My thumb moved in slow circles over her clit, and I loved how her body bucked under my touch. I looked up to see her watching me and I grinned. She blushed, but the excitement on her face communicated that she was ready, so I parted her lips and licked her. Her eyes went wide before growing hazy as I lapped at her. I kept my gaze on her, and she was doing her best to look at me, but when I put a finger, then two inside her, she lost the battle and threw her head back on the pillow.

Feeling my own need growing, I moved my face over her folds and began tasting, licking, sucking, and nipping at her clit, while pumping my fingers inside her. She grew even wetter and moaned as I felt her walls clasp my fingers. I pushed her harder, needing her to come in my mouth and on my tongue. My beautiful, fiery pixie didn't disappoint as she detonated. I lapped at her a little longer, loving the quivers and aftershocks before I moved up the bed.

"You're amazing. I knew you would be, but holy hell, that was…well… the best," she said, looking at me with hooded, lust-filled eyes. I loved compliments but that she knew I would be able to pleasure her had my heart thumping a little harder. I liked that she had been thinking about it because so had I.

"You ready for me again?" I asked, not wanting to work her too hard.

"Always," she murmured, rubbing her hands up my arms to my neck to pull me down for a kiss. I think her words had come out unconsciously, and my heart gave an almighty thud. I let her know how I felt by deepening the kiss, rubbing my now aching cock against her slick pussy. I put the condom on then nestled back between her legs. Up on my elbows, I looked down at her, taking in her eyes full of fire and lips parted in anticipation, before I slowly slid inside.

She arched then spread her legs wider, letting me in even deeper, and I hissed as her pussy clenched around me.

"Having you inside makes me want to come," she murmured.

"Don't do that. I want to take my time," I told her, rocking my hips slowly. I held my body off her, my arms tired, but I was conscious of how much bigger than her I was.

"I like the feel of you on me. I can take it," she said, pulling me to her for a kiss that let me know she wanted me there. I went with it, shifting to one elbow and letting her take some of my weight. I'd intended to take it easier this time, but she felt so fucking good the struggle to hold back was real. When she hitched a leg up to my side to get me in deeper, my resolve broke. I grabbed her thigh and started to move harder and faster, her breathing increasing in time with mine. Our rhythm was hot and smooth, as though we had been lovers for years, and before long I was ready to come.

"Pixie," I hissed as I tried to hold myself back.

"Erik." She tilted her hips up as I thrust deep inside her. It hit right where she needed and she came hard, clamping onto my cock. I joined her, hoping the roar that sounded in my head wasn't as loud for her as it was for me.

I took a moment to enjoy the feel of emptying myself into her as she pulsed around me. I stroked in a few more times before slowly coming to rest, breathing hard and feeling exhausted. I let her take my weight because I was spent and the feel of her softness under me was too good to give up. We lay for long moments, me nuzzling her neck while she slowly rubbed her hands up and down my back. When I heard her laboured breathing, I shifted to my back, pulling her with me.

"You good, pixie?"

"I'm better than that. You?" she asked, getting up on an elbow to look down at me.

"Same," I said, taking her in. She was smiling, giving me warmth and honesty that hit me hard in the chest.

"I need to take care of the condom."

"Let's shower, you gave me a workout, lumberjack. I don't get this hot and sweaty when I run," she joked.

"I thought I was a Viking," I corrected, getting out bed and waiting for her to join me.

"You're both," she replied, giving me a wink before leading me to the bathroom.

I didn't know if it was a gift or a curse that I had only two condoms on me. I wanted her, and watching the water run over her body in a hot, steamy shower had my dick perking up, but I was also tired and needed sleep. I could tell she was exhausted too, both physically and emotionally.

We fell asleep, my pixie in my arms, her back to my front, our legs tangled. This was something I had little experience with, but with Annie, it felt natural and I was surprised when I woke early Sunday morning to find that while we had changed sleeping positions, we were still connected.

Conditioned from my job, I was an early riser. Wanting to let her sleep, I left the bed, thinking she looked tiny amongst the pillows and sheets. I could almost miss her lying there if it weren't for the shock of black hair against the white cotton. I used the bathroom and had another quick shower to wake myself up properly. I could smell her all around me. The scent was pear and magnolia according to the shower soap. That I was aware of how she smelled and waxing poetic about it was utterly terrifying. We had shagged, sure, but I was taking it somewhere else entirely.

Needing some distance from how-much-I-liked-Annie overload, I headed to the living space to get the fire going and clean our dishes from dinner last night. I picked up her clothes that were strewn all over the floor, a good reminder of how hot and heavy it had been.

I looked through her cupboards for coffee only to find a truckload of Yorkshire tea. With nothing for it I put the kettle on and examined her fridge. If I thought I lived like a bachelor, then Annie outdid me ten to one. I managed to find some bread in the freezer, butter, and marmalade along with fresh fruit and muesli. My hankering for bacon and eggs would have to wait. I got everything ready for when she got up, made myself possibly the worst coffee I'd ever had, and moved to the French doors that opened out onto a small, half-completed deck.

It was a pretty spot she had here; the tall mountains at the back were half covered in sunlight, half dark green in the shade. I loved Wandiligong; it was a beautiful place and I was lucky enough to get to work here from time to time. I wondered why she chose here and not closer to Bright as her home base, but something told me it was because she was all about keeping people at arm's length. Now I knew a little more about her, I could see it was her way of protecting herself.

Her story was fucking tragic, and I *hated* that she had spent years punishing herself for putting her brother in a wheelchair. Clearly, she loved him, but him calling her surely forced her to relive what had happened. I didn't know how I would react if I was in her situation, but I would to call back to find out. Hiding from the past only made you think about it more. I knew that from experience.

I checked my watch to see it was nearly eight, and I remembered I was all packed and ready to head up to the cabin, given tomorrow was a public holiday. I still wanted to get up there, but I also wanted to make sure Annie was okay. Then I laughed. Who was I kidding? I simply wanted to be near her. The sex was amazing, but something had changed between us, and I didn't know what it meant. We were closer than merely lovers, but we weren't in a relationship either. My offer had been for good sex, and she had asked me to scratch an itch. I needed to slow my roll and stick to the plan. Good sex, good times, and then, good-bye.

Such bullshit since I spent the next ten minutes trying to work out how I was going to ask her to come to the cabin with me.

Chapter 10

It had been a long time since I had woken up feeling *that* type of sore. The good, achy, well-sated and well-orgasmed type of sore and this morning, I had *that* feeling so bad I wanted more. But as I opened my eyes and blinked away the sleep, I looked around my room to find it empty. When I listened for movement, I couldn't hear anything other than the light breeze ruffling the leaves outsides. So, I was alone.

At my realisation that Erik had gone, the disappointment weighed heavy in my chest and stomach. I knew I shouldn't be disappointed. His offer had only been for sex, no strings attached, and I'd taken him up on that offer. But I'd also exposed myself last night, spewing out my horrible tale, and that changed things. Well, it changed things for me at least because I felt connected to him after unleashing my horrible past. After that was done, however, I had proceeded to use him for sexual activity that led to my mental oblivion. I guess I had to own it and deal with it if his intentions hadn't changed.

I really had no good reason to feel betrayed that he wasn't still here in bed with me, but I still felt ill at ease. I should be pleased with all he gave me because he had certainly delivered. There was a reason he was considered a charmer and a lady killer, and that gave me pause for a different reason.

I'd only been with one man before in my life: Paddy. But Erik's prowess last night clearly demonstrated he had plenty of practice. He was also charismatic, fun, and handsome—a deadly combination. Paddy had been a charmer and had had a string of lovers before I hit town, but he had nothing on Erik. Erik had a way of connecting physically and mentally, making sure you were both in the moment and that the pleasure was mutual. I also felt his love of sex; he was completely open about being right there with you, wringing every last drop of pleasure from it. It was freeing because of his honest desire, and that had helped me let down my guard and be with him. At the time, it had also extinguished any lingering feelings of inexperience on my part, and I'd had the time of my life. Perhaps he'd want to do it again some time?

As I lay in bed contemplating how that was going to work in reality, my mind turned to how we had ended up together. Then I huffed out a breath as I threw my head back on the pillow, the guilt hitting me like a tonne of bricks. I was worrying about booty calls when I should've been thinking about why my big brother needed to talk to me. He'd obviously gone to considerable effort to reach me, and I knew I had to find out why. But my mind kept on straying to the big, blond, muscled Viking-lumberjack who had giving me the most pleasurable night of my life instead of the impending discussion with my brother whose life I had ruined. I'd worn my guilt like a shroud, but after one night with Erik, I'd started to forget how to hide behind it.

Unable to wallow any longer, I got out of bed and threw on my robe before heading into the bathroom. It was clear Erik had showered before he left that morning. I tried not to think about him in the shower and remember how he had looked with water and soap suds on his big beautiful body, but it was a struggle. He was enormous and not only because I was small in comparison. He had a huge, broad chest with a smattering of blond hair that got darker as it travelled down over hard abs to his glorious cock. That particular part of him was also impressive, not only in length, but in girth, and the way it sat nestled at the top of thick thighs. Watching him clean himself in the shower had been one of the sexiest things I'd ever seen.

The thought of him stroking his hard dick had me almost stumbling and breaking my bloody neck as I stepped under the spray. I needed to stop thinking about him naked or else I wouldn't get anything done and would most likely end up in a neck brace.

As I showered, I went over my plans, needing to return to the here and now and not spend any more time in fantasyland. First, I was going wait for Erik to make a move. The deal was sex with no strings. I needed to remember that and stop hoping he'd call me. Clearly he felt comfortable in my space, which was a good sign. Second, I was going to go on the hike of all hikes, come home exhausted, and have a soak in my bath. Third, after dinner I was going call my brother. My stomach dropped at the thought, but Erik was right: I owed it to him to call.

Once I'd showered, brushed my teeth, combed my hair, and moisturised, I put my robe back on and headed to the kitchen in desperate need of tea only to stop dead when I saw the fire was roaring, and the bench laid out with plates, bread, every condiment I owned, and a platter of fruit. What on earth? I snapped my head around, searching the space like I was possessed, to find Erik at the French doors, looking at me over his shoulder, cup in hand, smirk on his face. I must have continued my cartoon character routine as my eyes went wide as it sunk in that my melancholy was for naught.

"Good morning, pixie," he rumbled, his smirk turning into a smile that said he thought I was adorable and comical.

"Erik the Viking," I said, realising I'd never before made fun of him being a Monty Python character. He rolled his eyes at my reference, clearly having heard it all before.

"Let me put the kettle on. It's clear you dig fucking tea, but I wasn't game to make it." He strode into the kitchen to flick the switch while I stood rooted to the spot like an idiot.

"Toast?" he asked, pulling the bread out of the bag and holding it like he needed to make sure I knew what it was.

"Ah, yeah," I said like I didn't, in fact, know what it was. He put it in the toaster, then turned to me.

"Get over here, Annie. It looks like you're freaking out, but you don't need to. It's just toast," he said, putting on a show of confidence, but I could see him watching me, assessing my reaction. He probably thought I was regretting all we'd done last night given I was looking at him shocked that he was still present in my space. But I didn't regret it at all, and seeing him in my kitchen made my stomach feel the good kind of squishy. All I could think of was asking when we could compete in the bedroom Olympics again. But I was English. I should be reserved and polite. So, I managed to knuckle down and not lock in another bedroom date, but I also wanted to make sure he wasn't worried. I moved to him in the kitchen, planted a hand on his flat abs then leaned up to give him a quick kiss. A friendly sort of kiss. Sort of.

"Hey," I said, looking at him, letting him know where I was at. He seemed to relax and gave me a big smile that had me wondering if *I* had any condoms anywhere in the house.

"Hey," he said, coming back for a longer, deeper kiss that had me clinging to him, needing the contact of his hard body. Before the kiss got out of hand, which was where I wanted it to go, he ended it. I was pleased to note that at least he was breathing heavy and there was a hardness in his jeans communicating that we were on the same page. The kettle clicked off, breaking our moment, and he put his hands on my hips then lifted me up on to the bench. I let out a girlish squeal then swore at my inability to play it cool.

"You don't have to demonstrate how strong you are by picking me up all the time," I quipped.

"You didn't mind last night, especially when I was bouncing you on my cock," he said, giving me a wicked grin that had me quivering as he brought the tea, the pot, and the kettle over.

"No need to be so cocky," I sassed, but it was too breathy to be taken seriously.

"Besides, I like picking you up. It makes me feel manly."

"Darling, you have nothing to worry about in that department," I said, setting about making tea, realising too late that I'd called him darling. Shit. Maybe he didn't hear it. This was about sex, and I needed to remember that.

"Yeah? How so?" he asked with a teasing grin, not missing a beat.

"Well, you wear your masculinity very comfortably," I muttered, focusing on the task at hand, not wanting to go further down this path.

"Please, explain it to me," he said in mock confusion.

"Well, you have muscles," I blurted, sounding like a fool.

"I do, but so do you. How are they feeling this morning, by the way?" he asked, giving me a knowing look.

"Like they've had a workout." He chuckled at this, nodding his agreement.

"Lots of people have muscles, what else?" he asked, moving to me, parting my knees and stepping in close. I held my breath, looking directly into his gorgeous eyes, feeling a bit hazy as they glittered.

"You're tall."

"Height doesn't mean you're masculine."

"Well, you have a really big, thick neck," I managed and he laughed again.

"You make me sound like a professional rugby player," he fake grumbled. He was an Australian Rules Footballer and proud.

"You don't have that physique. You're more lithe than that."

"Lithe doesn't sound masculine."

"It can be. And you have a beard," I said, my eyes dropping to his mouth, my brain beginning to disengage.

"Hmm." He licked his lips.

"And you have long hair but don't look like a girl or a wanker," I said, not really paying attention to what I was rambling on about. I was caught in his snare, happily. At this comment, he smiled wide and showed me his white teeth. Like the idiot I was, I sighed.

"I do wank though," he said, his words conjuring images in my mind that had me shuffling forward, wanting his hard bits to contact my soft, now wet bits.

"You do?" I heard someone who sounded like me ask this question. He leant forward now, placing a small kiss under my ear and scooting me forward so I was flush against his erection. I groaned at the contact.

"Yeah. Sometimes, I do it thinking about you."

"Me?" I breathed as I let my head fall back, and I ran a hand into his still-damp hair.

"Yes, you," he said as he planted kisses up and down my neck as he worked at his jeans, then releasing himself.

"What about me do you think about?" I asked, some inner vixen taking over, thankfully leaving Annie the fumbling Brit behind.

"Your pretty pink nipples," he murmured as he started to stroke himself, the knuckles of his hands rubbing through my exposed, slick folds, flicking my clit with each stroke.

"I like your nipples too," I said, wondering where the vixen had gone because that sounded lame.

"I've been thinking about your tight, firm ass," he murmured.

"I think about your bottom too." Vixen gone. Shit.

"Yeah?" he purred, moving his hand a bit faster, and I sucked in a breath.

"Yeah." In the background, I heard the toast pop up but I couldn't have given the first shit.

"What else?" he asked, holding my eyes as he pumped himself and rubbed against me.

"How your eyes are blue like the ocean near the Maldives. I call them holiday eyes." I felt his body shake a little with laughter.

"I like your eyes too, they're bewitching. So, are my eyes, nipples, and *bottom* all you think about?" He kept moving, rubbing my clit harder and faster. My inner thighs tightened around his hips and I gripped his hair tight, my body getting close.

"That you're fucking sexy in your lumberjack outfit, especially when you smell like sawdust. And diesel fuel. And you also have nice arms. And legs. And chest. Jaw. And hips. Fuck. And. Beard. Did I already mention your beard?" I said ridiculously as I got closer and closer to the edge. As my core started to pulse, he found my mouth, kissing me hard as he pumped impossibly fast, bringing me to an earth-shattering orgasm. Two, three, four more pumps and he groaned into my mouth, his fist closing over the head of his cock while his hips jerked as he found his release.

I kept my lips pressed to his as we both came down, our breathing returning to near normal after being ragged. When I was in control of my faculties once more, I pulled back to look at him. His eyes were hazy with lust, but also with satisfaction and a little bit of humour.

"I love your dirty talk," he said, taking me in. No doubt I was looking at him like a punch-drunk teenager.

"What?" I asked, confused. I was pretty sure he was the one doing the sexy talk.

"Maldives? Sawdust? Diesel fuel?" He was grinning lazily, but as my lunatic ravings came back to mind, and heat filled my cheeks at how ridiculous I sounded, he gave me a flat-out smile.

"It was sexy," he said, kissing me with a conviction that suggested he did, in fact, find my words sexy. Well, that was a relief. He stepped back, nodded toward the bathroom before walking away, where I presumed he went to clean himself up. Once he was gone, I got down from the bench, needing a moment to steady my legs, before I put more toast on and finished with the tea. He returned as I buttered the toast and handed him a stack.

"Thanks," he said, taking it from me before taking a stool at the bench. We both set about getting something to eat, and as the post-orgasm euphoria left me, reality took its place. I was still not sure where we stood, and I still had to speak to my brother. As though sensing my thoughts, Erik spoke.

"When will you call your brother?"

"Around dinner time. He'll be awake then," I said, fear at what he might say gripping me once more.

"Are you okay to do that? You should take a day or two if you need it."

"No, he was calling for a reason. I need to front up to what I've done and call him back."

"You haven't done anything," he said, leaning into me.

"It's because of me that he ended up in a wheelchair. Not to mention how I ran away like a coward."

"Annie, you ran away because they made you." I could sense a little frustration in his voice, and I understood it. He didn't see it how I did. He hadn't lived it.

"Anyway, I am going to call him tonight. Otherwise, I will sit around obsessing over it."

"On that," Erik started to say almost hesitantly. It was a strange tone for such a confident man. "I'm heading up to my cabin on Dinner Plain this morning. I'll stay overnight given we've got tomorrow off. Did you want to…come with me?" he said as though he wasn't asking me away for the weekend. I swallowed hard. "No pressure, it's a good place to get away and you can call your brother in peace. But if you have somewhere to be—"

"I don't," I cut him off before I could stop myself.

"Okay. So, you'll…come?"

"Um. Sure. Sounds good," I said, feeling nervous. There was no need to feel nervous. We were grown-ups.

"Cool. It will take your mind off everything," he said as he lifted his mug to his lips. I nodded, knowing how well us spending time together last night had worked to take my mind off everything. The sex had been amazing and if our countertop session this morning was anything to go by, he had more tricks in the bag. I needed to remember he was *only* offering sex.

"You did a good job of that last night," I said, forcing a wink as I stood and cleared our plates. He gave me a strange, fleeting look as though I'd inflicted some pain, but he followed it with a cocky smile.

"Well, practice makes perfect, right?" he said, standing and helping me clear up. It was a weird comment, but I could tell from the way he focused on cleaning up that the conversation was over. Once breakfast was done, we headed to my car so I could drive him home. He'd then pick up his car and come back to collect me. We headed out to my car but when I stood at my open door, I saw him looking at me like I was insane.

"What?" I asked when he just stood there.

"Woman," he said as if that was supposed to communicate something other than my gender.

"What?"

"Woman."

"Why are we talking about my gender?" I asked, not sure why he was repeating himself.

"No," he said, sounding frustrated.

"No what?" I sassed, knowing I wasn't the one being cryptic.

"No I am not getting in that car," he growled.

"Why the hell not?" I looked at my car. It looked like it always did. I loved my Mini Cooper, it was red and black, and I always kept it clean and shiny.

"It's a Mini."

"So?" Clearly, I was not understanding him.

"And I have a dick. I think you're familiar with it, yeah?"

"Now you're *being* a dick."

"And?" he asked stubbornly.

"And get in the damned car." He was being utterly ridiculous.

"Firecracker, I am not getting in that car."

"Is this about you being masculine? Because I don't think this qualifies as a positive masculine trait. You're being ridiculous."

"I am not," he defended.

"Yes you are." I had my hands on my hips, incredulous that he was being this way.

"No, I'm not," he answered, putting his hands on his hips..

"Fine. I'll see you later," I said, getting in the car, starting the engine and slowly heading down the driveway. I saw him in the rear-view mirror, hands still on his hips, shaking his head.

As I reached the road, I stopped and he grabbed the bag he'd dropped at his feet and stalked down the driveway. When he reached the car, he yanked the door open, gave me a look that said I needed to keep my mouth shut, before starting to lower himself into the passenger seat. I say *started* because when he was halfway in, it became clear that he wasn't going to fit, not really. He grunted a few times, jerked the seat back as far as it would go, then folded himself in. His head was on the roof, tilted to the side, and his knees were around his ears. So, this was the reason he didn't want to get in. It was a good one. He looked utterly ridiculous, like a huge Viking-lumberjack pretzel in a clown car. I felt a laugh bubble up my throat, but he stopped me.

"Don't."

"Don't what?" I asked, feeling my body shake as I looked at him, tears threatening to spill.

"Drive. Just. Fucking. Drive," he growled, giving me a glacial side eye. I decided it would be prudent to do as I was told.

As we drove through Bright in the early morning, my interest at where he lived grew. He had a larger-than-life personality and knew everyone in the community so I assumed he lived somewhere people spent time with him. But when we pulled into the small driveway flanked by old units, I was completely taken aback. It wasn't a halfway house, but it was close. There were plastic chairs out the front of the units, and a few were occupied by old men smoking and drinking coffee.

"Right here," Erik said, pointing to a unit with a big land cruiser parked out the front. I pulled in beside it, looking at what must be his door to seeing nothing that said "home" in sight. I made a move to undo my seatbelt, but he was out of the car quickly, poking his head back in the doorway. His face was blank and his tone void of any emotion.

"I'll pick you up in thirty, and I'll get some coffee." Without waiting for my response, he went to his door, unlocked it then entered, leaving me scratching my head.

***

It was my turn to laugh when Annie tried to hike herself up into my truck. I had finished putting her bag in the tray to see her preparing to climb in. In her defence, I had bigger tires on the truck since I was off-road often. But it wasn't only humour I felt. No, the ever-present lust was there as I eyed her jean-clad ass. Lust. I needed to remember that this was about lust. Last night we had crossed a line. It was the line I had been pushing to cross for weeks, and the sex had been astounding. But part of me knew we'd done more than that. She'd shared her deepest secrets and fallen apart in front of me. I felt like I was one of the few people to have seen it and her openness with me meant as much as her trust in me to pleasure her sexually. But I wasn't sure if it meant that we were more than lovers.

After picking her up and putting her in my truck, then listening to her tell me she could do it on her own, and that I didn't need to compensate for a little dick with a big truck because I didn't, in fact, have a little dick (her words, not mine), we started out up the mountain in the sunshine. It was supposed to be sunny until late afternoon when a storm would come in. I expected that we would get our first real dose of snow and had packed provisions accordingly. During our drive we kept conversation light, sticking to safe topics like netball and football. She received a return call from a friend she was clearly worried about, and after she shared with me a brief tale of woe of her friend Hannah. It was interesting hearing her recount the events and her take on it—clearly she was all about relationships when it came to her friends, but not for herself.

As we drove through the town of Mount Hotham, she started to pay keen attention.

"How long have you had the cabin?" she asked.

"It was my grandfather's. He was a builder who helped put up the ski resorts. It started out as a shack, and Dad made it more liveable for my mother and me, but after she left, he let it slide. Since he died, I've been fixing it up. It's where I like to spend my time. I only keep a unit in town for somewhere to crash during the week," I said, trying to brush over where I lived. She'd been interested to see it when she'd dropped me off, but that was no place to take any woman, especially Annie.

"How long ago did your mum leave?" she asked hesitantly.

"She went home to Sweden a long time ago," I said, looking out the window, sighing. It was enough of a message for her to change tack, and I was grateful.

"Do you ski?" she asked as we headed toward the township of Dinner Plain.

"I snowboard and I have a snowmobile. But I also mountain bike and hike, which is perfect for the summer months up here."

"The best of both worlds," she said, and I smiled. I liked that she was into the outdoors. When we drove past the town turnoff, I could see her looking around, confused.

"My place is actually in Cobungra. I say Dinner Plain so people know where I am talking about."

"Australians have such strange names for places. Cobungra. Porepunkah. Wandiligong."

"We're strange people."

"No stranger than anywhere else I'm afraid," she said ruefully.

We were quiet once more before I pulled off the main road onto a dirt track edged by gum trees. Annie started to look around in earnest now, probably worried where I was taking her.

"Don't worry, I'm not an axe murderer."

"That's a relief." She laughed. "As long as you pinky-promise not to kill me, then that's fine." I grinned and offered her my pinky.

After a few hundred meters I turned into the cabin's drive and drove up to the shack. Well, shack wasn't fair anymore. It was a log cabin, set into the mountain with a large outdoor paved area to the side, overlooking a small dam. It was beautiful, especially with patches of snow all around. I looked at Annie to gauge her reaction and like most things she did, it was priceless. Her amethyst eyes were huge and her mouth was slightly parted but smiling.

"Wow. Erik, this is beautiful." Her appreciation of my place made me smile too. I was proud and her opinion mattered. Probably too much but I wasn't about to delve down that rabbit hole. I pulled under the carport, next to the giant woodpile, and turned off the engine.

"That's a lot of wood," Annie said as she opened the door and jumped down. It *was*, given the pile went the length of the carport and was stacked three rows deep.

"The house doesn't have any other heating, but you're right, my woodpile is obscene. My father, like many mountain men, was obsessed with collecting firewood. I picked up where he left off. That way, if there is a zombie apocalypse, I can stay warm."

"You might be hungry, but at least you won't freeze to death."

I handed her her bag, grabbed my own then the Esky with all the perishable food in it, and nodded for her to follow me up the stone steps to the front door. Setting everything down, I unlocked the door and walked in, but Annie wasn't following me. She was caught on the view of the dam, with some kangaroos barely out of the tree line enjoying the sun.

"They can be pests you know," I called out, but she didn't turn her head.

"People oversees think Australia is full of kangaroos and koalas. Or at least we hope it is. Then you meet Aussies in the cities and they say they don't see them that much. But if you leave the city, you do get a good dose of the wildlife. It's incredible." She didn't take her eyes off the view, seemingly mesmerised, and I moved to her.

"Come on inside and I'll show you around." She jumped at my words, clearly lost in the moment and not hearing my approach. With a slight blush she looked up at me with an unusual look in her eyes, like she was trying to figure me out. I didn't know why—it really wasn't that hard.

"Sounds good," she said, giving me a warm smile that reached her eyes and it, along with her soft voice, did a number on me. I was stuck looking at her, somehow caught in her snare. We stood for a long moment, gazing into each other's eyes until she blinked rapidly, like she was snapped out of a trance.

"Bloody holiday eyes," she muttered as she walked past me into the house, and I huffed a chuckle.

I showed her around and pointed out all I'd done. She was impressed with the high ceilings and glass that overlooked the pond, and wooden panelling and herringbone tile splashback I'd done in the kitchen. After I'd put the food in the fridge and listened to her gush about the stools I'd made from reclaimed timber, we walked down the hall and I pointed out the bathroom, the main bedroom, and the spare room.

"Erik, your home is beautiful. I love the use of wood; it belongs here but is also made for comfort. You didn't want to be a builder like your grandfather?" she asked as she ran her hands over the smooth wood panelling in the hall as we walked back to the kitchen.

"My dad started working for the plantations and got me a part-time job there when I was in high school. I liked being outside to work and the places we ended up out in the bush are pretty spectacular. I worked my way up but now I do more computer work than I'd like."

"I love being outdoors too, but the human body fascinated me and I started studying physio. I'm not into blood and guts so being a doctor was no good."

We talked about our careers as we unpacked the rest of the food and I put the kettle on. She seemed more comfortable with something to do, so I left out cold meat and bread for our lunch and she busied herself with that while I lit the fire.

Sitting at the small table in front of the big windows, we ate while making plans: we'd go for a hike around Victoria Falls then come back, and she would call her brother while I made dinner.

She nodded, the solemness returning to her face. I didn't envy her, but at least she wasn't alone.

Chapter 11

We had been trekking for a few hours before we reached the falls that were teeming after the rain, the spray icy as it hit my skin. Erik was fit and he had set a good pace considering he was recovering from an ankle injury. He shook his head when I'd insisted on taping it before we left, but he let me do it. I would be strung up in the town square if I allowed any more damage to the Bright Bruisers' star forward.

We'd tried to talk, but we were breathless, so we slowed down. I asked him questions about his renovations, yet another thing we had in common. I was surprised how easily we fit and had common ground to base deeper conversations. I'd thought he was simply a good time boy who was loved for his looks and his skill with a football. But as I'd been learning, that assumption was wrong and I shouldn't have been judgmental. He was a gentle soul really, cared about the environment, loved being part of the community, in addition to being a good listener and a respectful, generous lover. After a brief stop at the falls with a thermos of coffee and a KitKat, we walked back as night came in around us.

It was another of those times when the environment fit my mood exactly. It got darker and colder as we headed toward his cabin, and my eyes and nose stung as the air turned frigid. The wind picked up, and clouds descended, promising snow. We didn't talk for the last hour; Erik gave me quiet companionship as I went inside my head, running through all the scenarios of how my talk with my brother would go. He would most likely be angry still, and perhaps he wanted me to apologise. Maybe he wanted closure to know how much I regretted what I'd done. I could give him all that. I was more sorry than he'd ever know.

I fretted about how it would feel to hear his voice. I'd loved and idolised my brother, and I'd felt cherished because he'd always gone out of his way to make sure I was safe. I didn't deserve him, but I knew how good life was with him and I was selfish as I mourned the loss. Sensing the darkening of my thoughts as we got closer to the cabin, Erik reached out and grabbed my hand, holding it firmly in his.

"He's your brother, and if he's as great as you say, he'll still love you."

"I want to believe that, but the look on his face in that hospital bed tells me I'd be a fool to. And then there's my mother. That kind of nastiness is infectious. I hope he can eventually find it in his heart to forgive me, if that's what he is even calling about. He could be ringing me to say I owe him for what happened."

"Owe him?" Erik looked confused.

"Money maybe, or to press charges against Paddy. I'd do whatever he wants." Erik tilted his head to the side, considering my words, then frowned.

"Maybe he misses you."

"Maybe," I said without one ounce of conviction.

"Annie, I get that you blame yourself and I understand why he was pissed. But him calling now doesn't mean he hates you. He's had time to look back, and think about how you might have felt and the situation you were in. Maybe he realised that you honestly didn't think Paddy was under the influence," he said, peering at me in the near dark.

"You're a real optimist, you know that?" It came out a little snarky, but I didn't really mean it. I just wasn't ready to hope yet.

"I have my moments. Hear him out, it might not be that bad," he said, ignoring my shitty attitude. I really hoped he was right.

Once we went inside, I took a moment to have a shower and warm up, opting for comfortable yoga pants and a soft cotton AC/DC concert top. It gave me time to settle myself in his inspired, redecorated bathroom that was practically a wet room with concrete-like tiles and an enormous walk-in shower.

When I came out, I saw that Erik was busy in the kitchen making dinner, a radio playing Jack Jones somewhere. His choice of music suited him. I entered the kitchen, smiling at his apron that had a woman's body wearing a scant bikini made from the Australian flag. It was ridiculous and trashy, but the grin he gave me when he saw me was anything but. It was a cheeky, sexy look that was supposed to calm my nerves. I rolled my eyes, unable to hide my smile, then sorted through my handbag looking for my phone. Clutching it in hand, I took the glass of red wine he handed me and the soft kiss he planted on my lips before I headed to the oversize tan leather armchair in front of the fire.

It was as good a spot as any, looking out into the night as the sleet came in. I could see an acoustic guitar that look well loved beside a huge stack of crime novels. I wondered if they were Erik's until the phone in my hand started to feel like it was made of lead. So, I put the wine to my lips, and two large sips later I recalled Theodore's number, took a deep breath, and pressed the green button. It rang four times before I heard the voice I'd longed to hear for more than four years.

"Hello?" His voice was rough, clearly still hazy from sleep.

"Ted. Theodore… It's…Annie," I said, my voice sounding small and choked with emotion.

"Annie," he said then the line went silent. I didn't know if we had lost the call or not.

"Ted?" I called, hoping he was still on the line. I didn't want to play phone tag. My heart couldn't handle it.

"It's good to hear your voice. I've missed you," he replied, his voice thick with emotion.

"I've missed you too," I whispered. I didn't know what else to say. Did I ask him how he was? Was that a stupid question to ask from the person who'd injured him?

"How are you?"

"Okay, and…you?" I held my breath, not sure I was ready for the answer.

"I'm fine, all things considered." Shit.

"That's good, I guess," I hedged.

"It's been years, Annie. I had a hard time tracking you down, but I am glad you called back. I wasn't sure you would, given how we left things."

"Of course I'd call you back," I mumbled, feeling tears threaten.

"Annie, are you sure you're okay?" he asked, and I smiled as my eyes filled with tears.

"I wasn't sure why you wanted to talk to me," I admitted.

"I want to talk to you. You're my sister and I miss you," he said as though that were the obvious answer.

"Really?"

"Of course. I know it's been too long, and that when you left everything was all wrong, but you're my sister."

"Ted, I don't know what to say." I choked as the tears ran.

"Don't cry. I've been wanting to talk to you since you left, but I thought you needed time to process what happened with Paddy. I tried to give you space, but when I noticed that you'd left me money, and Paddy told me you'd paid for his rehab, I figured you wanted to be left alone."

"You spoke to Paddy?"

"He came to apologise."

"And you forgave him?"

"Eventually. I was pissed at him—he put us at risk and he hurt and betrayed you. I wanted to throttle him for a long time, but seeing him and how he has changed, I can't be that angry." I couldn't believe it.

"But we put you in a hospital…in a wheelchair," I sobbed, unable to hold back.

"Annie, no…" he started but the gates had opened and all my regret came rushing out.

"It's my fault for falling for his charm and being overtaken by my feelings. It's as much on me as it is on him. You were going to go overseas and save the world. And I put you in a wheelchair. I ruined your life. I broke you, broke us, broke everything. I'm sorry. I love you and I am so sorry I didn't do right by you. You have always done right by me, and I let you down. I…" I was rambling, but the words came as fast as my tears fell.

"Annie, listen to me. That isn't what happened."

"I was there, I saw you. Mother told me what the doctors said," I cried, verging on hysterical.

"Annie, stop for a minute."

"I'm sorry, so sorry. I've been sick with guilt ever since and I would do anything to take it back," I said on a wracking sob.

"I can walk," he practically yelled down the phone, and his tone caught my attention.

"What?"

"I didn't end up in a wheelchair. I had some broken bones and a long recovery, but I'm fine."

Wait. What?

"I don't understand." I ran my hands through my hair before grabbing a chunk and giving it a yank, trying to snap myself back to reality.

"I don't know what Mother told you, but I recovered fully. It took six months before I was running again, but I'm fine. I have some brilliant scars, but that's it." I couldn't speak. I had no way of processing what he was telling me.

"But I saw you, and she said…" I was stammering, still trying to make sense of what he was on about.

"What did Mother tell you? What did she say?" He sounded frustrated and I didn't want that.

"She said that you wouldn't walk and that it was my fault you wouldn't be able to work overseas. She said it was my fault," I whispered.

"You're bloody kidding. Why would she say that?" He sounded incredulous. He knew how Mother could be, but he clearly didn't think she was capable of this.

"She hates me." It was a simple truth, one I'd accepted years ago.

"No, she doesn't. She was angry and worried," he said, and I wanted to believe him. My tears had stopped, and I was exhausted, especially since my own mother had a role to play in my misery.

"She paid out my inheritance to make me go away," I told him quietly, but my words were met by silence.

"What?"

"She wanted me to go. Gave me the money hoping I'd never return."

"Oh Annie." The remorse and grief in his voice had me tearing up again.

"I came to Australia, got a job, and tried to keep out of all your lives. I didn't want to do any more damage."

"Listen to me, I'm fine. Paddy is fine. It was an accident, not your fault. I could have said no, I'm not getting in the car, and stuck to my guns. You would have listened if I had pushed it," I didn't say anything. I had nothing to say. My brain had stopped working.

"Annie, are you still there?" he asked after the silence stretched.

"I'm still here."

"Good. We have a lot to catch up on. I'm glad you called me back," he repeated, steering us back to safe ground. He was skilled at that, taking people away from places that hurt.

"We do. So, how are Mother and Father?" I asked, surprised I still cared. Despite everything, stupidly I still cared what they thought of me.

"Well, that's actually one of the reasons for reaching out. Mother is sick. She has cancer."

I felt my stomach plummet again, and I wondered how much more my brain could take. First it was crossing the line with Erik, then learning my brother wasn't in a wheelchair, and now I had to bend my head around the fact my mother was dying.

"What?"

"She has cancer. Bowel cancer. She has started treatment and it's going well, but her chances of being cured aren't good."

"Shit," I whispered.

"I know."

"Are you okay? And Dad, how is he doing?" My father was straitlaced, so to say we didn't get along was a gross understatement, but he and my mother were close.

"He is being tight-lipped, as you can imagine. I know he is taking it hard, but he has no ability to express it."

"How are you coping?"

"I think it's sad, and I can see she needs help but doesn't want to ask for it. I see them every second weekend now that I'm back, and I sit with her."

"Back?" I asked, hating that I didn't even know where he had been.

"I've been working with a charity ever since graduating. I have been overseas a lot, managing water security projects." I smiled. My brother was *the best* person I knew.

"Where abouts?"

"Malawi, Uganda, and Russia."

"Wow. You really did it."

"Yeah, I did. But I'm working at home now, keen to get some money behind me, maybe buy a house or something."

"Are you seeing anyone?" Women fawned over my brother, but he wasn't really into the short-term thing, and he didn't respond well when women were in his face. He was handsome, polite, caring, and quiet, and there was someone out there for him. That didn't mean I had to think she deserved him.

"No, not presently. I had been seeing someone on and off, but I didn't feel it was going anywhere. What about you?"

I glanced over to the kitchen to see Erik leaning on the counter. He had showered and changed. His damp hair was pulled back with one unruly piece falling forward. He wore a tight blue Henley and I caught a glimpse of loose lounge pants. They hung low on his hips and clung in all the right places. Generally speaking, men did not look sexy in sweatpants, but Erik managed it without even trying.

"Annie?" My brother's voice interrupted my ogling.

"Sorry, what was the question?"

"I asked if you are seeing anyone."

"Well…"

"You are," he said, and I could imagine him grinning and pointing at me.

"It's complicated," I hedged, not wanting to answer that Erik and I were only shagging, but that I was falling for him. Erik had music on but it wasn't that loud.

"It's new, and I'm not sure where it is going."

"I see. Have you had many, ah, boyfriends after Paddy?" he asked softly.

"No, none. I didn't want to lose sight of what's important again. I couldn't lose myself again," I said, being honest because despite the years, my brother knew me well. "You need to stop with that. You were young and in love. There is nothing wrong with it."

"Love makes you blind." I sighed as I stared into the fire.

"It does other things too, you know."

"I know," I said unconvincingly.

My brother changed the topic again, giving me a reprieve, and we discussed where we lived. He avoided bringing up Paddy again, and I was glad for it. One trip down memory lane was enough for the moment. After we'd spoken for almost an hour, I told him I needed to go eat dinner, and he said he would call me during the week. We exchanged email details to schedule the right time to talk. I hung up the phone feeling utterly exhausted but lighter than I had in years.

"How was it?" Erik asked, surprising me when he appeared at my side, filling up my wineglass.

"Really good," I told him, giving him a smile.

"Is he okay?" Erik asked, sitting down on the chair next to me and sipping his own wine.

"It turns out he isn't in a wheelchair. I think my mother exaggerated his injuries to get me to leave," I said, wincing as my heart tore open again.

"That's a shitty thing to do."

"It is, and now she has cancer. But I don't know how to feel about that. Of course, I don't want her to die or be in pain, but I can't muster the feeling of loss. She was lost to me years ago." I didn't know if it made me a bad person to say that, but I knew Erik wouldn't judge me.

"Fair enough. You should take time to process it all. You can feel grief or loss whenever you want, but give yourself time to think about it. That was a pretty heavy conversation, and it will take a while to deal with having your brother back."

"I know. I've missed him more than I thought was possible," I said, getting a little teary again.

"Hey, pixie, no more tears for a while," he said, putting his glass down, then taking mine from me. After placing them on the table, he pulled me out of my chair and into his lap so he could cradle me. I relaxed into his warmth and strength, tucking my head into his neck, I let a few more tears flow. I wanted to melt into him. He smelled good and his heart beat strong and true under my palm, a reminder that life was going on all around me.

My stomach also chose that time to remind me that I needed to eat, and as it rumbled loudly, Erik chuckled.

"Ah, excuse me," I muttered, unable to hold back a laugh.

"Come on, it's time for dinner. Then after that, since I have no TV, we will have to think of something else to do with our time." He set me on my feet then he stood and pulled me close then put his lips on mine. He proceeded to kiss me in a way that communicated what he had planned.

***

I was no good at sleeping in and I think I started with my father. We were always up with the sun and outside doing something. I don't have a lot of memories of my mother, not many vivid ones at least, but I remember her coming out to find us, and giving us a second breakfast on the weekends when we were up here as a family. Despite my limited recollection, that memory was a good one.

Now I lay awake as sun streamed in through the bedroom window, the storm having come and gone during the night. The wind had been wild for a few hours, but we hadn't really noticed. We were being wild inside the house, and the damned weather was the last thing on my mind.

Dinner had been good, and Annie had recapped some of her conversation with her brother before we talked about other things. It was incredible to see how much lighter she was now that the shroud of melancholy and guilt had started to lift. I found myself asking about Paddy, who sounded like an arsehole. It rankled me that she had been in love with him. It wasn't like we were in love, but I didn't want him to have that from her when he didn't deserve it. I guess that made me an arsehole too.

After dinner, we'd cuddled on the couch, watched the fire, and talked about travelling the world and where we had been. I liked the idea of going on a holiday with Annie. She sounded up for anything and able to roll with wherever the wind took her.

The thought was unbidden but once it was in my brain, it settled there. We'd even had a whiskey as we talked, something I rarely indulged in, but liked on occasion. We'd continued to talk about nothing in particular and sitting close, my hands on her, but as the storm really came in, our conversation had given way to touching, kissing, licking, and biting.

I smiled at the roof, feeling Annie snuggle into my side, hand draped over my stomach. I liked being with her. I had to stop myself laughing out loud as I remembered how last night she had reached into my pants and held my hard dick while telling me I was wearing the most attractive lounge pants she'd ever seen, which didn't have what she and her friends referred to as *dick-cling*. I don't know why, but I thought girls didn't talk about shit like that.

When we'd moved to the bedroom, it had still been fun, but she was moaning more than laughing then. I closed my eyes as the memories rushed back: her riding me as I leaned against the bedhead, her tits in my face, her hand in my hair as we'd come together.

We had lay in bed recuperating, but before long we were at each other again, and the sight of her grasping the sheets like a lifeline as

I hit her deep from behind flashed in my mind. I'd gripped her amazing arse as I'd driven into her small frame, her neck arching back as she moved to meet my thrusts, her hair a mess—the tattoo at her side looking alive as she moved with each thrust. It was a fucking sexy, fantasy, spank-bank-for-all-time montage and soon enough my dick was straining, ready for more.

I looked down to see Annie still asleep, but her eyes were moving, the sunlight clearly taking working its magic. She rolled away from me, hiding her face in her pillow, but the movement caused the sheet to drop down, exposing her back and spine. It was a sexy sight. She had such fine features, such smooth perfect skin, and a narrow waist that my calloused hands could span. Needing to touch and taste her, I rolled to my side, my front at her back, and I kissed her neck and roamed her skin with my hands.

I knew she was awake when she mewled and pushed her arse back into my now hard-as-a-rock dick. I pressed into her, letting her know what I wanted, and she reached an arm behind her to grip me behind my neck and pull me close. Then she moved her hands into my hair, gripping tight, and she pressed into me, holding me in place.

"I hear you, pixie," I muttered as I planted kisses behind her ear, then down to her neck. I slipped one arm under her to access her pretty pink nipples, rolling them in my fingers until they became hard. Then I moved my other hand down her taut stomach, over the small nest of dark curls above her sex, and delved right in.

I rubbed between her folds, loving the sounds she made each time I made a pass over her clit. It was a sexy, whimpering noise. I loved it so much that I focused my attention there, rubbing circles at her most sensitive part while toying with her nipples. Before long she was shifting restlessly, trying to ride my hand to get what she needed. It was hot, watching her, feeling her try to use my body for pleasure.

I felt my balls draw up tight, my dick ready to get into the fray. Knowing I needed to get condom before I blew over her arse like a damned kid, I rolled to my back, smiling at her protest as a I rolled a condom on.

"You're supposed to be marauding and pillaging me, Viking," she sassed, making fun of my Nordic heritage. I liked that she called me her Viking-lumberjack, despite the fact I didn't really see myself that way. I supposed I liked that she had given me a name at all.

"I'm about to, prepare yourself," I growled low behind her ear before I moved in close at her back that was still facing me, hitched her thigh up, and positioned myself at her entrance. I replaced my hand under her, grabbing a fist full of her tits, pushed down on her clit hard, and slipped inside her. She was slick, hot, and tight, and it felt amazing but I wasn't in the mood for slow and steady. After last night's long session and thinking about her this morning, I wanted to fuck her brains out. Not being one to procrastinate, I got on with it.

I pounded into her relentlessly, noting her grip the pillow as she moved her hips between my fingers at her front, and my dick entering her from behind. She was getting close, I could feel it in her desperation and the way her pussy gave little tremors, a warning of what was to come.

I wanted more, so I drove in harder and faster, pushing her down into the mattress as I leveraged up on my elbow to swing my hips faster. It felt fucking amazing and she was begging and cajoling, wanting me to move harder and faster. It was a heady combination, and when she detonated around me, I followed suit, roaring as my release left me. As I was finding was the norm with Annie, it was explosive, visceral, and unlike anything I'd experienced before.

In other words, completely addictive.

Chapter 12

We drove down the mountain at around four as the golden afternoon sun hit one side of the mountain and put the other into shadow. It always surprised me to see the tortured gum trees in alpine areas. This was so different to what I had grown up with and what the rest of the world associated with snow and winter.

I found myself smiling as Erik told me about his time growing up with Ben, and Fleur's deadbeat ex Reece. Clearly, they'd had a good time living in this area, mountain biking, riding motorbikes, fishing, hiking, and camping out. Happily, I was able to share the good parts of my childhood with Theodore. Now it wasn't as painful a memory.

It had been a great day, starting out with Erik banging the ever-loving shit out of me before cooking me breakfast. The man had talent in the kitchen and had paid a mind to my heritage, giving me a huge cooked breakfast including butter-poached tomatoes, garlic and thyme mushrooms, sausage, fried eggs, and thick, well-buttered toast. It was glorious, made even better by the gallon of tea I drank to wash it down.

After food, we went on a small walk around his property in the fresh but still shallow snow. It was such a beautiful spot and I got the sense that this place was Erik's spiritual home, not the dump he lived in during the week. It also became clear that it was a significant place for him growing up. He told me he had spent time here with both his parents, he and his dad tinkering around, his mother keeping hearth and home. He didn't say much more about it, only that he spent more recent time at the cabin with his father, who had been withdrawing from life. Erik, it seemed, had focused on being outside, doing things around the place, and making sure the house was maintained enough for his dad. When I'd asked him why, he'd taken a moment to consider that, and then said it was because he probably wanted it to be a happy place again. It was a heartbreaking thought, imagining a young Erik trying to keep his father happy, but having to watch him deteriorate. He hadn't elaborated but gave me enough facts and the feeling I shouldn't push for more.

After excellent coffee at Dinner Plain, we'd done another short walk out along a ridge with a sheer drop. It was beautiful, covered in snow, lit by the sun and peaking above the low cloud. I'd felt like we were on top of the world. I could see his ankle had started to bother him, so we headed back to the cabin to have lunch. I couldn't fit much in but the homemade beef and Guinness pies were to die for so I put in a good effort. After a lunch that size, we lay on the couch talking before we both drifted off in front of the fire, having one of those peaceful, lazy naps that left you feeling heavy and rested.

That laid-back feeling hadn't lasted long when I'd awoken because my hands couldn't keep away from his big, beautiful body. I took my time exploring him with my hands, then my mouth before it had been too much for him and he took me on the floor with an urgency that stole my breath. The man was a passionate lover, and every time we were intimate, my control fled and safely, I fell into abandon, going wherever he took me.

As the sun started to set we were reminded that life, and in particular work, was something we couldn't ignore. Begrudgingly, we'd both packed up and got the house ready before leaving, as though we both felt robbed that we didn't have more time in each other's company. Well, I had assumed it was a mutual feeling at the time, but the farther down the mountain we descended and the closer to reality we came, my confidence followed suit and started to plummet.

Being with Erik had been both comfortable and exciting. It was a good mix of being able to spend time with someone in a way that didn't require effort, and to anticipate how good they make you feel. I didn't have much experience with relationships, only Paddy. But when I reflected back to those years in London, we had shared a young person's relationship where you were out with people all the time but you went home with the same person every night.

With Erik it had been completely different. He was a man who was confident in his own company but was open to share it with me. He was also attentive and engaged in a way that made me feel like my time was valuable. Well, that's what I felt, not what he had disclosed. He had been quite clear about his proposition from the get-go, adamant in fact, and we'd both had enough orgasms this weekend to satisfy that itch. He'd never indicated that he wanted more with me, only that he cared about me in my current predicament. No promises were made and all the effort with food and wine? Well, he had already planned to come up to the cabin; he hadn't done all that for me. I'd do well to remember that.

I could not have a repeat of Paddy, of that mindlessness and complete abandon, being absorbed in another person and not seeing what was happening around you. I had started healing the wound with my brother. It didn't mean that my blinding faith in Paddy went away. Falling in love made you stupid.

This case, wasn't exactly the same. Erik wouldn't physically hurt me or the people I loved. But a one-sided love affair with this god? A man who I would have to see all the time? It would be almost as disastrous for me as it would crush my heart and drive me back into myself, and I'd already done that once. This helpful reminder squashed some of my good feelings and drove me to get ahead of the problem, to safeguard myself.

"Erik," I called, breaking the silence.

"Pixie. What's been on your mind? It's been whirring so loud I had to turn up the radio," he teased, again surprising me with how in tune he was with me.

"I was thinking about your proposition," I said conversationally, waiting to see his response.

"My proposition?" he asked, seeming confused.

"Yeah, the one you made in my office. About us, er…" I trailed off as realisation hit him.

"Fucking?" he asked, his tone a little flat.

"That's the one."

"What about it?" He didn't look at me, and I sensed he didn't like where this conversation was heading. Perhaps he was uncomfortable being reminded of how he'd been pushing me now he knew what had been on my mind? It was understandable.

"Well, from my perspective, you've been proved right. We are great in the bedroom." He didn't answer but nodded his agreement.

"And as you'd mentioned, you'd like to keep enjoying it as long as it lasts?"

"I'd mentioned?" he asked.

"That's what you'd inferred, as part of your proposition."

"I see. Well, yes, that's still true." He sighed.

"So, I'm suggesting we keep on, well, keeping on," I said awkwardly, and at this he looked at me with a brow raised, but no smile.

"So, you want to keep shagging. Is that what you are saying?" His tone made me hesitate. He didn't seem happy or unhappy and I couldn't figure out where he was at. This was what he'd originally suggested. Had he forgotten?

"Well, yeah. I mean, you were clear that you were up for some between-the-sheets action and that was it. I'm letting you know that I, well…that I concur." My earlier desire to get ahead of the problem seemed like a really bad idea.

"You concur." There was a ghost of a smile at his lips.

"Ah, with your offer. Let's be lovers as long as it lasts."

"Lovers?" he asked, as though he really needed to clarify what I'd said.

"You don't want that?" Shit. Had I misread everything? Did he want to end it?

"Yeah. I want that. Sounds like a plan," he said, giving me a smile that didn't reach his eyes. I didn't know what this reaction meant, but he didn't seem angry or offended.

We made the rest of the journey in a silence that was more strained than I would have liked, but when we got to my place and I invited him in, he said yes. Once inside he headed straight to the fire to get it going, while I pulled out the only real food source, other than toast, that I kept on hand—cheese. I loved cheese, and it went perfectly with wine so as the afternoon became a colder and darker evening, we sat in front of the television, watched movies, drank wine, ate cheese, and cuddled on my couch. It was peaceful and affectionate; maybe this *lovers* thing was going to be okay.

That night, after three orgasms and four sexual positions, we lay in bed and I prepared to sleep next to his big, warm body again. It took me a moment to come back from the brink of sleep when he got out of bed and started dressing.

"You're not staying?" I asked, blinking, trying to get some focus.

"No, got work early tomorrow," he said, not looking at me but focusing on buttoning his jeans. I wanted to whine and ask him to stay, liking it too much to have him sleep beside me. But the way he was getting dressed served as a reminder of the proposal he'd made and what we were actually doing. This was about fucking. I needed, absolutely *had* to keep that in my mind. Maybe him leaving was for the best. I didn't want to get crushed or attached in a way that would ruin me.

"Of course," I said, throwing the covers back to walk him out.

"Don't get up, I'll deadbolt it on the way out. You're beat, stay in bed," he said as he crawled across the mattress to me. It was a sight to behold, him on all fours covering over me like that. He had a perfect, too-long beard, his blond hair was mussed and loose around his shoulders, and his biceps were flexing under his shirt as they held his big body up. He was so damned sexy it was obscene.

He paused there, giving me a strange look again, before he leant down and kissed me on the forehead then moved away, calling a *good night* on his way out the door. I lay in bed, holding my breath. I had no idea why I did this, nor did it make sense when I heard the front door open and shut and tears pricked my eyes. I needed to get a grip. Lovers. Not love.

The next morning, I woke up feeling both positive and depressed as I went through the usual routine of running, eating breakfast, showering, and going to work. I was so preoccupied with Theodore and Erik that I only remembered that Leslie and I had planned to meet for a quick coffee before work so I swung into Wills Street to meet her.

"I want to say you look a bit rough, but you kinda do, kinda don't. What on earth is going on with you?" my friend asked, giving me her look that said she wasn't going to be fobbed off. She was completely correct, of course, and I told her all about what had happened with both Erik and my brother. When I'd mentioned his name was Erik, and unwittingly mentioned I refer to him as the Viking-lumberjack, she'd lost the plot. "Erik the Viking!" she'd hooted before threatening to text Hannah and tell her about Erik the Viking. She'd seemed unsure about the nature of our relationship, but I'd done my best to convince her, and myself, that it would be fine.

***

Tuesday had not started well, beginning with waking up without Annie by my side. I knew I was a damned fool for even thinking it, but two mornings of having her small, lithe body next to mine had made me want to reconsider my rules. I did not do relationships. Women played games. I was about the physical, a few laughs, and a see-ya-later. It had always been like that. Until Annie.

She'd come into my life, giving me sass, calling me on my bullshit, and I'd fucking loved it. Making matters worse was my reaction to her vulnerability. I'd gone all He-Man, wanting to protect her, to help shoulder her burdens. Then she'd let me in, showing me her secrets in a way that was honest and true. I liked that she trusted me enough to share like that.

This was what had really floored me. From that point on, the chemistry, and all we had in common, plus the ease of hanging out with her was taking me down a path of considering more. Of taking a risk, despite seeing what it had done to my father and Ben.

I'd been building up the courage to say something on the way home from the cabin when she'd brought up my proposal. I'd wanted to stop the car, and stop those words coming out of her mouth. I didn't want to hear my own words come back at me, I didn't want to think about all I'd said before Saturday night. But fuck me, she'd brought it up and I had to suck it up. I *had* said those things and I had to acknowledge that that was all she wanted from me.

I should be happy, knowing I'd dodged a bullet, and kept my promise to myself. Instead, I felt frustrated. Frustrated and pissed that because of my own desire to get into her pants from the get-go, I'd never know if there was more for us or not. That said, it may not have mattered given she wasn't considering anything but a sexual relationship. She had pigeonholed me as the charming lover with all care, no responsibility.

But that wasn't exactly true, was it? No. I'd pigeonholed myself.

My day had gotten worse when I'd arrived on site to get a voice mail telling me that two of my guys were sick. I'd had to pick up the tools and get the job done. My ankle was almost better, but the hiking over the weekend had given it a nudge, and today's work on the side of the mountain wasn't going to help. On my way home for a quick shower before football practice, I'd received another call that I didn't recognise, but it was an Australian number so I answered.

"Hello?" I sounded grouchy.

"Erik?" the young female voice said, almost timidly. Shit. Did I know this voice? I couldn't place it exactly. She sounded young, maybe a teenager, and she had a strange, slightly American accent.

"Who is this?" I asked as I pulled into my shitbox apartment.

"It's Freya, I've been trying to contact you. I need to…" I cut her off before this nonsense could go any further.

"Look, lady, I don't know who you are or how you got my number, but I am about to hang up. I have better shit to do," I growled as I cut the engine. I sounded like a dick but I didn't care. I wasn't in the mood.

"Daphne gave it to me," she said, voice shaking.

"Say what?"

"Daphne gave it to me, when I rang the government office." What the fuck? Daphne worked for the local council, but in her role there was no way she would give up personal details like that, or at least she shouldn't.

"She did what?" I was not only shitty, I was full-blown pissed now. This was either a joke, or Daphne was up to something.

"She told me…" she started to stammer but I cut her off.

"Actually, I don't want to know. Whatever bullshit Daphne is up to, I want no fucking part of it. She, and you, are dead to me. You hear that? Don't bother calling again. I won't answer," I ground out over her protests then I hung up. Maybe this was the reminder I needed to avoid women; they play games. On my way to football training, my phone rang again, and figuring it was Freya calling me again to try her bullshit, I got in first.

"Stop fucking calling me. I am not playing whatever bullshit games you are up to."

"Well shit, Erik. Here I was checking in, seeing where we were going for dinner on Friday, and you treat me like that. I thought we had something special," Ben said, and I sighed, feeling like a dickhead.

"Sorry, thought you were someone else," I muttered.

"Clearly, but now I'm intrigued and I want to know who. Either you had a fight with your English lass, Daphne has cornered you again, or the mystery caller turned up at your door with a baby," he said dryly. Sometimes I hated how well he knew me.

"Piss off."

"I would, but I'm enjoying giving you shit. So, tell me was it door number one, two, or three that has you all grumpy?"

"Doors two and three."

"Both?"

"Yeah. The girl who has been calling me is called Freya and it seems she got my number from Daphne."

"What the fuck? Why did you answer?" All humour from Ben was gone.

"Before, the number was blocked. This time it came from a different number. I asked her how she got my digits and apparently, this kid called the council and a woman called Daphne gave it to her," I told him as I pulled into the football ground and cursed. I was late and had to park in the muddy paddock.

"She can't do that," Ben said, all humour gone.

"No shit. She is up to something and so is Freya."

"Are you going to ask Daphne about it?"

"I don't want to. I want to ignore it. That'll piss Daphne off more," I said, getting out and trudging toward the club rooms.

"Let me ask my sisters, they know everything that's happening within a two-hundred-kilometre radius." Ben wasn't joking, his two sisters knew everyone and everything, but I didn't want them in my business. Once they started, they would be hard to rein in.

"Nah, I'll figure something out."

"Let me do a bit of digging, I won't set them loose in a way we can't get them back, don't worry."

"Ben—" I started but he interrupted.

"I promise."

"No ripples, you hear?" I needed him to know that I did not want this to get any bigger. Daphne already took up too much oxygen.

"Of course not," he lied before hanging up.

To say my mood was in the toilet when I walked toward the clubhouse was an understatement. In reality, it was buried beneath bucket loads of shit and waste. I walked past the netball courts on my way in, for some reason not wanting to see Annie. I didn't want to see her indifference, which made no sense. We were only fuck buddies, right? I also didn't want to see Daphne, not yet. But, like the rest of my day thus far, I didn't get what I wanted.

"Erik, hey. Can I talk to you after training?" Daphne asked, running up to me, detouring from running her warm-up laps. I didn't answer, I kept on walking, but I could feel her eyes on me. Unable to help it, I slid a glance across, looking for Annie, to see her looking dead at me, concern on her face. Every time I saw her, it was like a hit to the chest. She was stunningly and unconventionally beautiful, and I wanted to walk up to her and kiss that look off her face, but we weren't about that. Then she mouthed the question "you okay?" and I nodded, giving her a grin back. It was the first time I'd smiled all day.

I set about spending time in the gym, then heading out to the field to speak with the coaches and join in some drills. I would be back playing next week if all went well, and I wanted to get my hands on the ball. It helped take my mind off the drama, and when we were done, we showered up, then headed inside for dinner. I was in a marginally better mood until Daphne pounced on me as soon as I entered.

"Erik, I really need to talk to you," she said, trying to smile, like everything was okay. I shook my head, intent on not getting into it here with her. I was not in the right frame of mind to do this. When she put her hand on my chest to stop me walking away, I looked down at her. She wasn't necessarily nervous, but rather calculating.

"Stop," I ground out, moving my eyes around the room to see who was looking. The answer was simple. Everyone was, including Annie. Her eyes were on Daphne, and she didn't look pleased. Fuck.

"Erik honey, it's me you're talking to, and I'm your friend. Remember?" she asked sweetly. It was the kind of sweet that made your teeth hurt.

"Friend? You're fucking kidding me, right?" I wanted to laugh.

"Look, I know that we are over, but I still care for you."

"Is that why you did it?"

"Did what?" she asked, blinking.

"Don't bullshit me. I know what you did."

"Erik, I didn't do anything," she said, going for tears. Out the corner of my eye, I saw Annie, flanked by Fleur, Bel, and Jade, move forward. Fucking hell, this was going to be a mess.

"No? Nothing to do with someone trying to get their hooks into me?"

At this she paled a little, and I knew I had her. I was ready to blow my stack about her passing off my details when I felt warmth at my side. I looked down to see Annie standing beside me, looking at Daphne like she thought she was crazy.

"This is because you can't keep your dick in your pants," Daphne said, looking at Annie. I wanted to grab Annie, but I was too concerned by Daphne's face. She'd gone from looking confused to calculating. I was going to ask her to explain when I heard Annie's voice and I stiffened, waiting for the impact.

"Hey, Daphne, are you talking about Erik's dick again? I've seen it too. I get it, but I kind of think he doesn't want you to talk about it. It's personal, you know?" Annie said conspiratorially to Daphne. Daphne glared at her, then at me.

"Do you know about her?" Daphne spat.

"Know what?" I didn't know a damned thing about Freya.

"Do you know that she used to run with drug addicts and that she almost killed someone?" Daphne said, smirking like she had played her trump card. What was she talking about? I was about to ask when I noticed how stiff Annie was. Then the penny dropped. Daphne wasn't talking about Freya. She was talking about Annie. She had been the whole time.

"Watch your fucking mouth," I growled, my control slipping. Daphne had the sense to look concerned. Clearly her plan was backfiring.

"Yes, he knows. If you have something to say about it, then own it and say it to me. Not to him. To. Me. Unless you're too much of a coward," Annie said calmly, but I could hear everyone suck in a breath.

"Well. I..." Daphne stammered. I put my arm around Annie, pulling her close, making the statement.

"Erik, I was looking out for you. As a friend. I wanted to know who you were getting involved with. I care, remember?" she said quickly as she too took in the room.

"I know exactly who I am getting involved with. It's a nice change actually, being with someone who is honest," I fired back.

"I'm honest, I am. I promise I had your best interests at heart," she said, edging away, as though she were the injured party.

"Did you have my best interests at heart when you gave out my number to someone calling the council?" I fired off, and she froze, her eyes going huge.

"Erik..." she started, but I was done with the circus.

"Shut it. I don't want to hear another word from you. I don't want to know why you did that, or who this person is. You need to drop whatever game you're playing. I'm done. Done," I said quietly, but she didn't mistake me. She knew I was serious and she nodded as she walked off.

I let go of the breath I'd been holding, feeling Annie do the same. I looked down at her, hoping she was okay after all that Daphne had said. But she looked at me with big eyes. "You sure know how to pick them," she said, giving me a sassy grin. I didn't know what to say to that, and I could feel my jaw drop open. Was she making a joke? "And she is so awkward. It's like watching someone with a shotgun, aiming at their own foot then pulling the trigger," she said, shaking her head in disbelief.

"Ugh. She needs to save her drama for her llama," Fleur chimed in.

"She is quite possibly the worst mean girl I've ever seen," Annie said to her, nodding in agreement.

That was the last straw. I couldn't help it. I burst out laughing. "You never cease to amaze me," I said to her, pulling her in close for a hug as our bodies shook with laughter.

"I am kind of amazing," she sassed into my chest.

"No shit," I said.

Chapter 13

In the light of day I wasn't too angry, despite Daphne's little tanty the night before at training. She'd been telegraphing her intentions all night, so I was prepared. I wasn't surprised either. I knew she would Google me. There were articles written about my brother that also mentioned my name, but after speaking to Theodore, it didn't feel like it was such a big deal anymore. Besides, it was the truth, what was I going to do about it?

Daphne's plan had backfired more than she could have imagined; when I'd seen her accosting him, I'd rushed to his side, ready to throw down. He wasn't going to be tainted by anything I'd done; he was too good for that. But then he'd defended me in public and put his arm around me. Thanks to Daphne, we'd outed ourselves and the fact we were...close.

When I'd walked into the clinic this morning, Fleur had given me a knowing look that was verging on smug, then demanded that I tell her everything. Not feeling the need to be closed off after having started to mend the wound with my brother, I'd taken her to Cherry Walk for Persian Love Cake and spilled my guts. She didn't seem too surprised about how things had progressed with Erik, only that he'd taken me to his cabin. To her, this seemed significant, but I wasn't sure why; people obviously knew he had it.

She was a little taken aback that we were only having a sexual relationship but said nothing when I adamantly defended it. They were Erik's terms and I wasn't about to rock the boat and become another Daphne.

After Fleur was satisfied with the new state of play and we returned to the office, Geronimo had graced us with his presence and his overt and obvious effort at taking his turn cleaning the kitchen. Despite his palaver, nothing seemed to be able to ruin my mood. This was in part due to the fact that my mind kept wandering to Erik and his impending appointment. I found myself thinking about all that he'd done to me in the shower, then cursing myself for blushing like a school-girl.

During the day, these sex-induced lightning strikes happened at the worst times, like when I was working on Mr Stephenson, who was eighty and was boring me to death with details of his prune regimen for bowel movements. I'd been zoning out thinking about Erik taking me against the wall again, when he'd asked me if I was going into early-onset menopause given the blush I'd been sporting. Being caught out had only made more blood rush to my cheeks. It was like I was in heat.

Soon enough Erik's appointment time came around, and I found myself eager to see him, touch him, and kiss him. All. Over. I knew I needed to keep it in check, but I couldn't, especially when he sauntered into my room, giving me a lazy perusal. It was so slow and salacious that I began to think he might have been remembering our morning too. Or he had early-onset Man-o-pause. If that was even a thing. I should ask Geronimo. He looked like he would know all about that.

"Hey, pixie," he said, closing the door and coming to me. He took off his woollen beanie, and his hair hung loose, all mussed from being covered all day. His beard was a little wild and he smelled like pine needles, the outdoors, and that sexy sweat smell that men get, before it becomes heinous body odour. He was too desirable for words, so I didn't give him any. I nodded to my bench, inferring I wanted him to sit. He gave me a grin then did as instructed. Then I locked the door and returned to him to kneel between his legs. His eyes went wide before his grin turned into a full-blown, lusty smile that made his bright blues sparkle against his tanned skin.

I made a show of taking off his boots, inspecting his ankle to make sure it wasn't swollen or discoloured anymore. At some point I was going to have to look at it properly, but I had my sights set on his other body parts. Next, I worked his belt buckle undone, then undid his pants to expose his now hardening erection in his underwear. We were still silent but when I gripped him over his underwear, the sound of the intake of air into his lungs filled the space. I decided that I liked affecting him like this. It evened up the playing field because when he touched me, I was at his mercy. His ability to ensure we both had immeasurable pleasure made me feel cherished and free to let loose. Now, I wanted to give him that.

I freed him from his underwear, gripping him at the base of his now hard cock as best I could. It was a bit of a struggle given my hands were small and he was thick. I gripped tight, licking the length of him from base to the tip with the flat of my tongue, before swirling around the head as he hardened further under my touch. I repeated this a few times, the taste of him strong in my mouth. He adjusted on the bed, leaning back into his arms but dropping his chin down, and when I looked up at him, his eyes were glued to me, and in particular, what my tongue was doing. His eyes were dark with desire, intense and focused, and his hair had fallen forward to partially cover his face. He looked utterly male in his lust-driven rapture.

I straightened a little and pulled his dick forward to meet my mouth, taking him in shallow at first with a strong suck, then taking him deeper and deeper until he hit the back of my throat. He groaned with pleasure as I held him there, and when I rubbed my tongue beneath the head, he hissed.

"Fuck, pixie. You keep doing that I'm going to come in that pretty mouth of yours." His voice was rough, breathing ragged, but I nodded, letting him know that was my intention. I kept at him, taking him deep, sucking hard and using my tongue when he was fully inside my mouth. His breathing increased and I felt his thighs flex as he grew closer to release.

"Annie, baby, I'm going to…." He trailed off but I moaned with him in my mouth. This was enough of a signal and he came hard, his groan low and deep as he pumped into my mouth. When he was done, I stood and moved between his legs into his open arms. His hands roamed my body lazily at first, as he regained control of his breathing. Then he went from roaming to groping, squeezing, and rubbing. I wanted more, and my head fell back as he expertly lavished attention on my nipples.

"Wait," I murmured, hating to put a halt on where this was going but knowing I had another appointment.

"Wait? I'm not sure I can," he growled low as he kissed me below my ear.

"Next time, book a double appointment. I have Mavis coming in after you. She's my last appointment," I said, stepping back from him. I needed the space or else I was going to let Mavis wait outside and listen to Erik drill me on the physio table.

"Do I get a discount if I make you orgasm?" he asked cheekily as he took me in. No doubt my eyes were a little hazy and my lips swollen.

"Only what your health care covers," I said, shaking my head with laughter.

"How about I take you out to dinner tonight instead. I'm starving and I need my energy before I spend the night fucking your brains out," he said as he stood, and did up his pants.

"Sure, but I want to be home to call my brother by nine," I heard myself say, my body quivering at the thought of him fucking my brains out.

"Perfect, I'll go shower and come back to meet you?" he asked.

"Sure. We can hang while I call him, if you want?" My voice was unusually high-pitched, but I was unsure if this was what we were doing. Would he stay over again?

"Cool, I have some work to do anyway. I'll pack some clothes for tomorrow." I loved that he wanted to stay at my place, but I didn't want him to feel it was the expectation.

"I can stay at your place if you want."

"We're not going to the cabin tonight, pixie," he said meaningfully.

**

On my way home from Annie's office, I could not wipe the grin off my face. As soon as I'd walked in, seen that look in her eye, I knew she was feeling like I was. I ached to see her, needed to touch her, and had to have more. The blowjob of the century didn't hurt either. I pulled into my shitbox apartment, more than okay with spending the night at Annie's, only to find a couriered envelope stuck under the door. I let myself inside, threw it, my keys, phone, and wallet on the bench and headed straight to the shower.

After that was done, I called to book a table at Elm, wanting to take Annie somewhere nice. Then I got dressed, packed my gear for tomorrow, and headed back to the ratty couch to chill before she shut up shop. I nabbed the envelope as I sat down, tearing it open to see a handwritten letter inside. I'd been expecting something about Dad's estate at best, another speeding fine at worst. I had not been expecting a handwritten letter from Freya. The note was short and cryptic.

Dear Erik,

Please I need to speak with you in person. I promise I mean no harm. I have news for you that is important and I think we should speak face to face. Next time I call, please do not hang up.
Freya.

What the fuck? Who was this chick and what on earth did it have to do with me? Surely, this was something to do with Daphne and the bullshit she was going for. With a little time to spare, I decided to call Ben to see if his sisters found out anything about what Daphne was up to. He didn't have much to report, other than Daphne saying she was going to prove that she was the better woman. That was both ridiculous and alarming.

When it was time to leave, I contemplated bringing my guitar. I hadn't played in a while and could practice when Annie was on the phone. Being a grown-up now, I took my work computer instead, knowing I needed to check my emails and get on top of some project plans. When I walked back into the clinic, Annie was talking with Fleur, who was desperately trying not to grin when I arrived. Annie was ready to go with her bag, and when I followed her out the door, I turned and winked at Fleur. She laughed softly before shaking her head. We made the short walk to Elm as the night grew dark.

We sat at a table by the fire, and talked about food, my love of cooking, and her love of eating. It reminded me why I could cook— my mother had taught me. She knew that there was more going on in my head, but I told her that I'd been forced to cook because Dad was only good at opening a can, not the positive memory of my mother.

Annie went on to talk about her friends, and I could tell that she loved them, and they cared about her same way I cared about Ben and Fleur. I respected her even more when she explained she'd wanted to give her friend Hannah advice, but held back so Hannah could get there on her own. Ben sure as shit didn't take that tack, but he did have me thinking. Eventually our conversation turned to past relationships, and given I knew about hers, she asked about Daphne.

"That girl has issues," Annie said, savouring her dessert in a way that made me want to talk about anything but Daphne.

"She's up to something, that's for sure. I fucking hate games and she knows it. I don't understand why she thinks playing them *with me* will work," I grumbled, my head hurting thinking about the shit that must have been going on in that mind of hers.

"I've forced her hand. It's the jealousy that has brought forward her timeline. She tried to get information from me, but I didn't give her much so she moved on to discrediting me. It's a classic bitch manoeuvre," Annie said. I didn't like her assessment of Daphne. I didn't like it because it was true.

"We broke up years ago and I wouldn't really call what we had a relationship," I told her as I rubbed my face.

"She doesn't see it that way, and while you were doing whatever you did after you broke up, she felt confident enough that *that* was just shagging, and was no doubt waiting for you to be ready to settle down with her."

I didn't like hearing Annie talking about me *doing whatever I did.* She had already thought I was chasing skirt and while that was all I was offering the other women I'd slept with, everything felt different with Annie.

"She should know better. Everyone knows what my mother's games did to my dad," I found myself saying.

"What happened?" She looked hesitant and to be honest, I didn't like talking about it.

"My mum up and left one day, saying that my dad didn't love her, but I don't think that was true. He was fucking miserable after she left. I was young but he told me she said one thing but did another and that women play games to get what they want. I couldn't understand; she was supposed to love me and instead of taking me, she left me with my dad, who slowly started to drink himself to death. If it wasn't for Ben and his family, I'd probably be in a gang or something," I told her, leaning back, focusing on the table. No doubt there were questions on the tip of her tongue, but whatever she saw in my eyes let her know I didn't want to take it any further.

"Well, looks like we both have mummy issues," she said, giving my hand a squeeze, letting it go.

"I don't like people not being honest about their intentions. It's why I can't stand what Daphne is doing," I admitted, and she nodded.

"That's completely fair. You warned Daphne about something last night, what?" Annie asked as our bill arrived. She was momentarily distracted by my speed with the credit card, and I was grateful for that.

"She's up to something, giving my number out to people. I want nothing to do with it," I said, standing. Annie gave me an assessing look, then stood and talked to me about hiking trails, my ankle, and her obsession with violent, bloodthirsty action movies on our way home. I wondered if she could get any better.

When we got back to her place, she made tea, pulled out the most enormous tin of biscuits I'd ever seen, and turned on the TV. When it was time, she called her brother, sitting by the fire facing me while I worked on my laptop. I tried not to listen to her talking, but it was hard not to.

Clearly she was excited to talk to her brother. It was infectious. They talked about people they knew, she asked him about his job, his love life, and where he was living. She was quiet for a while, only giving cryptic answers, and I supposed she was talking about her ex. I wanted to say I didn't care, clearly he was a douche, but something about it irritated me. Perhaps it was the fact that she thought to moderate the conversation for my benefit. Did she still love him? I didn't get that impression, but then she'd only recently reconnected with her brother.

My ears pricked up even further when the discussion turned to her mother, and her saying she didn't want to go home to see her. I could tell he was trying to persuade her, and there was part of her that wanted to say yes, although I thought it was about seeing him, not that old bag who had tried to destroy her relationship with her brother. I should have expected this, but I liked the idea of her going home about as much as I liked her thinking about Paddy. I wanted to say something to her, ask what her intentions were. But I remembered our deal. Then I got pissed all over again; I had no right or claim on her. We were together to feel good while it lasted, but in that moment, it felt anything but good.

Chapter 14

The week continued drama free with Daphne ignoring me. Erik and I had kept our routine going, one that started with orgasms and ended with dinner, more orgasms, and naked cuddles with a sexy, blue-eyed, blond-haired, ripped Viking-lumberjack.

He'd stayed over every night since our dinner out, and I was fast getting used to seeing him naked and him making me coffee in the morning. Sometimes, he did both at the same time so life could be worse. I knew I was playing with fire, getting used to this kind of good, but I didn't much like the idea of not having him at my place. Now it was Friday and I was geared up for a quiet night in with Erik cooking dinner then watching action movies until I received a call from Hannah, who was in a complete tizz, asking me to collect her dogs because she needed to go see to Howard. I was happy for her, although the way she'd come to that decision, via a drunken sleazebag, a brothel manager, and a coke-addicted rich kid conspiring against them, was crazy beyond words.

I didn't mind looking after her dogs again. Patsy and Eddie were familiar with my place and good enough company if you could handle Eddie's snorting and Patsy's strangely human mannerisms—the dog looked at you like she knew what you were thinking. Erik was down with dogs and when he'd arrived, the girls took a shine to him immediately. Hannah and I believed her dogs were in fact hussies who were highly skilled at manipulating men into doing their bidding. This was proven when I saw Erik share his T-bone steak with Patsy, who just sat there looking at him, using her superhero talent of persuasion. He coddled them, cooing with the voice we all reserved for fluffy animals and babies. It was beyond sexy, like when firefighters took photos with puppies for calendars. It made me want to buy him a damned dog.

I sighed heavily. I needed to pull my heart back. It was more than the orgasms he gave me or how he cuddled dogs. It had been building the entire week. When we were home together cooking dinner, talking about our days, our plans for getting to the game tomorrow and spending time with our borrowed fur babies, it was like we had been together for years. It was easy, and I felt at peace. Watching us become domesticated, my mind wandered to what was next, which I figured for most people was marriage and kids. I knew Erik would be an amazing father. Me on the other hand? I wasn't sure if I was cut out for kids. The image of Erik holding a baby in those big muscular arms made my chest ache and my core pulse. I needed to get myself together.

"What's on your mind, pixie?" he asked, quirking a brow and giving me a sexy half grin.

"Ah…." If I said babies, that would be weird and creepy. "You," I hedged.

"Me?"

"Yeah, you. You and me. And…" I said, blushing harder now. I sounded like a bloody idiot.

"Me and you. Huh. Well, I can tell by the way your eyes are hazy and you're biting your lip that those thoughts are good," he said, shutting the door after the dogs came back inside, then moved into my space until our hips touched. At the contact, I shivered.

"Cat got your tongue?" he asked when I stared at him, lost in his eyes. "Hmmm, I think it has. How about we fill that tub of yours, and you can show me what you were thinking about and I can show what I was thinking about," he murmured as he kissed me, hot and wet, pushing his hardening erection into me. Some part of my brain told me to sass him with a quick-witted remark about grown men and bubble baths. Instead I sighed, climbed him like a tree to wrap my arms around his shoulders, legs around his waist, and whisper, "Let's have a bath after you fuck me." Erik then demonstrated that he was open to suggestions, and we had a bath after he took me on the bathroom cabinet.

I hadn't thought he could get any sexier, but when I'd looked in the vanity mirror to see his naked torso, slick with sweat, clench as he relentlessly powered into me from behind, I knew there were no bounds to his magnificence. His calloused hands gripped my hips tight, and his hands were so big that they almost met in the small of my back. He was grunting too, with each thrust that had me barrelling toward orgasm. When he opened his eyes and focused on mine, the hunger and desire was strong enough to make me come harder than I ever had, and he followed immediately.

The next morning as I lay in bed sated, waiting for Erik to make coffee, I got an early call from Hannah. She was bursting with happiness, having worked things out with Howard.

I'd gone to get the dogs back to Hannah while Erik set about making what he called the pre-game breakfast of champions. I'd thought about him coming with me, but for some reason, I didn't think I should share him with my friends yet. If we were a fling, I didn't want Hannah to get her hopes up. Besides, she would see through me in a heartbeat, and I didn't want to explain why I was invested and he wasn't.

Any further intentions on my behalf of not letting people get the idea that Erik and I were more than what we were went up in smoke when Erik insisted that we go to the game together. He then proceeded to stop and chat to people as we drove around the ground to find a park. Needless to say, we were not in the Mini.

"I don't give a shit that people are looking at us. I'm not ashamed, are you?" he asked as we pulled up. I shook my head; of course I wasn't ashamed. What I didn't want was for people to think we were an item, when I wanted that but all we were really doing was fucking. That made me like Daphne, fooling myself that there was more to it. What we had was good, and I needed to enjoy it while it lasted. We were friends with benefits, and friends shared rides; it was that simple. Fleur wasn't convinced, however.

"Things are good with you and Erik, as per your arrangement?" she asked, grinning.

"It's working out fine," I said honestly, ignoring the fact I wanted to renegotiate.

"It must be nice to have someone like that," she said then blushed at her own inference.

"Have you been with anyone recently?" I asked, wondering what love life Fleur managed with her son.

"Not since Tate's conception."

"Holy shit." I should've tempered my disbelief, but I was astonished. How could no man have seen how amazing she was in over a decade?

"It's no big deal if you never really got started. Besides I've been completely focused on Tate. It's been tough, with lots of ugly moments, and the idea of another complication doesn't seem like a good idea.," she said, trying to sound rational. I let her have that.

"What's Ben's sad love story?" I asked, wanting to know more about Erik's BFF.

"He was engaged to his high school sweetheart, but she did something that changed him and he called it off and moved overseas. He only recently came home. It was sad; they'd seemed in love," Fleur said.

Hearing about Fleur's, Erik's parents, and Ben's woes, I wondered if relationships ever worked, but after seeing Hannah with Howard, attending Molly's wedding, and knowing Leslie and Carol, they sometimes *did* work—if you were willing to take the risk.

After our game, I showered quickly and headed out to the pavilion to watch the Seniors finish their football game. I hadn't ever seen Erik play, and given the Bright Bruisers were beating the visiting team, Erik was on the field, getting back into the swing of things. Growing up in England, I knew about our football, which people here called soccer—a clear distinction from their beloved Australian Rules Football. I was glad to see the women's code doing well too, but right then, I was watching Erik and completely objectifying him. While I usually wouldn't think short shorts, long socks, and tank tops were particularly sexy or masculine, on Erik they looked divine.

He had his hair tied back, and his strong arms and legs were on display as he ran and tackled his way around the field. Everyone in the crowd was talking about how it was good to have him back before finals and even after a lengthy injury period, it was obvious that Erik was the best player on the team. When he kicked a goal, I found myself cheering and giving Fleur a high five. We laughed when someone yelled, "The Viking Returns," which was followed by a few beer-laced "Yarrrs."

It wasn't long before the siren sounded and the players, after many man hugs and bum pats, walked off the field. I couldn't take my eyes off Erik, whose sweaty body was now gleaming in the late afternoon sun. I should've averted my gaze; I was no doubt drooling but when he looked up, he gave me a huge, sexy smile. I was glad I didn't miss it. When he winked, I rolled my eyes. He was incorrigible.

"So, you're really an item?" Jade said, and I turned, seeing my teammate beside me with wine in a plastic cup, looking at me expectantly.

"Pardon?" I asked, as though her statement were preposterous.

"You and Erik?" Bel added, joining her with a Diet Coke.

"Not exactly…" I started to say. I didn't want to get into the details.

"Looks like it to me," Fleur added unhelpfully, smirking. I was about to set them straight when Bel spoke again.

"I reckon Daphne thinks the same thing," she said, her stare focused in the distance. We all turned to find Daphne, with her posse, giving me a *we'll see* look. I smiled and waved at her, as though she were a long-lost friend, and her face turned from smug to confused. She was too easy to mess with.

"So, are you coming to the mid-season ball with him?" Jade asked, and I turned to look at her, honestly confused this time.

"Ball?"

"Yeah, it's in two weeks. It's a fund-raiser and an excuse to get dressed up and drink a lot. We're all going," Bel said but what she was really saying was that I'd better go too but a ball wasn't really my thing, especially with all the drama that would be sure to follow Erik and me.

"It might not be a good idea," I muttered.

"What's not?" I spun around to see Erik standing behind me, a sweatshirt on, standing there with ice strapped to his ankle.

"Annie doesn't want to go to the mid-season ball with you. We really want her to come, perhaps you can persuade her," Fleur said, her eyes twinkling.

"Why don't you want to come with me? I'd be a great date. I'll pick you up and everything," he said to me, giving me another damned wink.

"Well, it's just that I'm a nice girl and you might try to take advantage of me," I said primly, and he laughed.

"Pixie, I promise I *will* take advantage of you." Now it was my turn to blush, and while I wanted to sass him back, I was too busy thinking about exactly how he was going to take advantage of me.

"Great. Now I need to figure out what to wear," Jade said, and the conversation moved to dresses, but my mind was stuck on Erik when he came up close behind me and whispered in my ear, "I'm ready to go when you are. I fancy another bath." He planted a wet kiss under my ear that had me shivering.

"See you later, girls," I said without thinking, grabbing my bag. Erik didn't say a word, he just chuckled as he followed me to his truck.

**

"So...?" Ben asked as I sat down beside him at the bar. It was Wednesday night and I'd left Annie's clinic after my final appointment. She was catching up with her girls for dinner so I'd called Ben. It was a good chance to check in and I'd do anything to avoid my shitty apartment. I'd managed not to spend one night there for at least a week and a half, sleeping every night in Annie's enormous bed, with her little body wrapped around mine.

"So...what?" I returned, not responding to his stupid fucking grin. He was a smug bastard sometimes.

"Tell me, how are things with you and the physio? Clearly your ankle is healed."

"Ankle is fine, played on the weekend," I told him before taking a pull of my beer.

"I heard. That said, I've heard a few other things too," Ben said, grinning into his beer.

"Like what?" I grumbled. I should be used to people talking about it me. I'd heard a lot about my dad growing up, and now people talked about my carousing, like they knew what was really going on. It didn't mean I had to like it though.

"That you arrived at the game with Annie, and left with her. One report claimed that you winked at her from the field. Another said you sleep with her netball briefs under your pillow at night."

"What?" I laughed because he'd made the last part up.

"Is any of it true?" I couldn't help but grin at him.

"All of it. Except I wear the briefs to bed."

"I knew it." He laughed, giving me a nudge.

"Where did you hear all that?" I asked, mildly interested. I knew it hadn't come from Daphne, because it was accurate.

"My sister Evelyn was at that home game, to spy because she'd heard from Melanie that Daphne was in a tizz at work over something that went down at the clubhouse and she'd wanted to see the source of Daphne's pain in the flesh." Ben shook his head at his sisters' antics. They meant well but they were way too excited by bullshit like this.

"Annie handled Daphne like a pro. Being with her... It's different."

"Different?" Ben's brows raised high on his head, not believing what I was saying.

"Yeah, different."

"You mean together," Ben said flatly.

"No, we're friends with benefits and we're enjoying the friends *and* the benefits parts," I said, trying for conviction, but clearly Ben didn't buy it.

"Sounds like more than that, mate," he said, looking at me strangely.

"It's not, I assure you," I huffed. I needed him to be on board, for my sake, but he wasn't going to like it.

"Why?" he asked as our food arrived.

"I don't do relationships, you know that."

"Bullshit."

"It's what we agreed to," I told him, sounding defensive.

"And it's what she wants? She wants you to sleep with her, and hang. That's it?" He sounded disbelieving and it was starting to piss me off.

"Yeah, that's what we both want," I snapped, and he stared at me for a long moment before letting it drop. I was glad he let it go, but I knew he didn't buy it for one second. Sad thing was, neither did I.

The last week and a bit had gone like clockwork. I'd spent every night at Annie's, cooking when we were home, travelling to and from practice together. We had breakfast every morning, then went to work, texted during the day to check in, see what we wanted to do that evening then chilling on the couch before having the best sex of our lives. We went to another away game together, stayed for drinks afterwards and came home together, like it was what we always did.

It wasn't until I was lying in her bed at night, her body draped over me that I felt my words burn holes in my gut like acid. It was a shitty feeling, only surpassed by memories of listening to her chat to her brother and talk about Paddy. This guy sounded like a douche. I was also wary that her brother was turning up the pressure, wanting her to return. They would talk about all the things she missed about home, and how much fun they'd had. She didn't say outright that she wanted to go home, but I knew she was thinking about it and it did not make me happy, which was ridiculous and unavoidable.

It was on my mind when I was walking off the field at our last home game, watching her watch me with eyes that told me she liked what she saw. Hating the idea of some other dude entering her life again, I'd let everyone know, especially Annie, that there wasn't room. It had only been a wink but as I suspected, everyone had seen it. She'd seemed unsure at first, but interestingly, she didn't shy away from the idea that I wanted everyone to know I was with *her*. So, what did that mean?

When she came home from dinner to find me in bed reading, she'd wasted no time in stripping off, before jumping on me like she was desperate for me to be in her. My body reacted in the same way, and as we made love, my restless mind stopped hassling me. It wasn't until she was asleep on top of me that it started to whir again.

Chapter 15

"Why are you only telling me this now?" Hannah asked, looking flabbergasted and a little irritated.

"You were busy with Howard." I sounded defensive but it was the truth.

"What about me?" Molly asked.

"You just got back from your honeymoon," I said, and this was also true. Clearly, the cat was absolutely out of the bag and my friends were not happy about it.

"We're your friends, you should have told us you were seeing someone," Hannah huffed as she poured more wine for everyone. We were at her house as we often were but that was usually on a Thursday evening. But given that Molly had recently returned from her honeymoon and I had practice on Thursday, we'd had to reschedule. Now it was Wednesday night, after my final appointment with Erik and I'd dragged Fleur along—she needed to meet the women who would be at her back from now until forever.

Hannah loved any excuse to cook for us all and had made fancy burgers and fries for everyone. It felt like a party now that Molly was back and Leslie and Carol were finished setting up the new community hub in town. Instantly, the girls fell in love with Fleur. Both Fleur and Hannah had a keen interest in homegrown vegetables and were already planning to make tomato sauce and curry paste in the summer.

The party atmosphere dimmed when Hannah had asked me about the lumberjack, and I'd blushed, stammered, and tried to divert the conversation. None of them were having it but Fleur and Leslie watched me speculatively. But I knew when I was backed into a corner so I'd spilled, telling them we were only friends with benefits but it was great. Then Fleur had said that Erik was my date for the midseason ball and they all looked at me like I had grown wings. I wasn't really into getting all fancy for a *ball* but this news sent

Hannah and Molly into a frenzy. When I mentioned I didn't have anything to wear, they went utterly berserk. Then Fleur, bless her hand-knitted woollen socks, said everyone should come. She didn't realise that these lunatics needed no encouragement to party. So, for the last thirty minutes, we had been on a dress-renting website and paid an extraordinary amount of money for express shipping.

It was only after that excitement that Hannah and Molly were now sharing how hurt they were. I felt bad because I could have told them about Erik, but I hadn't wanted to. After Erik and I spending all our time together the last week, laughing, fucking, eating, fucking, cuddling, and being practically attached at the hip, I was more nervous about my own feelings than ever. I was getting in deep and the rouse that I was content with being friends with benefits was increasingly harder to maintain. It was hard, but that didn't mean it wasn't absolutely necessary. When he'd had enough, not only would I be destroyed, but Hannah, Molly, Leslie, and Carol would tear him to shreds. Really, I was doing this in his best interests, certainly not because I was a coward. Not. At. All. As they asked more questions, I did my best to play it down, but this only partially satisfied them. I would need to do better but the effing ball wasn't going to help.

"So, how did you two hook up? Was it at the clinic when you treated his ankle?" Carol asked, not feeling sorry for me taking the flack from Hannah and Molly.

"Well, not exactly," I said, knowing I needed to tell them about Theodore. They were going to like this even less than they liked me not telling them I was shagging someone. I didn't want them upset with me, I'd missed spending time with them and we were close, really close, so I decided to spit that out too.

"My brother called me," I said. Hannah's mouth dropped open and Molly shook her head in confusion, her blond curls bouncing around like springs.

"What?" Hannah asked, eying her wine suspiciously as though she had had too much and it was impairing her ability to comprehend my words. I wanted to laugh; their reaction was comical, but there was nothing humorous about it. I told them, starting with the voice mail, then to Erik's role in being there for me and finally about my reconnection with my brother. The further into my tale I went, the more solemn the room became and when I was done, no one said anything about me hiding it from them. Clearly, they understood how intense life had been for me.

"And Paddy? Is he okay too?" Molly asked.

"Yes, and he wants to reach out to me and try to mend fences. Theodore is pushing it, but I don't want to, or need to."

"Maybe he needs to. If you were as in love as you remember, it must be cutting him up," Hannah said, and she was right. I'm sure he did feel like that. But I didn't know if I wanted to deal with his needs while I was managing my own.

"I'll speak to him, but I don't need to travel down that road right away. It brings up things that I have put in my past. It all makes me nervous actually."

"What do you mean?" Carol asked, concern etching her features.

"He has such a hold on me. I was infatuated with him to the point that I believed what I wanted to, not what was real. That loss of control can be scary," I said honestly.

"Not when it's with the right person," Hannah said. That might be fine for her, but that didn't mean it was for me.

I'd left Hannah's feeling rejuvenated from the time with my friends. It was a good reminder that being lonely by choice was stupid. These women were at my back, and I needed to remember it. They were so supportive, in fact, that they had all bought tickets to come to the midseason ball. This kind of support scared me a little. When we were together, we were a strange sort of crazy and I didn't know how Erik or the other netball girls would handle it. I drove Fleur home, and she thanked me for sharing my friends. I didn't like the idea of her being lonely either and now she had met everyone, there was no turning back for her—they were hers now too.

After leaving Fleur, I drove home, loving that Erik was waiting for me. When I found him in bed, hair loose, shirt off, and reading glasses on, I lost the plot and pounced on him. He had me straddling his hips as he sat on the edge of the bed, driving in so deep that I could still feel him there in the morning.

Thursday and Friday went by in a blur as my phone was constantly blown up by messages from Leslie, Carol, Hannah, Molly, and now Fleur. It started with details about hair, makeup, where to get ready, borrowed handbags and strapless bras for Saturday. Then it went to Erik the Viking, and Hannah sent video after video of Monty Python's Eric the Viking. I could imagine her hooting with laughter. It was worse when Carol sent through some pictures of the Whimsical Woodsman, a hairy, middle-aged lumberjack who took photos of himself in his undies, holding a chainsaw.

I rolled my eyes at each new message, but Fleur found it hysterical and was in tears when I'd stepped out for lunch, threatening to show him. I made her swear not to, but I could clearly see she was lying through her teeth. Turncoat. At training on Thursday night, Daphne was quiet but I could see she was watching me, especially when Erik carried my sports bag to the car after we'd finished dinner. When she learned that all my friends were coming to the ball, she was going to flip her lid.

After a relatively peaceful day at work on Friday, I'd decided to stay in for the night because Erik had planned to catch up with Ben's family for Ben's mother's birthday. He'd said I should come, but I was too afraid. To me, this was definitely more than shagging, although the nonchalant way he'd asked, I didn't think he saw it that way. If I went, it would be more people whom I would have to extricate myself from and even I had the sense to say no. I'd told him that I'd had such a good time with the girls, and that he needed time with his friends too. He'd given me a strange look, not quite irritation but something else, before he'd let it go.

So, after eating cheese and crackers for dinner, I didn't bother with television while I waited for Erik. Instead, I went into my front room and cleaned it. I'd always avoided the space because it held the links to my brother, the evidence of what I'd done. Now, it didn't seem as scary and after everything was in order, I pulled out my collection of keepsakes and went through them. I laughed at the photos of Theodore and me growing up, playing soccer in the backyard, a trip to the beach, visiting Buckingham Palace, and even one when we'd snuck out to see Oasis in concert without our parents knowing.

There were also a few images of Paddy, Theodore, and me in London. We were always smiling, always with a drink in hand. I remembered that Paddy had been attentive, but looking at the photos now, I noticed that we were always touching. He had a hand on my knee, or our fingers were entwined. We looked young, in love, and infatuated. He was handsome with light brown hair, green eyes, and a broad, confident smile. I'd thought he was the best-looking man

I'd ever seen, but now he paled compared to the masculine beauty of Erik, who was brawny, rugged, and chiselled.

The more I looked at the old photos, the more surprised I was at how besotted I was with him. I couldn't imagine myself like that anymore, so open in my affections, and that made me sad, like I'd lost something. Not wanting to dwell too long on that morbid thought, I pulled the best pictures out and took them with me back to the kitchen. I would scan them and send some to Theodore for a laugh. Maybe I'd even frame a few and put them up around the house.

After my trip down memory lane, I drew a hot bubble bath and waited for Erik to come home. I was always eager to see him, but today it felt like it had been too long since breakfast. I was on the precipice of dozing off when he walked into the bathroom with another strange look on his face. He wasn't upset or worried or irritated as he had been earlier. Now he seemed distracted.

"You okay, handsome?" I asked, hearing my words tainted with sleepiness.

"Good. I'm good. You?" he asked, coming farther into the room to stop by the tub.

"I'm great. Are you going to join me, or should we hit the sack?" I asked, becoming more alert and noticing that he looked like there was something weighing on his mind that wasn't pleasant.

"Let's get to bed. Looks like we've both had a big day," he said, and I wasn't sure what he meant. My day hadn't been any bigger than usual.

"I'm sorry?" I asked.

"You cleaned out your front room," he said, clearly concerned for how that might have impacted me. It was thoughtful but unnecessary.

"Yeah, I did. It was time." I smiled, hoping to allay his fears.

"Are you okay with everything?" he asked, like *everything* meant something more than it did.

"I am. Why?"

"No reason, just a lot of memories to bring up," he said, and I nodded, agreeing with him. There were a lot of memories but many of them were good ones. Something about his mood told me that there was something else going on. I stood up, ready to get out and talk to him about what was really on his mind.

"Will you pass me a towel?" I asked as I stood there, letting the water run off me. Erik took a long moment to answer as his gaze travelled over my naked body.

"No," he muttered as his eyes grew hazy and he drew in a deep breath.

"Please?" I grinned, loving the fact I had this effect on him

"No." His beautiful voice was huskier now as he bit his lip and I shivered in response.

"Why not?" I teased.

"Because you are sexy as fuck any time, let alone when you are naked, wet, and your skin is a pretty shade of pink," he said, grabbing my hips with his large, calloused hands that almost spanned my waist. When he moved his gaze from my body to look at me, I could see his lust and desire, and it was intoxicating.

"What are you going to do about it?" I asked, running my hands through his loose hair, gripping it tight and giving it a little yank.

"It's time for some pillaging I think," he said as he scooped me up, threw me over his shoulder, and hauled me to the bedroom. Then he kept his word and pillaged me into the early hours of the morning.

***

As usual, I woke up before Annie. She didn't sleep late, not really, but I woke earlier. And like always when I slept next to her, I woke up hard and needing her. It was an unconscious need, something that my body called for in my sleep and added fuel to the fire in my brain. Before Annie, life had been simple. I played football, spent time at the cabin, got laid, avoided Daphne, and worked. But now? Now things were messed up in a way that was both good and bad. It had been great to talk to Ben last night because without his help I would be even more confused.

According to Ben, my interest in Annie had clearly set Daphne into motion. From what his sisters had learned, she was not happy that I'd pursued Annie and that Daphne had focused her anger on Annie, and not me. Seemed stupid, but according to Ben, it was normal. None of it was normal.

Melanie had also heard from a friend of Daphne's who worked at the council that it was Geronimo who had told Daphne about my interest in Annie in the first place. Seemingly he had heard something I'd said to Annie and mentioned it to Daphne, although I had no idea how they were ever in the same space. At least it explained how Daphne was on to my feelings for Annie before we had technically "hooked up." This was the downside of small towns, and Ben's sisters were in the thick of the gossip network, and although Melanie had settled down a little, Evelyn was still a little rogue. Annie should consider herself lucky she was a "non-native," as she put it. It meant she wasn't directly connected to the rumour mill.

Ben said our couple-like sparring in public and the most recent showdown with Daphne when she'd brought up Annie's past made for a very public confirmation that we were together. This was no surprise, but neither was the news that Daphne was overheard at work playing the injured card, hurt that she had tried to help me and that she was simply misunderstood. That was the end of Ben's news and none of it was helpful or unusual. Daphne was obvious and I didn't care much about it.

It was her connection to this Freya that really bothered me. To start with there were texts and hard-to-hear voice mails that were not from any number I could call back. Then after I spoke to her demanding she leave me alone, she had sent a letter to my home address. Daphne must've given out my number and my address.

Since then there had been a few texts and another voice mail, but this time from a number I could return. Ben, who was not just a pretty face, suggested that she had been calling from overseas, but was now in Australia. He seemed to think it was relevant; I didn't. I didn't want a stalker based here or abroad. End. Of. Story.

Ben and I had gone through my days of travelling, but there was no one I recalled with that name when I was backpacking through Europe. Something in my gut told me it wasn't about that. Ben suggested I talk to Freya and I had considered it. But Daphne being involved made it feel like a trap, leaving me with one option. I needed to talk to Daphne. This fact made me more than unhappy, but as I'd driven to Annie's place, my dissatisfaction with the status quo between Annie and me had taken front and centre in my mind. In the twenty minutes it took me to get to her place from Ben's family home, I'd cursed myself for offering a friend-and-sex deal. Knowing what I knew now, and how we were together, I wanted more. Shit. We were already *doing* more.

There were times when I thought she was feeling the same. Quiet times, when we were at home watching television, on her beloved hiking trails, or when she first woke up, that I reckoned she was like me: falling hard. She was open, letting her body and heart dictate her actions, not her head, and she would idly caress me, give me a kiss just because, or tell me something personal, not because she was prompted but because she felt safe.

But then she would realise and retreat. It wasn't a physical retreat, and she didn't become cold or distant; she became cautious and guarded. It was the same feeling I got when she spoke to her brother. When she still talked in hushed tones about returning home or Paddy, I felt like she was keeping a part of herself from me. She didn't need to hide that from me given the bloody agreement we had, but she did. I was also not loving that she'd only recently told her friends about us. If they were as tight as I thought they were, her hiding what we were doing from them didn't sit right with me. I couldn't make her want more from me, but fuck I wanted it. I craved it. I was desperate for her to feel for me what I felt for her.

So, it was with this and Daphne on my mind that I walked into her house and headed to the kitchen to find her. That's where I found the photos and my chest tightened painfully. They were photos of a young Annie. She was still beautiful but younger and freer. I wished I'd known her then, to see her at full flight without the burden of experiencing misplaced guilt for years. I thumbed through the pictures, surprised she had gone through that front room so soon after reconnecting with Theodore. She'd told me that she used to go in there to torture herself and I'd been alarmed at the depth of her self-loathing.

From the images, it was clear who Theodore was and that they were close. I was glad she had that back. Then I came across the photos of who must be Paddy the douche. He looked smarmy to me, like a cocky motherfucker who knew he was batting above his average. I was being irrational—I knew it—but I did not like the way he was all over her in the photos. It was possessive and creepy. Then there was the fact that he was a fucking drug addict who almost killed her and her brother. The fact that he did that and still got to have her love made me want to punch his lights out.

I drew in a deep breath, needing to stop. I was being a jealous arsehole and I had no right to. One thing I knew for sure, thinking about this, Freya and Daphne made me dog tired, and I could hear the ghost of my father rattling in my brain telling me women weren't worth it. I was not going to be like him, a drunk who neglected his parental responsibilities or got torn up for the right or wrong reasons over another woman.

So, I took a deep breath and walked toward Annie's room, assuming she was in bed when I saw the bathroom light on, door ajar. I peeked in to find her in the bath, almost asleep. The sight of her, at rest with a small smile on her face, her tiny feet poking over the edge with nails painted black, her hair pushed back from her face showing her dark lashes resting at her cheeks, made my heart constrict. She was a complex person: sassy, loyal, righteous, vulnerable, and like this, an angel. What the fuck was I going to do?

Chapter 16

Hannah and Molly were certifiable. They had gone bonkers and I was not sure how to launch an intervention. I knew Carol was with me because she was looking at them like they had morphed into aliens with an unhealthy love of hair straighteners and eyeliner. Leslie was going with it, seemingly happy to be fluffed about, and Fleur was smiling softly, no doubt secretly enjoying the ridiculousness and girl time. Me? This made me more nervous than I already was, which, to put it mildly, was at a catatonic level.

We were at Molly's house attached to the winery, getting ready together. The men, consisting of Howard and Dave, who had been conscripted to attend, and Erik, who had agreed to come for a drink before we went to the party, had been banished to the tasting rooms because we were doing important, female-only things like applying flipping mascara. I wasn't sure about the importance of this, however; getting drunk on red wine sounded pretty fucking important to me. But no, I was here on the couch in Molly's enormous bedroom with my nails drying, my hair sprayed to within an inch of its life, wearing my underwear and a robe, getting my makeup done by Molly.

"It's not a wedding. Or a debutante ball. Or a prom for that matter. We are only going to the club rooms for drinks and dancing, and to help raise money for the club," I grumbled.

"Shhhh. I can't put on your eyeliner and listen to you bitch and moan. You want to look like the drag version of Cleopatra?" Molly snapped, reminiscent of her days as a bridezilla.

"Of course not, but you need to get that it won't be that fancy and we don't want to look over done," I said.

"Anne Elizabeth Clarke, we need to look our best. Especially if Daphne is going to be there," Molly chided.

"Not to mention your hot-as-shit Viking-lumberjack," Hannah threw in, and I desperately tried not to smile. But I did.

"He's not mine," I muttered.

"Of course not. You're only shagging him. I get it," Hannah threw over her shoulder as she slipped into a red lace corset dress that was figure hugging, emphasising her assets and falling below her knees. Hannah looked like a 50s bombshell, and with her hair out and full of bounce, I could see why Howard couldn't keep his eyes off her.

"That's right. We're just shagging," I confirmed, but she rolled her eyes.

"You're spending every night together and taking long walks in the woods. What's next, pina coladas and getting caught in the rain?" she sassed, and it was my turn to roll my eyes.

"No. I draw the line at pina coladas."

"I can't imagine Erik drinking a pina colada, but I'd love to try one," Fleur chimed in, smiling at me as she put her own dress on. She'd gone a little more conservative than Hannah, wearing a soft pink dress with shoestring straps, a sweetheart neckline that managed to restrain her plentiful chest, and a chiffon midi overskirt. She looked like a princess, especially with the classy chignon Molly had given her. Beautiful was an understatement.

"You've never had one?" Molly asked, looking at her, slightly alarmed.

"I don't drink a lot. I've had a child since I was eighteen and there is no way I want to deal with Tate and a hangover."

"You're not selling this kid business," Molly grumbled, and I laughed. She was trying to fall pregnant because Dave was desperate for a big family. She had pretended like she was neither here nor there, but we all knew she wanted lots of kids too.

"You'll romp it in love," Leslie told Molly with a warm smile and I sighed. As much as they were pains in the ass, I loved my friends.

"You're done now, Miss Annie. We all need to get dressed so we can grab at least one drink before we head off," Molly said, clapping her hands. Molly loved to be organised, and after coordinating her own wedding like clockwork, wrangling a few ladies wasn't exactly like herding cats for her, although you wouldn't know it by the stern look she gave me. I sighed and stood up, taking in everyone else in the room.

Carol looked sharp in a black tuxedo, Leslie wore a kick-arse blue maxi dress with long sleeves and intricate stitched detail, and Molly wore a long-sleeve, emerald green dress with a ruffle skirt that was short and showed off her holiday tan. She was as short as me, and as we always did when we went out, we wore the highest heels we could manage. Hers were gold, which only enhanced her tan. Her curly hair was piled on top of her head to show off the gold collar she was wearing. I was the last to suit up.

"Annie, your turn," Molly told me as I loitered, not ready to get dressed and look in the mirror. I wasn't a vain person nor did I have low confidence. I also knew I wasn't a shrew. But the stakes seemed higher tonight not only with my friends meeting Erik and being on show at the ball. It was because I was going *with* Erik, and he had never seen me really dressed up. I knew it was ridiculous, but I was nervous. Reluctantly, I stepped into my dark purple jumpsuit. The pants were tight and hit me at mid-calf, my sexy, strappy black sandals that wrapped around my ankles on full display. The top was looser with a deep V at the front that exposed a considerable amount of chest and décolletage. It came to a thick halter-neck band around my neck and exposed my whole back. It fit me like a glove and Hannah let out a low whistle when I turned to show the crowd.

"You look like a sexy badarse in that outfit," she said, waggling her eyebrows as she added jewellery. I didn't feel sexy or like a badass. I felt nervous and anxious to see Erik's reaction.

"Come on, vamp, let's get a drink," Molly said. We filed out of her room and as we walked into the tasting area, all talking ceased. I was at the back so I wasn't sure what was happening when I heard Dave speak.

"Shit. You cannot go out like that," Dave said, looking at his wife.

"Excuse me?" Molly asked with her hands on her hips.

"Too beautiful. The other men will be driven mad," he said, grinning as he came and gave her a kiss. Hannah walked to Howard, giving him a smile full of promise.

"You all look lovely," Howard said to the room while not taking his eyes off his woman, and I smiled at his politeness. I knew Erik was at the back; I could see him but I was avoiding looking directly at him. I rubbed the back of my neck uncomfortably. Why was this so hard?

"You better get over there," Fleur whispered as she walked past me to the bar to take a glass of Prosecco Dave was holding for her. With nothing for it I swallowed and looked at him. He was standing closer now, looking incredibly handsome in a black suit with a black shirt, no tie. His hair was pulled back and his beard was trimmed low, showing off how chiselled his face was. He was breathtaking, and I found myself licking my lips as I took him in.

"Pixie," he murmured as he came to me. It was only when he was in front of me, hand on my hip, that I really looked into his eyes. Gone was the lazy blue gaze, replaced by hunger and appreciation, making my heart beat too fast.

"Stunning," he murmured before coming in and planting a soft kiss behind my ear. He smelled amazing too, his woodsy, spicy smell even stronger, and with my senses being overwhelmed, I was lost. Shivering at his touch, I gripped his lapels as I had a sudden, desperate urge to take him to the wine cellar and tear all his clothes of. It was as though my brain was momentarily disengaged, and I was driven by something more primal. Did he realise how gorgeous he was? But instead of being sexy, I opened my mouth.

"You too. You look hot, I meant, amazingly handsome, hot. Sexy. Yes. Sexy too. And sharp. Sharp like a bad-arse. I was going for bad-arse too but you nailed it. A bad and hot-arse, woodsy-smelling Viking-lumberjack sex god," I muttered like a madwoman, but being in his arms like this, his body close, his head bent to mine intimately, I couldn't help it.

"I want to kiss you then fuck you, right now. Let's skip the ball; I don't know if I can take being close to you without touching you inappropriately," he chuckled in my ear.

"Try to be sneaky about it," I heard myself say, and Erik laughed outright at this. I wasn't trying to be funny though, I meant it.

"Annie, Erik, a drink?" Molly asked, coming over and bringing me back to reality with a fresh beer for Erik and a glass of red wine for me.

"Thanks," I said as I leant back and took the drink from my friend, who was giving me a suspicious look. Hannah was in the background watching me too, and when she caught my eyes, she mouthed the question *just shagging?* I tried to glare at her but it didn't work.

We had time for one drink before we headed to the ball, which was held at the club rooms. They'd performed a miracle, transforming the big open space into a sophisticated party venue. Dark flowing material covered the walls, with giant indoor trees strategically placed to soften it. The lights were dimmed, but dark corners were lit with art deco lamps, cocktail tables and tall stools strategically placed around the room with candles and flowers giving it an intimate feel. Music with a heavy bass played in the background as waiters served platters of food and drinks. We'd garnered lots of attention when we entered, not only because there were new faces and we were dressed up to within an inch of our lives. No, people were looking at Erik and me, who were hip to hip, his arm possessively splayed across my naked back, partially covering my tattoo.

"Wow, you look amazing," Bel said as she came over and gave us a hug. "You scrub up okay too, Erik," she understated.

"Thanks, Bel, you're looking lovely," Erik returned easily, and she grinned. We were joined by Jade and some of the other club members I knew. I introduced them to my friends and they thanked Hannah, Molly, Leslie, and Carol for coming and supporting the club. Howard and Dave hung back, doing some sort of manly thing where they sized up the other men. Erik was great; he introduced them to Ben and a few of his friends, and the night started to fire up as more alcohol was consumed.

"Annie, you are both kidding yourselves. There is nothing *booty call* about the way he looks at you, or the way you go all doe-eyed when he smiles," Hannah said when we were standing around a table we'd commandeered and the men were off doing, well, manly things.

"Leave her alone," Leslie said softly, seeing my discomfort. I think she knew that it wasn't me who didn't want more.

"It must be my hair and makeup," I said, trying to diffuse the situation.

"I'm not sure that's all it is, although you look very sexy," Hannah said, taking Leslie's warning on board.

"Look, who knows where it will go, but it isn't what we agreed to. If something comes of it, great. If not, then no harm done," I said quietly, not wanting Daphne's minions to overhear.

"Agreed? Did you sign a contract or something?" Molly asked, confused.

"No, they're just our terms of reference and…" I started before Fleur cleared her throat and looked at me with big eyes. I looked around to see what had caught her attention to find Daphne walking over with her friends. Daphne looked beautiful as always, but tonight she had gone for classy and demure, with a simple little black dress, killer red heels, and her gorgeous hair free and glossy.

"Fleur, Annie. We're having a team photo, if you're free now?" she asked politely. Strangely, her words didn't hold any malice or mischief.

"Hi, Daphne. These are my friends, Hannah, Molly, Leslie, and Carol," I said as everyone awkwardly looked at each other.

"Nice to meet you. You all look so stylish," she said, giving each of my friends a small smile.

"It's a pleasure to meet you," Hannah said, sticking her hand out, and Daphne took it, giving it a pathetic shake. Hannah would not like that; her handshakes were firm and direct.

"We better go while the photographer is free," she said and turned to walk away.

"What was that about?" Molly whispered when she was out of earshot.

"No idea, but she is up to something," Fleur said as we walked off to have our team photo.

As the night wore on, we all relaxed into dancing and drinking. I don't know if Leslie had a word to Molly and Hannah, but they dropped the Spanish Inquisition and let me be. I understood their confusion; I was confused too. I would have been more sure if it weren't for Erik's distance sometimes, the fact he hadn't talked about his mother, which was clearly an issue for him, or when we were getting into serious territory and he steered us toward sexy times, not deep and meaningful times. Last night was a perfect example; something was on his mind when he'd come into the bathroom, but he'd distracted me in a very pleasurable way.

I'd pushed all that worry to the back of my mind, aided by a little red wine, and when the music ramped up, we'd hit the dance floor, our group expanding to include Bel, Jade, and Fleur, who were a little perplexed about our enthusiasm.

"They need more time to get used to us," Molly had said when she saw their happily confused stares.

"Or perhaps more booze," Hannah had added, and I'd laughed, nodding in agreement, glad to have my friends with me. Erik had hovered on the edge, talking to his teammates, and Ben, Howard, and Dave, although whenever I looked for him, it wasn't long before his eyes met mine and he smiled. We hadn't spoken much until we took a break from dancing to have a drink and rest our legs. As we were talking, Erik at my back as I perched on a stool, his hand started to do some sneaky and inappropriate touching at my lower back. I was ready to call a taxi and drag him to my place when his name was called out by one of his teammates at the stage, holding a guitar.

"Come on, who wants to hear Erik sing? The band is getting back together so give him a cheer and get his arse up here," the man said, and I spun around to look at Erik, who was shaking his head but smiling.

"Piss off," Erik mouthed at him, but the crowd had gotten involved and were chanting his name.

"You sing?" I asked him, surprised but not shocked. He could probably do anything.

"Yeah, Pixie." He gave me a small smile but before I could ask him if he could play guitar too, a teammate grabbed him around the shoulders and propelled him forwards. I watched him go for a beat before I looked at Hannah and Molly, who gave me big eyes, then at Fleur, who looked confused.

"You didn't know?"

"No, he's never mentioned it," I whispered.

"Well, you're in for a treat." She grinned.

Erik took the stage and my heart squeezed hard then started to pump harder. So hard, I thought the girls could hear it. He took the guitar handed to him by a band member he clearly knew, then completely shocked me when he sat down and adjusted the microphone. Damn, he was going to sing and play. Time for my ovaries to explode.

He opened with an awesome version of "Free Fallin'" by Tom Petty, going into "Fool for You" by the John Butler Trio. At the end of each song, the crowd erupted in applause. But I didn't make a sound. I couldn't. My eyes were glued to him, watching those blue eyes twinkle with enjoyment, his broad smile making his golden beard and hair glisten in the spotlight. I knew all the women in the room, irrespective of sexual persuasion, were thinking about that handsome, beautiful manliness in a black shirt with the sleeves rolled up, his tanned arms holding the guitar and his confidence filling the space.

"You're fucked," Hannah said in my ear, deadly serious, and she was right. I was fucked. I'd had a taste of this man, and the more I sampled, the better it got. I was well and truly in the danger zone. When he started to sing "Wonderwall" by Oasis, he gave me a wink and I shook my head in disbelief.

As the song ended, and I pulled in a deep breath, trying to use oxygen as a lifeline out of my deep, emotional musings, he started up with "Horses" by Daryl Braithwait, and the crowd erupted, especially my Australian friends. This song was like an end-of-the-night sing-along ambrosia, and people stood, signing in time with Erik. I felt myself stand but it wasn't a conscious action. I was hypnotised.

"You're more than fucked. A singing, sexy, thoughtful, Viking-lumberjack. Holy shit," Molly said.

She was one hundred percent correct. I. Was. Fucked.

And completely in love.

***

I wouldn't have said I was nervous about meeting Annie's friends. I had enough social skills to talk to people, and living in a small town, you get used to rubbing up against arseholes, wankers, and douche bags alike. That said, none of her friends were anything like that, nor did I expect them to be.

I felt a little uptight about the whole night because yet again, we were being a couple. Mixing friends, pre-dinner drinks, turning up at an event together. It was becoming obvious to everyone except maybe Annie that we were heading in a romantic direction, not a straight-up sexual one. The shitty thing was, I think maybe she did see it heading that way, but was avoiding it. Yet again, something was holding her back.

Howard and Dave seemed like good people, different than the guys I usually spent time with, but that was okay. Howard was quiet but exuded authority and intelligence. He looked like a GQ model in the fanciest fucking suit I had ever seen. Dave on the other hand was casual, cheerful, and funny. The girls were like Annie in the sense they knew their own mind and were happy in themselves. Hannah and Annie shared a fiery attitude and they all seemed to care for each other about things that counted. They'd taken Fleur in as well, and I was happy for her to have some women at her back again. But, while all was peachy in the group, I could see her friends watching us speculatively and I wondered what she had told them about us.

When she'd finally come into the tasting room, my chest had seized and my stomach had dropped. She was fucking sexy any time, but seeing her strut out, her hair looking like my hands had been in it, pouty glossy lips, dark sexy eyes, and all her creamy skin itching to be touched, I had to force myself to stay put and not drag her off somewhere and fuck her brains out. Something about her called to me, both emotionally and physically, and I couldn't imagine ever not desperately wanting her. She wasn't my usual type, that was for sure, but I supposed I didn't have a type until I met her. Daphne was beautiful in a bombshell kind of way, and other women I'd slept with had been a variation on curves, big hair, and pretty faces, but Annie. Fuck my life. Annie was something else. She was brilliant, interesting, striking, delicate, almost ethereal, and I was sucked in completely.

Her reaction to seeing me in my fancy duds had been the same, and for a moment there we were both lost for words. Then I'd felt it: the thing between us morphing yet again into something more primitive and absolute as we were suspended looking at each other anew. Then she'd gripped me like she needed my support to stay upright, and I'd thought she had come to realise what we had. When we'd headed into the club rooms together, I thought I was lucky to have her on my arm, and even though we weren't together all the time, I felt her gaze on me often, and I loved it.

So I was surprised and fucking disappointed when I'd come to check on her drink status only to overhear her telling her girls about our agreement being a terms of reference. Sure, we had started out that way but that wasn't how I saw things now. She was hanging on to that like a lifeline, not willing to take a risk. I was gutted. They were my words and she didn't want to commit to more but was content to lap up what we had and take what I was offering for as long as it lasted.

Daphne had heard Annie say that too; she had been walking toward the girls from the other direction and seeing me stop and listen. She did the same as she kept her gaze on me with a small smile on her face. I didn't like that look one bit, and no doubt she thought that when Annie and I eventually went up in smoke, she would be able to move right in. She was delusional like that, but I couldn't worry about it. She would do whatever the fuck she wanted to do. She was the least of my problems anyway. I had to figure out how I was going to manage being in love with someone who didn't feel the same. It made me feel tired, angry, and sick, and suddenly I reminded myself of my father.

Chapter 17

I'd barely stepped out of the shower when I had the life scared out of me by someone knocking on my door. Other than Erik, who came in without knocking, I didn't have visitors. I wasn't merely curious about who was at the door, I was annoyed. I threw on my clothes, brushed my hair out of my face, and headed to the front door to give them a serve. I could see two shadows in the leadlight glass but no one recognisable.

"Whatever you're selling, I am not interested," I said as I swung the door open. The man with his back to the door turned to face me and I froze solid. What on earth?

"Hey, Annie," my big brother said. Well, I thought it was him, although it could have been an apparition.

"Ted?" I whispered.

"Yes, it's me." My handsome brother gave me a small smile as we stood there looking each other over.

"It's really you," I said, reaching for him and pulling him into a hug.

"It really is." He laughed as he wrapped me in a hug. I clung to him as tears filled my eyes.

"What are you doing here? How did you get here? I don't understand," I said, not letting him go.

"I had a few weeks off work and plenty of points," he said, pulling me away so he could look at me. "It's good to see you," he said, emotion clogging his throat now.

"I've missed you," I said on a sob before hugging him again. As he always had, he squeezed me tight and told me it was all okay. Eventually my tears turned into laughter as I realised how ridiculous I was being. Theodore was here and I was crying all over him, in my doorway.

"What's so funny?" he asked, his face looking amused but confused.

"Me. I'm sobbing all over you when in reality, I am so fucking happy you are here. Come in," I said, stepping into the hallway, opening the door for him. He hesitated a moment before he spoke.

"I'm not alone."

"You're not?" I was unsure what he meant, but remembering that I'd seen two shadows, perhaps he had a friend with him?

"No..." he said, stepping to the side to reveal another man from my past, standing a few feet back. I blinked slowly, trying to comprehend who was before me. Paddy looked older and different. He still had sandy hair and a handsome face, but his body was now that of a man's and his face had changed. It wasn't that he was haggard; he looked as if he'd experienced hardship.

"Hi, Annie," he said nervously. This was something else I'd never seen on him before; he was always confident and assured. Now, he looked uncomfortable and ready to bolt, no doubt unsure if I forgave him. The look on his face communicated real remorse and if Theodore could do it, so could I.

"Paddy, hi," I said, moving to him, giving him a hug. He took a moment, then returned the embrace.

"It's good to see you too," I said when I pulled back.

"Thanks. I wasn't sure if..." he started but I shook my head.

"Come on, let's go inside." I turned and walked into the house, not ready to talk about all that yet. I wanted to enjoy my brother coming to visit first. They followed me down the hall into my kitchen.

"Take a seat, I'll put the kettle on," I said, moving about my kitchen. When I looked back, Theodore was looking around smiling, and Paddy was looking out the French doors into the garden. It was cold but sunny, and the mountain range shone in the background.

"So, tell me about getting here. When did you arrive?"

"Yesterday, we drove up from Melbourne last night late," Theodore answered distractedly as he continued to inspect my place.

"Where did you stay?"

"A motel in town," he muttered as he ran his hands over the stone of the fireplace.

"You should have told me, I could have picked you up and you could have stayed here, unless you don't feel comfortable," I said as I made tea.

"I thought maybe it was better," Theodore murmured, nodding at Paddy. Clearly he wasn't entirely comfortable with Paddy's presence. "Annie, you need to let it go. That's why I'm here, why Paddy is. We need to move on," he said, grabbing my hand across the counter. I looked up to see him watching me, his eyes concerned but without any judgment or blame. I turned to watch Paddy, who looked sad, remorseful, and uncomfortable. He hadn't forgiven himself, and perhaps Ted was helping him to move on too.

"Okay. I'll try," I said, giving them both a watery smile. We spent the rest of the morning at home, catching up. When it was time to go to work, we all headed back into town. I didn't have an appointment first up, so I convinced Fleur to meet us for a quick burger at Tomahawk. Fleur was being her usual cute and lovely self; trying to talk to Theodore and Paddy about the area but coming across as shy and nervous. She mentioned we played netball together, but Paddy interrupted her.

"Annie plays netball?" He seemed surprised by this but he shouldn't have. I'd played sport all through school.

"Of course she does. I bet she's good too, am I right, Fleur?" my brother asked, and Fleur blushed at the attention.

"She's been best on court every game since she started filling in. I had to persuade her to play though," Fleur said nervously.

"How did you do that?" he asked her. "Did you threaten to beat her with a stick? That's what I would've done," he continued, giving her a grin, and she smiled, shaking her head. "Why didn't you want to play? You never back away from a competition," Theodore said, teasing me.

"Lots of reasons," I said as I rolled my eyes.

"Erik was one of them, surely," Fleur said, and I nodded.

"Erik?" both Theodore and Paddy said at the same time. Their tone was intense, verging on concerned.

"Erik, the man I've been seeing."

"Why would you want to avoid him?" Theodore gave me a suspicious look and Paddy's face went blank.

"Well, I fought going out with him. I was avoiding relationships but he was relentless," I said, not wanting to continue given Paddy was here, but needing them all to know that I'd met someone.

"I see," Theodore said, assessing me.

"What's he like?" Paddy asked uncomfortably. I really didn't want to talk about Erik with him.

"Well, he's funny, and thoughtful. He is a great cook, plays the guitar, and looks like a Viking-lumberjack," I said, trying for glib.

"Sounds great," Paddy mumbled sarcastically, which pissed me off. We were long since done, and there was no need for him to be like that. Fleur picked up on it too.

"He really is. Great I mean. He grew up here and I've known him for a long time. He is brilliant at football and from what Annie has told me, is quite the skilled carpenter," she said, and I grinned, appreciating the support.

"I can't wait to meet him," Theodore said honestly after giving Paddy a quelling look.

"You'll have to meet all my friends too," I said, thinking about Hannah, Molly, Leslie, and Carol, who would be very interested to clap eyes on him. I really needed to make some calls.

"Line it up," Theodore said. Thankfully our food arrived and we could move on from Erik. After lunch, I worked all afternoon, and texted Erik before I finished, asking him if he was around tonight for dinner at the pub. I wanted to see him and introduce him to Theodore; I thought they would get on like a house on fire. Erik took a long time to answer my text, saying he had to work late. When I'd replied that I would see him later, his return message said he would try. If he didn't come over, that would be the first night in weeks we'd been apart.

I tried not to be put out; no doubt he was busy. My brother and Paddy were happy to head out for dinner and catch-up. After dinner, we left Paddy in town at the motel and I drove Theodore to my place and we set up the spare room. When I'd told him how I'd used that room before, we'd had another moment where I was in tears and he held me; our time apart had been terrible for both of us.

Ted crashed early so I sat on the couch, pulled out my phone, and filled in the girls about Ted and Paddy, then texted Erik, asking him to let me know if he could make it that night. After dozing on the couch, I saw a text from Erik saying he was beat but that he would see me tomorrow at training. Nothing he said was rude or inappropriate, but I was hurt. I'd wanted to share my exciting news with him personally, but he was unusually absent. I thought we had moved beyond our agreement, especially after the weekend. But perhaps I was wrong. Needless to say, I didn't sleep a wink.

***

I was in a bad mood and everyone at work knew about it. Yet again, people I worked with had to steer clear because I was pissed off, and the source of my irritation was a damned woman.

Part of my shitty attitude was residual irritation from the weekend. Annie and I had headed to the ball a couple, but when there, she had made it clear to her girls that this was still about the stupid fucking arrangement we had. We had spent the night together as usual and followed it up on Sunday by going for a hike, chilling out, and making dinner. But now, the better it was when we were together, the shittier I felt because I knew I was more invested.

Then when Daphne had conveniently bumped into me on my lunch break on Monday and told me she'd heard that Annie's brother was in town, she'd bloody loved the fact I was surprised. I didn't want to give her that, but my confusion and uncertainty had been a gut reaction I couldn't hide. I'd spent the rest of the day trying to let it go, waiting for Annie to tell me. But she didn't. She had tried to reach out to hook up, but nothing more than that. Maybe it was all I should expect. What I didn't expect was to drive past the pub to see her not only with her brother but also that fuckwit Paddy, laughing and having a good time.

I headed straight home before I really lost my shit, and after a shower I calmed a little. She must have been ecstatic that her brother was here, so I should cut her some slack. She texted, asking me if I was coming over, but by then I was past being able to adjust my mood, so I put her off. She had reached out as per usual the following day as though nothing were amiss and I had responded, despite the fact I was tired after tossing and turning, not liking how it felt to sleep alone. Now I was driving to training and would see her for the first time since early Monday morning when I'd made her breakfast before going to work. I wanted to see her, but she still hadn't told me about her brother or her ex.

It was a full house at the grounds, with both juniors and seniors having practice. I saw her Mini, and I felt the customary excitement to see her. I couldn't control it, the need to see her, touch her, be with her. But now that feeling also brought on a sense of dread, like what we had was on borrowed time. I pulled up, grabbed my bag, and walked toward the clubhouse to get changed. She was on the netball court, along with her team, and at the sight of her, my chest tightened and my gut clenched. Despite my need to step away from her, I couldn't. I wanted her too much. As soon as she saw me, she jogged over, and I was a little surprised. We normally didn't connect like this in front of everyone.

"Hey," she called giving me a smile when she made it to me.

"Hey," I replied, stopping and smiling back, knowing it didn't reach my eyes. She looked like she wanted to touch me but didn't. I felt exactly the same, my hands itching to feel her skin, my lips wanting to seek out hers.

"You okay?" she asked, giving me an assessing look. I wanted to say no. No, I'm not fucking okay. But I didn't.

"Why wouldn't I be?" I asked, my question coming out harsher than I intended.

"Well, you've had a lot of work on. I haven't seen you," she said, looking a bit confused. I wanted to say that not seeing me was on her, but yet again the words didn't come out. My lack of answer hurt her and I sighed. I was being a dick and I knew it. Despite how she felt, I still wanted her more than anyone.

"Yeah, it's been a bit frantic. I'll catch you after practice?" I asked, giving her a real smile. She assessed me a moment longer, but then nodded.

"Sounds good, I have a lot to tell you," she said, grinning excitedly, and I nodded.

"Sure you do," I muttered, not liking the reminder of her brother and ex's presence and me being the last to know. This point was driven home when she walked off and Daphne whispered to one of her friends, "Trouble in paradise," loud enough for everyone to hear. I sighed again in frustration but Annie walked past Daphne, glaring at her.

Practice was brutal and the weather had turned icy. It was well into winter now and there would be fewer chances to get up to the cabin to do any work, given the snow. Football had been my lifeline during winter because it kept me busy and out of my apartment. I had been thinking about how much Annie being on the scene was going to make this time of year that much better, but now I wasn't so sure. After we finished, I took a shower while being ribbed by my teammates about Annie and my new relationship status. I could normally take the heat; it didn't really matter what they thought. But today, I found myself defensively arguing that we were only hooking up and it tasted like acid in my mouth. They could fuck the hell off.

As I headed out of the door from the change room to grab dinner, I ran into Annie, who was standing there waiting for me. She gripped my shirt so she didn't fall and instinctively I put arms around her, pulling her close.

"You took your time," she said as she looked up at me, her eyes twinkling with mischief.

"I'm naturally dirty," I said without thinking before giving in and kissing her. It was meant to be a sexy, teasing kiss but before long it was a deep, intense kiss that was about reconnection and feeling. Thankfully my teammates filed out, almost knocking us both to the ground and effectively putting a halt on our reunion. A few told us to get a room, but most people smirked and slapped me on the back.

"Skip dinner here, come to my place. I have an unexpected visitor, and I want you to meet him," she said excitedly, and I drew in a deep breath, wanting to say no, but in the end nodding because I wanted time with her, for as long as I could.

I followed her to her place, convincing myself to be open minded. Maybe it would all be fine. Her brother would be all right, the ex a bigger douche bag than she originally thought, and they would fuck off back to wherever they came from. Then I could try to convince Annie we should expand our arrangement. But how pathetic did that sound? I shouldn't have to convince her—she either felt it or she didn't, right? I got down from my truck, unsure whether to bring the bag with my clean work uniform in or not, to find her waiting, looking enthusiastic.

"So, I have a visitor. It was unexpected but I'm excited for you to meet him. He turned up yesterday and I have been trying to tell you, but we haven't been able to be face to face," she said as I followed her to her door and through it.

"Oh yeah," I muttered, thinking a text heads-up would've been better as we walked down her hall to the kitchen area, where a man stood at the stove.

"We're home," she said, sounding fucking happy. This was huge for her.

"Great," the man said, turning around only to stop dead when his eyes landed on me. I stood a little taller as we eyed each other. There was no doubt this was her brother; they looked alike and he was certainly giving me a big brother's assessment.

"Theodore, this is Erik, who I was telling you about. Erik, this is my brother," she said, her eyes bouncing between us both. Reluctantly, we both moved forward to shake hands and size each other up from a closer distance. He was shorter than I was, but he was a fit-looking guy and was now eying me speculatively. I gave a small smile, and he followed suit.

"Hey, nice to meet you," I said.

"Same. Annie has been talking about you, and I guess you know a bit about me given you were there when we, ah, spoke on the phone," he said, his fancy British accent sounding much stronger than Annie's.

"Yeah, I'm glad I was there," I noted.

"Me too," he said honestly, letting go of the drama. I nodded again, thinking he might not be a complete tool bag.

"I've made dinner. It's nothing on your skills, I'm sure, but Annie had been craving sheppard's pie and even I can cook that," he said, handing me a beer from the fridge.

"Neither of us can cook really," Annie said, grinning at her brother. "Our parents were very plain eaters and we had the same seven dinners every week for as long as I could remember."

"Some kids would get excited about Christmas because of the presents. We were just happy to eat something other than overcooked meat and three veg," he added.

"I'll sort it next time," I said, finding myself loosening up. "So, when did you arrive?"

"We arrived in the country on Sunday and drove up here. We didn't spring it on Annie until yesterday though," he said.

"Spring is about right. I thought you were travelling salesmen or religious fanatics trying to recruit me when you turned up at my door," Annie said.

"We?" I asked, unsure if I'd been imagining seeing Paddy.

"Paddy and I. We go a long way back and he was involved in the accident. He was intent on making amends with Annie," Theodore said as he dished up the food.

"Right," I said, unable not to sound flat.

"He knows who Paddy was to me and what he did," Annie said quietly, and Theodore's eyes moved to mine.

"I see," he said, sounding unsure.

"Where is he now?" I asked, needing to know.

"He is staying in town, giving Annie and me space to catch up. That was the only way I'd let him come," Theodore said, giving me a look that communicated he felt where I was coming from. I relaxed, happy to know it wasn't an outright hostile takeover.

We sat down at her dining room table and spent the rest of the evening talking about nothing too serious. Annie seemed overjoyed to have us both getting along, and part of me relaxed a little. It turned out he was into mountain biking and was going to explore some of the local trails. I got the feeling Annie was waiting for me to offer to show him around, but I couldn't. This was the guy who'd brought her ex back to her, knowing he had almost killed her and that she had a new man on the scene, albeit one she was just shagging. He was also no doubt here to convince her to go back with him, so I wasn't ready to start a bromance. Not by a long shot.

What was clear was that he loved Annie, and that the two of them had always been close. We ended the night laughing about Annie's antics growing up, and the more outrageous the stories, the more I believed them. By ten p.m. we were all yawning and I stood to clear the table before leaving. Annie followed me into the kitchen, close at my heels.

"Where's your bag?" she asked, trying not to sound nervous.

"In the car. I'll let you two have some space," I said, not looking at her.

"But I, I…well. I want you to stay," she said as she pushed up beside me at the sink, moving under my arm so we were hip to hip.

"It's late and I don't want to, you know, make anyone uncomfortable," I said as I rinsed the plates.

"You won't. Besides, I've missed you," she whispered as she stilled my hands under the water.

"Yeah?" I asked. Now it was my turn, trying to hide my apprehension.

"Of course." She gave me another confused look. Clearly she didn't see anything had changed between us. So, at least we had that.

"Okay, I'll get my bag out of the truck. You sure your brother won't care?" I asked, not sure what Theodore's take would be.

"Of course not. I've been talking about you and he knows we're, well…" She trailed off, at loss for words. I wanted to laugh, it was a valid point. But it wasn't funny.

"Right, let me go get my bag," I said.

"Okay," she replied, leaning up to plant a soft kiss on my mouth before giving me a sexy smile that made my chest hurt. Without being able to help it, I leaned in for another deeper kiss that betrayed exactly how much I wanted her.

Chapter 18

Waking up with Erik, feeling warm pressed against his smooth skin, smelling him on my sheets, and hearing his even deep breathing had set the world to rights again. It was scary how much I'd missed him, given it had been less than forty-eight hours, but I supposed when you loved someone, you always missed them when they weren't near. I'd had a hard time reading him when I'd seen him arrive at practice last night. He'd seemed restrained, his carefree attitude that was usually intoxicating kept in check. But after we had physically reconnected, he'd started to return to normal, and it had continued through dinner with Theodore. Then we'd gone to bed, and spent time kissing and touching before making love and it was like it always was. Amazing. Now I headed to work feeling lighter and happier than I could remember, and Fleur noticed straight away, beaming at me.

"How did it go?" she asked, knowing I had introduced my big brother to my big not-quite-a-boyfriend.

"Okay, I think. They puffed out their chests a little but that's to be expected. After that was out of the way, and Theodore understood that Erik knew what had happened and knew about Paddy, it seemed fine. We are all going to have dinner tonight at the Brewery. Would you and Tate like to come?" I asked, hoping she would say yes. I wanted to include her and I knew her superpower of extreme loveliness would put Erik at ease when Paddy was around.

"Oh you don't need me there, it will be good for you to spend time together," she said.

"You are part of my life here too, Fleur," I reminded her, and she beamed.

"I know, but I don't want to intrude. And I have a child," she said as though that were reason enough not to invite her.

"So, lots of people have them. It would be good to get to know him better too. Erik already knows him and Theodore is great with kids," I said, and she blushed a little. I could understand why: Theodore had a way of making women feel special. He was polite, warm, and gentlemanly; no doubt he had an effect on Fleur.

"Well, if you think it would be okay. Tate will love it; he needs man time."

"So do you," I said, wagging my eyebrows at her.

"I can help you with that, Fleur," Geronimo said as he sauntered into the reception area.

"With what?" she asked, giving him a confused look.

"With man time," he said, trying for a sexy smile. It was pathetic.

"Thanks for helping, Geronimo. You know someone who can fit the bill then?" I asked, and he was momentarily confused before he gave me a flat look.

"I was referring to myself," he muttered as he walked away, and I had to fight not to laugh. Fleur put her head in her hands.

When we finished work, we both decided to head to the Brewery for a drink before the others joined us. It was cold and we nabbed a spot near the fire, Tate joining us and doing his homework like a good boy. It was clear he thought the world of his mother; she treated him respectfully and with so much love that it made me realise how bad my parents were.

"It's nice of Hannah and Molly to organise a dinner party on Saturday," Fleur said as we sipped at our wine.

"We all have a lot to celebrate. Hannah is engaged, Molly got married, Leslie and Carol set up a community hub, and my brother is in town," I said, grinning.

"Do I have to come?" Tate asked, looking stricken.

"No, you don't," Fleur told him gently, with an edge that let him know he was verging on being rude

"You can if you want," I added, but he shook his head like we were asking him if he wanted the plague or SARS, and I laughed.

"I'm good but thanks. Can I stay at Ethan's place?" he said very politely and I smiled.

"His mum already gave me the okay," Fleur told her son, and his relief was comical.

"So, you will be footloose and fancy free. We can pick you up and drop you off," I told her, and she nodded.

***

"Good evening, ladies," I heard my brother say and we looked up to see him standing there, looking as he always did—put together and appropriate. Tonight he wore a button-down shirt, dark jeans, and a heavy green sports coat. He gave me a kiss and Fleur a small smile. Fleur was too busy blushing to respond, so he turned to Tate, held out a hand, and introduced himself.

"Hi there, I'm Theodore, Annie's brother."

"Um, hi. I'm Tate. Fleur's my mum," the young boy said, hesitating before offering his hand.

"Hey, Annie," Paddy said, leaning in to give me a kiss. It was awkward but I was trying to be good about him being here. I wanted him to feel forgiven so he could move on.

Everyone took a seat while we waited for Erik, and Paddy and Ted told us about their day and the trails they'd discovered.

"Erik." Tate's voice rang out above the conversation and we all stopped to watch Erik saunter over to our table. He looked sexy as always, but tonight he looked particularly drool-worthy in a cotton check shirt, a navy military-style jacket, worn denim jeans, and boots, his hair pulled back from his face, and he'd had his beard trimmed again. As soon as we were alone, I was going to jump him—it was imperative. I needed to feel him against me again, to have him surround me. I grinned at him as I stood to give him a kiss when he made it to me.

"Hey, thanks for coming," I said quietly, trying to catch his eyes. I couldn't however because he had his eyes trained on Paddy, who was watching us avidly. Ugh.

"Evening, everyone," he said before taking a seat.

After I introduced Paddy to Erik we returned to our conversation, and Tate spoke quietly to Erik, desperate to spend time with his football hero. Paddy watched, like he was waiting for something to happen. But nothing did. We ordered more drinks and dinner as we talked. Well, really, Theodore and I talked, trying to include everyone. Erik was quiet, Paddy weird, and Fleur seemed shy in front of the group but was attentive to Tate. When it was time to leave, we all stood, said our good-byes, and headed outside. Fleur left straight away, while I drove Theodore home and Erik headed to his truck before heading to my place. Paddy wandered off toward his motel and I let out a huge sigh of relief. I'd wanted Erik to meet Paddy and see that there was nothing more between us. Now that was accomplished, they probably wouldn't see each other again until Saturday night.

***

Paddy, the fucking douche, still wanted Annie. That was clear as day. He'd watched us like a hawk, seeing how we were together. I'd wanted to touch her to stake my claim, really give him something to see, but I didn't. I was battling yet again with the fact that I was in too deep and I had no idea what claim I had on her. Being with her last night had reaffirmed my feelings, and as usual her actions were saying one thing but who knew where her head was at.

At least I'd survived dinner, saved in part by a kid who wanted to talk to me about football. It wasn't too uncomfortable, other than the fact Paddy was a creeper staring at the woman I loved. As I walked to my truck, I figured that I only had to survive one more dinner with the wanker on Saturday and then hopefully he would fuck off back to wherever he had come from. I could do that. Well, I thought I could until he approached me as I walked up the street. Clearly he wasn't just a wanker, but he also was fucking crazy.

"Erik?"

"Yep." I sighed heavily, stopping and turning to look at him. He came up close to me, verging on entering my personal space, and this pretty boy gave me a fake smile.

"So, what's the real go with you and Annie?" he asked, putting his hands in his pockets as though we were shooting the shit on a freezing cold winter's night.

"What?" I bit out, not in the mood.

"Well, what's really going on? I mean I get why you're into her, but you already know how I know that," he said, and I wanted to growl. I hated that he'd been with her, but I didn't need to bite.

"I have no fucking idea what you're talking about. There is nothing going on," I muttered.

"Then why are you playing games?" Um, excuse me, motherfucker?

"Why are you fucking interested?" I returned, stepping toward him.

"Because I actually care about her." I looked at him for a long time. Maybe he did care about her, or was it guilt? Who knew.

"And you think I don't?"

"No, I don't. You're just shagging her. It's been made clear that's all you are to each other, yet you come out with her fucking family and pretend to be something you're not," he said, moving farther into my space. It made the difference in our height and size more pronounced. As I'd thought—fucking crazy.

"Her family? You're the arsehole pretending to be something you're not," I said, standing to my full height.

"I am, or I was," he said darkly.

"And let me guess, you want to be again?" I inched closer, but he held his ground.

"Yeah, and I'd do right by her, not be in it for kicks," he said, pushing closer.

"What, like you did right by her last time?" At my words, his jaw clamped shut and he was dying to hit me. But instead he stepped back. It was a low blow but also the damned truth.

"I get that you're *the man* around here. Everyone says it, even Annie. But Theodore is here to bring her home, where she belongs. She won't be able to stay away, they're too close. Stop leading her on and let her get on with her life," he said before turning and walking away.

I watched him, adrenaline pumping through my veins. I needed to calm the fuck down before I went to Annie's. I walked around town before going back to my car and heading over. When I arrived, I could hear Theodore on the phone in his room so I headed to the kitchen to find Annie making tea.

"Hey," she said, giving me a sexy smile. I wanted to smile back, I really did. But my conversation with Paddy was replaying in my mind. He thought I was playing games, which was clearly a fucking joke. His comments about Annie returning to England were not, however, and maybe that was why she only wanted the physical relationship. Sure, she might feel something more for me, but she knew that she was going to return home. Maybe I never had a chance and this felt like a hit to the gut.

The feel of her at my side snapped me out of my downward mental spiral. She wrapped her arms around my waist and peered up at me, communicating clearly what she wanted, and like a damned fool with no control when it came to her, I wanted to give it to her.

"Your brother turned in for the night?" I asked.

"Uh-huh," she said as she moved her hand up my chest to wrap around my neck and pull me in for a kiss.

"What did you have in mind?" I whispered at her lips.

"I need you inside me," she practically moaned into my mouth, and just like that, I was done for. I nodded, then kissed her, pushing her against the counter and grabbing her legs to wrap them around my waist. We fit together as we usually did: perfectly. I walked her to her bedroom, our lips close but not touching.

"You looked fucking sexy when you walked in tonight. Fuck, I wanted to cancel dinner and head home," she whispered.

"You could have," I said dryly and she laughed.

"Don't worry about Paddy, he'll be gone soon. I have been talking to him about you, he knows the score," she said, releasing and gripping my hair in the way she did that sent a sensation all the way to my now hard cock.

"And what's the score?" I said as I put her down on the bed. She ripped off her shirt, exposing another sexy black sheer bra. This one was so sheer I could see her pretty nipples through it. I took my shirt off and crawled over her, rubbing myself against her core.

"Let's just say he knows what we are to each other, and there is no place for him."

I wanted to ask what we are to each other. I fucking should have but I said nothing, not wanting to hear it yet. Instead, I tore her jeans and underwear off, unzipped my own, freed myself, and drove in, losing myself and my pain inside her hot, wet pussy.

Our lovemaking was urgent and intense, as we both greedily absorbed each other's moans and murmurs of pleasure. Needing to be deeper, I pulled out so I could fully remove my jeans. As I stood, I looked down at her on the bed, naked and sweating, legs spread for me, my bite marks on her neck and breasts, and her eyes hooded and low as they roamed my now naked body. It was one of the most life-altering things I'd ever seen, because Annie was it for me. No one would ever do it for me like she did and while it made my dick throb painfully with a desire to be back inside her, it also made my heart sink. I wasn't sure how long I would have her for.

I came back over her, taking her again, and we moved hard and fast, our eyes connected as we rushed to the precipice and fell over together, each of us speaking the other's name as we were overcome with ecstasy, before we collapsed in a pile of limbs, exhausted and ready for sleep.

The following morning, I woke before her as usual, rubbing her naked back as she sprawled over me, snoring lightly. I loved it when she did this; it was fucking cute and when she was unconscious like this, she nestled into me like she couldn't get close enough. At least I imagined that was how it was for her.

At the start of the week, I'd considered talking to her about *us,* but then everything had turned south and I was becoming surer that I would be exposing myself for no good reason. She hadn't told me about her brother and Paddy being here. I'd heard that from someone else. I also knew they were here to take her home, and while I didn't have any siblings, I got that she would be seriously considering it. Again, not that she had discussed it with me. They were family and I couldn't compete with that. Then there was all that Paddy had said.

As I lay there, with her on top of me, loving the closeness, I knew it was time to let it go. I'd been kicking myself for ever making a proposal in the first place. I'd made my bed and now I was lying in it. But no more. I was not about to torture myself any longer; she wasn't where I was at. If she was, she would be handling things differently. She would not be telling everyone we were just shagging. She would be talking about where she was at with her brother. She would get that I was putting myself out there. So, I would see this thing out, get my fill of her then when the time was right, I would break it off and we would be no more. I only needed to survive her brother's visit. I wasn't about to be a dick while he was here and ruin their time together.

She stirred on top of me, clearly having woken up, moving so she was straddling me, and I smiled despite the pain caused by her unconscious action. This was my Annie with her guard down, open to possibilities.

"You been awake long?" she asked as she did every morning.

"Yeah, pixie," I said, kissing her neck and holding her tight, not wanting the moment to pass.

"Good," she murmured as she moved on top of me, my dick stirring to life again.

"Why is that good?" I asked, smiling.

"Because I need to ride my Viking-lumberjack," she said, pushing up to sit up.

"Yeah?" I asked, taking in all her beauty as she blinked sleep from her eyes. Annie looked amazing with crazy bed hair, swollen lips from last night, and little bite marks from me on her perfect tits. Her tattoo rippled at her side, and her belly button ring winked at me. The longer I admired her, the harder my dick got.

"See something you like?" she asked, giving me a wink. I nodded as I lifted her up and drove her onto me. She gasped, throwing her head back. This was another favourite image of her. When we were connected, she was open to me and in the moment, free and unguarded. It was how I wanted it to be all the time, but she wasn't going to give me that. So, I would take it now, while I could.

Chapter 19

I was glad we had a home game this weekend. It meant more time at home with Theodore on Saturday and ample time to get ready for dinner. Theodore and Paddy had insisted on coming with me to the game early, and Erik went along with it despite the fact we had to take two cars.

We'd been together every night except for dinner Friday when he caught up with Ben, and we had touched base during the day as usual, but I still had the feeling that something wasn't quite right. Erik was in the room with me, but he wasn't present. I could feel it in the reluctance of his responses and the lack of fervour in his embrace. He was going through the motions, but I didn't quite understand why.

That wasn't exactly true. I did have an inkling and it was what I had feared all along. This was coming to an end for him, and my brother's presence, along with the inclusion in my friendship circle, had pushed us into relationship territory, which wasn't what he wanted. I contemplated talking to him about it, but whenever I went to say anything, words didn't come. I rationalised my cowardice by convincing myself that I didn't want drama with Theodore and Paddy around. They would notice and get involved, making it worse for Erik. So I pretended everything was okay, waiting until it wasn't.

Despite my acceptance that it was going to end, I was still at home getting ready to head to Molly's, obsessing over my appearance. I shouldn't have cared, but right or wrong, I wanted him to want me. It was intoxicating when he looked at me like I was beautiful and sexy. So I did something I didn't normally do unless I was under duress: I wore a dress. It was a black maxi dress with a big slit up the front and long sleeves. There was a low V at the front and it was skin-tight. I wore black and silver pointed ankle boots with big silver cuff bracelets and silver hoop earrings.

"You look lovely," my brother said as I walked into the kitchen. He was sitting there sipping a beer, reading the local paper.

"You too," I said, and he did. He wore a white button-down shirt, dark jeans, and tan boots, his wool coat sitting over a stool.

"So, Erik will meet us there?" he asked.

"Yep, he will pick up Fleur on the way," I said, going through my bag to remove all unnecessary items.

"That's good," he said, smiling.

"That Erik is helpful or that Fleur is coming?" I asked, teasing my brother. I knew he wasn't unaffected by Fleur's charm.

"Both, of course," he said, giving me a wry smile.

"He really is a very good athlete," Theodore said, returning to the paper, open on an article on Erik.

"He is. He probably could've played professionally."

"Why didn't he?" Theodore asked curiously.

"I think he was looking after his dad, who was sick, and time passed him by," I said, figuring that was a safe way to talk about it. I didn't know a lot about Erik's past. Fleur had mentioned bits and pieces, Erik had skirted the issues, and people around town had mentioned it, but I didn't really know how he felt about it. I'd hoped he would tell me but nothing had come yet, and probably wouldn't. It was all well and good for him to hear about my past, but wasn't willing to share his.

"Sick in what way?"

"Not sure," I lied.

"You don't know?" he asked, looking confused. My heart sank a little further as I realised the extent of his under-sharing. "He knows about all our history though?" Theodore pushed and I inwardly flinched.

"Yes, I told him that." I tried hard not to sound defensive but a little of it snuck out.

"Why won't he talk about his dad?" he pushed, sensing my apprehension to answer. So I sort of lied again.

"I think it's painful for him, and we are new of course," I hedged because the real reason was that he wasn't as invested as I was.

"Right." He didn't say any more; he didn't have to. The fact that I was more invested was more than an elephant in the room. It was the whole menagerie.

We picked up Paddy on the way through town and arrived at the winery as Erik and Fleur, and Leslie and Carol pulled in. It was a bigger gathering than I thought, with Molly's mum and stepdad attending, along with Howard's cousin and, sadly, Molly's in-laws. It was an unusual mix to say the least but if Molly and Hannah had anything to do with it, it would go as smoothly as it could, lubricated by excellent food and plenty of booze. Theodore, Paddy, and I loitered as we waited for the others to catch up. Leslie and Carol reached us first, giving me a big hug. Paddy hung back as my big brother went into gentleman mode and even though he wasn't their type, I could tell they thought he was better than sliced bread.

Erik and Fleur walked up to us and I knew immediately that something was very wrong with Erik. Fleur smiled shyly before Theodore offered her an arm and walked toward the house, Paddy trailing behind. I didn't move, needing to get a better read on Erik.

"Hey, you okay?" I asked as he neared me. He was wearing a green shirt and black jeans tonight, and his hair was still wet from his post-game shower. I leant in to give him a kiss, and not only did he *go through the motions*, he stiffened momentarily as I tried to deepen the kiss. It was only a split second but it hurt my heart and I reared back.

"I'm good, just tired," he said, and while he did look tired, I didn't think his response had anything to do with fatigue.

"You didn't have to come," I found myself saying around the lump in my throat. I desperately wanted to cry, which seemed extreme even for me, but knowing you wanted someone who didn't want you back, and who was trying to back away gently, seemed worthy of shedding tears.

"I said I'd come and I'm here. Should we go in?" he asked, walking toward the door.

"Sure," I said, walking quickly to keep up with him.

We headed into the function area where Molly got married. It was far too large for our party, but she had set up a long table in front of the open fire, and everyone milled about having wine and eating something that smelled amazing that Hannah was offering. I took a deep breath, then plastered a smile on my face as I introduced Erik to the people he didn't know, and was introduced to Howard's young cousin Clara. Bruce, Molly's stepfather, greeted Erik with a hug. Before long, Erik was absorbed in a deep conversation with Dave, Howard, and Bruce about the ski season.

Molly and Hannah were busy with food and drinks, Leslie and Carol were doing the hard yards with Molly's in-laws, and Fleur and Theodore were happily chatting over a wine barrel close to the fire. Fleur was saying something that made her blush and my brother laugh, and I wanted to join them, but I didn't think I belonged there. In fact, I was on my own and unsure I belonged anywhere.

"Annie, would you get some more red wine out of the cellar? We want the GSM 2011 Green Acre release," Molly called to me, and I wanted to hug her for giving me a reason to be busy.

"I'll give you a hand," Paddy said, joining me, and I gave him an uncomfortable smile, wishing he had something else to do. But then, he was in the same boat as me, not fitting in.

"This way." I nodded to a hall that led to the industrial part of the winery. We walked past Erik and the men, and I gave them a small smile. Erik was watching us, his look a mixture of irritation and frustration.

"So, how are you liking Australia?" I asked as we headed down the dimly lit hallway.

"It's great. I mean it's cold and I expected it to be hot and all beaches, but what I have seen is beautiful."

"You have come to the alpine region in winter. You could go up north and see all the beaches that you want. You would be with every other Brit backpacker getting burnt on the beach in their winter," I teased and he laughed.

"Bright is great too, but a little smaller than I expected for you," he said as we turned into the cellar and I started looking for signs that would lead me to the Green Acre releases.

"Well, it's small, but I like being able to get outdoors and the town itself has everything I need. My home is here now, and I have great friends as you can see."

"Your home is here?" he asked, sounding surprised.

"Yes, that house is important to me. It gave me a sense of purpose after everything happened. My friends are solid and I have a healthy business so I'm happy."

"But don't you miss England?"

"Of course I do, but if I moved back, I would miss here."

"What about Theodore?"

"What about him?" I stopped and looked at Paddy to find him giving me a serious, assessing look.

"Well, don't you want to be close to him?"

"Of course, but I have put down roots here. We can visit each other as often as we like and talk regularly," I said, wanting to remove tension from our conversation but seemed unable to. I had successfully avoided spending too much time with Paddy. I didn't know why but I needed space from him, and after my interlude with Erik, I needed space from everyone.

"It won't be the same," he said flatly.

"Nothing stays the same," I huffed, and his features were overcome by pain for a moment. "Paddy, what is really on your mind?" I asked, needing to cut through the shit.

"I, well. I still have feelings for you. I know I've made mistakes but I can assure you I have changed and I know, I *know* that things can be as good, if not better than they were before. You and Theodore are like family to me, the best people in my life, and I want that back," he said, moving in close to me, gripping my hands.

"Paddy, I…." I started to say but stopped. I didn't know what to say.

"I know you are established here now, and that you're seeing someone, but we both know he isn't in it for the relationship. He practically told me so after dinner this week. I want everything with you. House, kids, minivan, whatever, and I know you, I know how important loyalty and family are to you. I know because they are important to me too," he said, bringing my hand to his mouth to give me a kiss, staring at me with such conviction that I felt his plea.

"Paddy…" I started again.

"Don't say no, think about it."

"I don't need to think about it," I said, feeling tears fill my eyes.

"Annie," he said urgently.

"No." It came out as a sob, but it was the absolute truth.

"No?"

"No, I don't want to go home, and I don't have those feelings for you anymore. I'm sorry if you came here hoping I would, but I don't. I let that go a long time ago. I forgive you for what happened, it was a crazy time and we all had our parts to play, but I'm different now. I've changed and I'm sorry," I whispered. I wish I had a better way to say it, but I didn't.

"You have changed. I can see that. So can Theodore," he said, sounding more bitter than hurt.

"What is that supposed to mean?" I asked.

"Well, we both see you're putting up with whatever the he-man in there is giving you. We know you are settling for something less than perfect. You can't blame us for wanting more for you. But as usual, you'll do whatever you want irrespective of what anyone else thinks." He walked out and I stood trying to control my emotions. His words had hurt. His comments were like little barbs tearing at my soul. The worst was the fact that he thought I was settling for second best. It hurt the most, because it was true.

***

Annie had been down with that motherfucker for too long, and I was about to go and get her when he appeared, looking furious, beelining straight for Theodore. I waited a few minutes and then Annie appeared, looking blank. It was the look she had tried to give me when she was hiding what was fucking with her head. I wanted to go to her, to pull her against me and make her tell me what had happened so I could comfort her. I could guess what had taken place: Paddy had made his move and it clearly hadn't worked out.

But something else must have happened to put that haunted look back in her eyes and I couldn't help it. I moved to her and grabbed her hand, unable to stop myself touching her. I pulled her close, but when she looked at me with sadness and acceptance, my stomach fell because I knew *I* was the reason. After all I'd done and all we had been through, she was kicking me out of the fortress. I needed to end it. I was causing us both pain—it had to be over. Tonight. My chest hurt with a pain that seemed so deep and permanent that it made me fill sick, but I had no other option. We were no longer enjoying what we had. In fact, it was tearing us both apart.

I didn't say anything and neither did she; we held hands as a long moment passed, sounding the death knell, and then we re-joined the conversation but neither of us contributed. When the food was ready, we all sat at the table and Annie and I pretended that everything was fine but we both knew it was the opposite. I talked to Howard and Bruce across the table, and she focused on Hannah and Leslie. Every time we accidently brushed legs or hands, she stiffened and it killed me a little more.

"Annie, you sure you're okay?" Hannah asked, eyeing her suspiciously. I liked her friends, liked that she had them, but they saw everything. I needed to exit before it became a matter for public discussion.

"Yeah, just tired," she lied, and I looked at her, noting that she was biting her lip and digging her nails into her hands.

"Are you keeping her up all night, Erik?" Hannah asked me, grinning.

"Not exactly," I said, giving a small smile, not wanting to go down this path because fuck me; I *was* responsible. I'd taken it too far. We made it through the rest of the torturous dinner, when we adjourned to the patio outside that had two fire pits going. I hung back, waiting to see where she went so I could talk to her. I stood with Dave, Howard, and Bruce as we talked about nothing important while I nursed my beer, scanning for her, but she was nowhere to be found. I did see Fleur and Theodore inside by the fire, talking and laughing. It was nice to see Fleur laugh and be without the burden of the past. But Theodore was heading back to England and I hoped he had a mind to that.

After more time passed and Annie hadn't emerged from the big room, I decided to look for her. If she was alone, I could talk to her before it got any more awkward. I headed inside under the guise of going to the bathroom, but after looking everywhere, including the bathroom and cellar, I went for the front door to circle around the outside of the house. It was a frigidly cold night now, and the full moon illuminated the winery and Mount Buffalo in a ghostly silver. I had almost circumnavigated the entire building before I found her. She was against a huge oak tree, facing the forest at the back of the property.

"Hey," I announced my presence, not wanting to frighten her.

"Hey," she croaked. I could hear in her voice that she had been crying, and my gut tightened. I hated that she had been crying, and I wanted to comfort her, but the resignation I'd seen earlier stopped me in my tracks. That and the fact that I needed to protect myself from falling more in love with her.

"Look, Annie. I..." I started.

"Don't."

"Don't what?"

"Don't say it. I get it. It's over and you want to get out of here before it gets any worse," she whispered.

"It's not that, it's that I don't want to pretend anymore," I said, and she sucked in a breath. This was the hardest thing I'd ever had to do. It was harder than giving my dad's eulogy to a bunch of people who knew he was a drunk arsehole, harder than having to tell people at school why my mum wasn't around anymore, harder than explaining to Fleur that Reece had skipped town without giving a shit about her. I loved this woman, and she didn't return the sentiment, but we both were struggling doing the ending if her tear-soaked face was anything to go by. But I could do it. I had to.

"We can wait until after tonight and you can tell people on your own, but I can't keep going until your brother leaves. It's too hard," I said, reaching for her hand. She let me hold it for a moment, and it was shaking and ice cold.

"No, don't do that. If you need to go, do it. It's fine. I'll take Fleur home too," she said, looking off into the distance. I stepped in front of her, but she turned her head to the side to avoid looking at me, her jaw determined.

"Annie, I'm trying not to be a dick here," I said, the frustration at her reaction getting to me. This was on her too, not just me. She clearly was quite happy putting on a show for people, but I didn't do that.

"It's not working," she hissed.

"What?"

"You *are* being a dick. I expected it though. I guess I should've been prepared. But you need to go now, before it gets any worse for me. I'll see you around," she said, looking at me briefly with eyes that were hurt and angry before she stalked off, leaving me alone. I didn't know what the fuck was going on with her, but this was what she wanted, had wanted. I got that the timing wasn't great but I was breaking inside, and she was only concerned about herself. Her disregard for where I was at turned my pain into anger. I wasn't up for being used as a rent-a-boyfriend, and that was too fucking bad. Tonight had been so unbearable that it couldn't continue. She would have to deal.

I drove home slowly, trying to stem the blood flow from the gaping wound in my chest and clamp down my anger and fury at the situation I'd created for myself. I'd done what needed to be done to fix it, but it did not make me feel any better. In fact, I felt worse. On that note, I decided to do something I hadn't done in years and promised myself I would never do. I stopped at the pub and bought a bottle of whisky, then went home and drank until I passed out.

Needless to say, the next morning when I woke up with a pounding headache to someone knocking at my front door, I felt like death. When I answered, though, and was face-to-face with a young girl who looked like me, I wished I was, in fact, dead.

"Hi, I'm Freya."

Chapter 20

I'd gone back to the party after Erik had left, after lurking outside for a few minutes fighting tears. I'd stood in the cold night hoping he was going to come back and apologise, but he didn't. Why would he? Knowing I needed to pull myself together so I could go home and fall apart more properly, I'd done what I'd practiced after I thought I'd put Ted in a wheelchair—I shut my sense and my emotions down. It was scary how easily I could do that, and once my hurt and rage were safely stowed away, I returned to the party, knowing I would have time soon enough to feel that way.

The closer I got to the house, the more in control of my heartache I was. But my efforts did nothing to stop how pissed off I remained; he couldn't have waited until tomorrow? Was it that fucking hard to be near me? My brother had only been here less than a week and before that he was more than happy to have his hands all over me. It wasn't like my brother's arrival had caused me to turn into a yeti. It was with this anger bubbling under the surface that I'd told everyone Erik had to leave, given he had a heap on the following day and that he said to say thanks. Hannah and Molly looked at me like they wanted to hug me, but they knew I didn't want them to. Hannah told me tomorrow we were all having breakfast and that we would discuss it then.

Wanting to go home, I'd sought Fleur out to find her sitting close to my brother, looking at him as though he hung the moon. I agreed with her; my brother was amazing, but he was leaving, and I hoped that she was protecting herself from that sort of hurt. Although I wasn't really qualified to have hopes in that department. When I'd told them that Erik had left, Fleur looked confused but my brother gave me a look that said he thought Erik was a major arsehole and he wanted to beat the tar out him. Well, I guess that made two of us. Paddy smirked, which irritated the shit out of me, and everyone else gave me a wide berth.

Saying our farewells, we piled into my Mini, Fleur and Theodore in the back, Paddy in the front, everyone quiet. When Theodore and I walked into my kitchen, he looked at me as my mask slipped, then put the kettle on. I stoked the fire and sat on the couch, knowing my brother wasn't going to let me go to bed without talking this out. When he handed me my tea and sat next to me, I turned to him, seeing concern and love on his face. I started to cry.

"Annie," he said as he put an arm around my shoulder and I cried into his shirt. "What went wrong?" he asked when I blew my nose and tried to shake the tears away.

"Don't hate him," I said, and he raised his brows.

"What did he do?" He was being protective and I loved him for it, but it wasn't required.

"Nothing. He didn't do anything. We had never agreed to more, but I couldn't stop myself. He felt the full force of that and didn't want us to pretend to be something we weren't. So, while I'm hurt and humiliated, it was my own doing." At my confession, I broke down again, letting all the could-have-beens and what-ifs pour out of me like a depressing river that was taking my hopes and dreams with it.

"Annie, nothing is that simple, and he could have cut himself loose at any time," he said when I had calmed myself, and I nodded.

"Nothing is ever that simple," I echoed his words, and he gave me a sad smile.

"What can I do? Do you want me to challenge him to a duel? I don't think I'd fare that well in a fistfight given he is built like a behemoth," he said.

"A duel? Have you got your musket with you?' I smiled at his attempt at levity. He knew what I needed.

"Sadly I don't. I could manufacture a slingshot though. A rock between the eyes might do it. Or I could commission Paddy into helping me," he said, grinning, but I couldn't hide my grimace.

"Don't talk to me about Paddy," I sniffed ungracefully before sipping my tea.

"He spoke to you then? He has as good a timing as the Norseman," he muttered, holding his cup to his lips as he frowned.

"That's a fucking understatement. So, he told you he was going to try to convince me to get back with him?"

"No, but he didn't have to. I know for a fact he wants your forgiveness, and that is the only reason I allowed him to come with me. But when we got here, I saw the way he watched you, and how he reacted to Erik being on the scene."

"He only wants me because he thought someone else did?" I didn't want to get back with Paddy, but that idea made me feel worse.

"Of course not. But I do believe his feelings about you are wrapped up in his path to redemption, and he can't quite separate the two yet," he said, and I could tell he was unhappy with Paddy.

"Well, he didn't redeem himself in my book. He was kind enough to point out that Erik didn't want a relationship, and that I shouldn't settle," I sniffed, feeling the tears rise.

"Well, we agree on that. You shouldn't settle for anything except for perfect. You deserve the very best and you always have. That doesn't mean Paddy needed to tell you or suggest himself as a replacement." My brother was pissed now and I understood why. At least I knew he would take care of it.

"It's not really about settling. It's about loving someone who doesn't love you back. It's a terrible feeling, especially when the worst thing they did was break up with you at an awkward time. Aside from that, Erik hasn't been a horrible person. In fact, he's one of the best people I know. He doesn't feel the same way for me." With this melancholy, woebegone assertion my whole body sighed under the weight of the sadness, and my big brother hugged me again.

"I'm not sure about that," he said as he held me, but I didn't believe him. If Erik wanted me, he wouldn't have stiffened at my touch, and he wouldn't have walked away.

The following morning, I was up early for a run, my brother joining me. He was impressed with my fitness, but he was not sure about me running in the rain, in deserted woods in the wilderness. I told him I'd been doing it for years now and he told me that he'd picked his nose since he was two but that wasn't necessarily a good thing. He was going for humour with me, and it was the right thing to do. Any serious questions right then would have shattered my defences. I needed time to reinforce them, not that I would get that at breakfast with the girls.

I dropped him in town to meet with Paddy for breakfast, picked up Fleur then drove out to Hannah's. I was glad Fleur could come; I was telling the girls where I was at and I wasn't into repeating myself. She was quiet on the drive, and I knew she had something on her mind. No doubt it was about Erik and all she knew about him before me. But I didn't encourage her; I wasn't ready to have a deep and meaningful yet. I needed coffee. And booze. And a heart transplant.

Hannah, Molly, Leslie, and Carol were all there when we arrived, setting the table and pouring coffee. Howard was on his way out the door. On his way past me he stopped and to my surprise he pulled me into a strange sort of side hug.

"You should know, Annie, that if he doesn't realise what he has in you, he's a damned fool," he said as he gave me a brief, awkward squeeze before setting me away and giving me a kind smile before walking out the door. This threatened my edict on not crying because as Hannah had said many a time, Howard was the shit. Once I made it to the kitchen in one piece, Molly thrust a coffee into my hand and gave one to Fleur as Hannah ushered us to sit down. She must have been up early because the table was covered in magazine-worthy food including fruit salad, pancakes, baked eggs, roasted vegetables, chorizo, and haloumi. Fleur's eyes went wide at the spread and Hannah noticed.

"What? We need to eat." she said as though it were perfectly normal to think we were going to eat our body weight in breakfast. We all sat down and people tried hard not to look at me but the conversation was stilted so I decided to get it over and done with.

"Look, I know you all thought Erik and I were more than a fling and I can see why. But we weren't and he never promised as much. It may not have been a good idea, but other than having shitty timing, he hasn't really done anything wrong. If anyone is in the wrong, it's me for knowing he didn't want more but pushing on with the family and friend routine before we'd agreed to it," I said before I bit into a hunk of chorizo, hoping the hot spicy meat would magically hold tears at bay.

"You were having more than a fling," Hannah said, giving me a stern look, and I could feel the heat rush to my cheeks.

"Perhaps I was, but he wasn't," I told her, feeling stupid.

"Annie, I saw how he looked at you," Molly said, shaking her head in frustration.

"Look, we had amazing chemistry and the sex was off the charts, but I started to confuse love with lust. He said it was about sex, and he kept his word," I defended before putting more food in my mouth. I'd decided I *was* going to eat my body weight in food; it gave me something to do. Everyone was quiet as they took in my words, how I sounded backed into a corner. I didn't care what they thought, I wanted to be left alone.

"Did your brother and Paddy have something to do with his fast exit?" Leslie asked after a while, and I nodded.

"It probably forced his hand. Meeting not only my family, but my long-lost brother is significant in any relationship. Paddy sure as shit didn't help, but I don't think Erik saw him as a real threat." At least, I hoped he hadn't.

"You can't know that, and he may have seen your brother as a threat," Carol added, and I paused mid-chew of pancake.

"Why?" I asked around my food.

"Maybe he thought they were here to take you home," she said. I thought about this, but I'd never mentioned it to him.

"I don't want to go home. In fact, here is my home, not bloody England. I certainly never mentioned it," I said, but as I looked around the room, I saw everyone relax. Had they all thought I might leave? They needn't have worried but my chest warmed a little. "I love my brother, I really do. And I am glad to have him back in my life, but aside from him, my family is here," I said, not liking the lump in my throat.

"What about your mum?" Leslie asked.

"I am thinking about visiting her, but I feel like she only wants to ease her guilt before she dies. I'm not sure if I'm ready to forgive her," I said, not sure if that made me a bad person.

"Whatever you decide to do is right," Hannah said, and I gave her a grateful smile.

"You can't help who you fall in love with." Leslie's sage words said with a sad kindness hit me deep. She was right. I was a lost cause from the beginning and I would remain to be one.

"I wish you could, but you're right. You can't. And in Erik's defence, you can't make yourself fall in love with someone either," I added.

"I don't think that's right," Fleur said quietly, and everyone stopped and looked at her.

"Not the part about not helping who you fall in love with. But that he doesn't feel something more for you," she said, almost afraid of the response she would get.

"He was quite clear last night," I told her.

"Well, I don't know about that. I only know you went to his cabin and he helped you with your brother. He also spent all his time with you, at the football club no less. That doesn't say fling to me. Especially when it comes to Erik. I can't imagine him doing any of that without knowing what it meant," she said, and everyone was quiet.

It seemed they all agreed, but I saw it differently.

***

My life was fucked up beyond recognition. The girl looking at me had my eyes and it was freaking me out. At least my hangover was receding, but now it was replaced by a tapped keg of what-in-the-actual-fuck.

"Um, did you hear me?" I heard her, but I had no idea what I was supposed to say. *Hello, sister. Long time never see?*

"Yeah. Come in," I muttered as I stepped out of the doorway and walked inside. She hesitated a moment before following me into my miniscule living room. She was looking around with wide eyes and apprehension, and I couldn't blame her. This place was a shitbox. I closed the door, which plunged the room into darkness, and I heard her suck in a breath. I fumbled to open curtains so I wasn't standing in the dark with my *sister*. Grey light illuminated my ratty couch, my guitar, and the empty liquor bottle on the table. My dishevelled appearance and the scene before us didn't make me look good. Shit, I was failing at being a big brother already.

"Coffee?" I asked, not wanting to see the wariness on her face.

"Okay."

I went to the kitchen and put the coffee on. Then I made a half-arsed attempt at putting away some dirty dishes and wiping down the countertop. I'd spent so much time at Annie's that I hadn't been paying attention to this place.

Annie. Fuck.

Thinking about her made my damned chest ache, and I did not need that when I had an unexpected family reunion to deal with. It was almost funny. Annie had experienced this almost a week ago, but at least she knew her brother.

"I'm gonna take a quick shower. Be back in a minute," I called out as I walked into the bathroom to try to get my head straight. The shower helped a little, and I returned to the living room to find her sitting on the couch, looking at her phone.

"Let's try this again," I said awkwardly, not knowing where to start.

"I'm sorry?"

Well, what did I expect? English wasn't her first language, since she'd grown up in Sweden.

"Let's start over. Hi, I'm Erik," I said, holding out my hand, and she nodded, giving me a small smile before taking it.

"Hi, I'm Freya. I'm your little sister," she stated the obvious, and I sucked in a breath. I had never imagined a conversation like this would be possible.

"Right," I said, running a hand through my hair.

"I brought my birth certificate and photos of me with our mother as proof. Do you want to see?" she asked, reaching for her backpack.

"No," I snapped, and she pulled up short. I did not want to see images of the woman who had abandoned me. It was bad enough having this girl who looked like me standing in my apartment. But I would check out the birth certificate. Later.

"Sorry," I mumbled, remembering I'd offered coffee. "Milk, sugar?" I asked as I poured two cups.

"No thanks. Black." Well, aside from our looks, we had coffee in common. I guess it was a start.

"Can I ask what you're doing here?" I asked as I put the mug in front of her and sat in a dining chair.

"I wanted to meet you," she said nervously.

"And you've been calling?" I guessed.

"Yes, but you seemed reluctant," she answered, looking up at me as though I might bite. This young girl didn't deserve my anger.

"Sorry. I've had a lot going on and I had no idea," I said lamely as she glanced at the empty bottle.

"Are you like your..." She was trying to ask if I was like my dad.

"No. I'm not. He didn't start to drink until after Mum abandoned us," I said, and she winced. Man, I was an arsehole. "Shit. I'm sorry. I, well. I meant it, but you don't need to hear that from me," I added, scrubbing my face, trying to get it together.

"It's okay. She told me about what happened. What she did and why. I don't necessarily agree, but I understand."

"What's there to understand?" I asked, interested to hear why abandoning your child was comprehensible.

"Why she left."

"Why she left her son," I amended.

"Look, I'm here because I want to reach out and find out why my mother is broken. I want to fix it, so we can all get better. I also want to know my family," she said, lifting her chin despite her wariness.

"Maybe this can't be fixed," I stated. There was a lot that was broken around here.

"Of course it can. Anything can be fixed."

I let out a humourless laugh. She was young and clearly believed what she was saying, but from where I sat, it didn't seem likely. But I could get to know her. We were family.

"Come on, let's go get some real coffee," I offered, and she put the mug down. My waning hangover needed greasy food. I knew we would be seen, but Freya gave me something to focus on other than Annie and the tears in her eyes the night before.

Over breakfast, Freya told me that she was sixteen, and had stolen her mum's credit card to purchase a ticket to Australia when her mother thought she was at school camp. I had to laugh because the kid didn't seem the type, but it was clear she was going to be in deep shit. Apparently, she'd called her mother from Singapore and told her what she had done. I should have thought of her as our mother, but it still didn't compute. Freya had been adamant that she was boarding the plane to Melbourne no matter what, so she'd transferred money to her account. I found myself smiling at her gumption.

She took a moment to call her mother while we waited for our food to arrive, and I didn't know how to feel. She spoke in Swedish, but she said my name, and from the tears in her eyes it clearly was difficult for them to discuss me.

I didn't know what to make of that and thankfully my breakfast arrived, giving me something to do. She was talking to the woman who had abandoned me, and when she hung up, she looked at me with sympathy. I'd thought ignoring my feelings was the way to go, but now I had a chance to know more about what had happened, albeit via a sixteen-year-old girl, and I found myself yearning for answers.

"How did that go?" I asked.

"Better than I thought. She is glad I am safe and that I made it to you. She is also happy that you are not an alcoholic," she said then winced at how that sounded.

"Thanks, Mum," I muttered, and Freya frowned.

"I don't think we see why she left the same," she said, her mouth twisted to the side.

"I know we don't," I told her on a sigh.

"Well, I'd like to hear about what you remember. I can't imagine not having her close, but she told me she thought you would be okay without her."

"Of course she fucking did. Maybe my dad was right." Deep-seeded anger and betrayal that had always lived in my heart were coming to the fore.

"Your dad is why she left," Freya said defensively.

"That may be so. But that doesn't excuse leaving her son behind without an explanation," I countered, and her shoulders slumped because it was the truth.

"I know it doesn't. But she knew you would be safe with him," she said softly.

"Of course I would be safe. Why wouldn't I be?" I asked, not liking where she was going with this.

"Maybe we should talk about it later," Freya suggested, looking around at the full cafe.

"Fine," I agreed, and we ate in strained silence.

I took the time to rein in my anger. When I partially managed it, I looked at Freya again, and she gave me a watery smile. It looked like I had managed to get everyone in tears, and that thought squashed rest of my anger. Sighing, I got up to pay and she did too, pulling out a fifty-dollar note.

"Kid, I got this," I told her, appreciating the effort.

"But I don't want to be a burden," she said in a small voice. I cursed myself for being a prick. This wasn't her fault. I put my money on the table and motioned for her to follow.

"You're not a burden, and this isn't your fault. I'm sorry. I had a shitty week and wasn't expecting to meet my sister and have all this come up again."

She watched her feet as we walked to my truck. "Look, I was going to drive up to my cabin today to check the place over. Did you want to come? Your…I mean our mum spent time up there before she left. There will be snow, but I'm coming back down the mountain tonight."

"Mother spoke about it. She said it was beautiful. I was going to look for you there if you weren't home today," Freya said, and I felt myself smile.

"You're pretty brave, you know that?"

"Brave or stupid. I'm not sure." She laughed.

"Everyone can be stupid," I said as I reversed out. I wished Annie was here. She would know what to do, how to handle Freya.

As we headed up the mountain, Freya distracted me from the pain by asking me lots of questions. It was strange introducing myself to a family member, but clearly Mum had no idea what I did or who I was.

I learned Freya was in high school, loved English literature and roller derby, and didn't have a boyfriend because she was in love with the heroes from her novels. Good for her. Relationships weren't worth it. *Liar.* When we pulled up to the cabin, the ground was covered in snow and sun was making the pond shine.

"It's pretty, but the trees look like they're from another planet. The cabin looks nicer than Mother described too," she said as she followed me inside.

"I've repaired it," I told her.

"It was broken?" she asked, and I laughed at her literal interpretation. Her English was impeccable, but sometimes she missed the subtext.

"Pretty much. My dad spent a lot of time here, but was in no state to repair it. After he died, I started rebuilding it," I explained as we entered the main room. "Let me light the fire then I'll give you a tour," I said, focusing on the mantel.

"I'm sorry he died," she said, and I looked at her. "That meant you've had no one." "Thanks, but he'd checked out a long time ago so I was used to it. What about you? Where is your dad?" I asked, unsure if I wanted to know the answer.

"She isn't married. Father is older and, after a few years of living with us, decided he didn't want a young family. He left us with money and each year he sends me a card at Christmas and my birthday. My mother wasn't upset really, she accepted it, saying you can't change people."

"He sounds like a prick." I struck the match and watched the fire come to life.

"Not really, only weak," she said, and I smiled.

We spent the rest of the afternoon at the house. I made us lunch and she told me part of what she had come here to say. She wanted me to know our mother loved me, and that she left me here because my father had threatened her. Freya didn't elaborate, and I was glad. I wasn't in any state to process that.

She was uncomfortable as she spoke, but it was clear she believed Mum when she said she left to save her own life, and mine. I was too astonished to know what to think. My dad was grumpy, sure. But threatening the woman he loved?

It didn't seem possible.

Chapter 21

Knowing my time with Theodore was short, I made sure we continued our exploration of the area, not that I'd felt like being a tour guide. It hurt to breathe and whenever my mind wandered to Erik, I wanted to fall apart and sob. I wondered if I should approach him and convince him that I could do just sex. I craved him enough to consider it but then my brother's and Howard's words rung in my head. I deserved better and I figured if he felt for me a fraction of what I felt for him, he wouldn't have given up so easily. This stopped the urge to call him but made me oppressively sad.

After breakfast on Sunday we'd visited the historic gold town of Beechworth. He'd not said much about Paddy, other than he still wanted forgiveness, but was going to head off for a few days to see the sights. Theodore had not pushed any conversation with me about Erik. We had wandered through the shops, chatting about nothing of consequence, and I honestly wasn't up for anything more.

Monday morning he was the same as we headed out to Harrietville for a vanilla slice and quick walk around the town at the base of Mount Hotham before I headed into the clinic for clients. He loved Harrietville and seeing the snow on the mountains as we headed through the lush green valley. I was glad he could see the appeal of living here; the natural beauty and plethora of places to eat and drink was not lost on him. He also didn't ask me to come home again. I knew he wanted me to, but he wouldn't push it if I was truly happy here. And I was, or I would be when my heart stopped bleeding and Erik was part of my past. Maybe I should put everything that reminded me of him in the front room and take to locking it again. Given I'd had two relationships in my life and both had failed miserably, perhaps I should lock myself in that room and avoid people all together.

When I arrived at work close to lunchtime, I was in a manageable state of depressed apathy. My fury with Erik's poor timing had dissipated. Clearly he couldn't wait to be rid of me and instead of that pissing me off, it had crushed my self-esteem. Theodore accompanied me to the clinic, keen to use the WiFi and check in with work. I was also sure he was there to keep an eye on me and plan my ongoing management with Fleur.

"Hey." Fleur was standing as we walked in. She gave Theodore a small smile but her focus returned to me, full of concern.

"Hey, Fleur," I said, looking at her, letting her see that I was hurting, but not catatonic. She looked worried, and while I appreciated it, it wasn't necessary. I had to wait until the heartache dulled a little.

"I need to talk to you," she murmured, giving my brother another small smile as he took a seat and pulled out his computer.

"Truly, Fleur, I'm okay. Sure, I'm hurt but as I said yesterday, he's done nothing wrong. I got carried away, and you know how great he is. It was bound to happen." I tried to give her a smile, but it didn't reach my eyes.

"How great who is?" Geronimo said as he walked down the hall from his room toward us. He had a cheery grin on his face. I wanted to give him a punch in the mouth and knock a few teeth out. Now there was something that might lift my mood.

"Not you," I muttered.

"What's that, Annie?" he asked, smirking at me, and I wondered what was wrong with him. Normally when I insulted him he knew it and became defensive.

"Nothing," I said, and he stood there watching me, effectively blocking my path.

"You are in a bad mood today," he said, and I huffed in irritation. "I can understand why. I feel for you, I really do," he said with mock sincerity and I stiffened.

"Geronimo," Fleur exclaimed, and he looked at her, a little less smug. People must already know Erik and I were over, but the attention surprised me. I expected this to unfold after netball practice tonight.

"I'm sure you really feel sorry for me," I deadpanned.

"I do," he said, giving me a sympathetic nod, which irritated me.

"That's good. I often feel sorry for you," I said, and his eyes narrowed.

"Is it difficult wanting something you can't have?" he asked cattily, and I stared at him.

"Well, I guess we both have experience with that," I said to him, then looked at Fleur and back at him. He was being an arse but I should've stopped baiting him.

"At least what I want isn't sleeping with a pretty blond behind my back," he said, happy with himself at landing what he thought was his victory blow. But I just blinked. What did he say?

"Excuse me?" I hissed, stepping toward him, but the weasel stepped back.

"Geronimo, that's enough," Fleur said, moving to me, her voice firm. Theodore stood and walked forward, so both he and Fleur were flanking me. Geronimo finally showed some intelligence and looked for an exit.

"It's all right, Fleur, Geronimo must have had too much kombucha."

"You don't know?" he asked.

"Don't know what?" I sighed, frustrated that we were still talking.

"That Erik has a new piece. He took her to breakfast yesterday, then to his cabin and she stayed at his flat last night," he said, putting his hands up in mock defeat. I wanted to pummel him, but I couldn't move. I was stuck in place, trying to make sense of his words. Erik was with someone? Was that why he left the party abruptly? He'd hoped to get out of it sooner because he'd already lined someone else up. It seemed unbelievable but if there was smoke, there was fire, right?

"Fleur, did you know about this?" I asked, not taking my eyes off Geronimo who was still inching his way back down the hall.

"I heard this morning. From a few people. Annie, I'm sure there is another explanation," she said, but her words held zero conviction.

"Motherfucker," I muttered before shoving past Geronimo to my office and slamming the door. I took a moment to breathe deeply. The anger that I'd worked through came roaring back, but I didn't have time or the physical and mental space to address it. I worked all afternoon with clients, stowing my anger and fury, trying to strap it down so it didn't eat me alive. I only had Theodore here for a few more days; I needed to focus on that. After? Well, I could lose it completely then. Fleur and Ted tiptoed around me, which was a good thing. The floodgates needed to remain shut; no one was ready to see that kind of ugly-hurt.

I headed to practice that night as ready as I would ever be. Theodore insisted on coming, promising he was only there for backup if it came to a fistfight. He didn't need to worry; while I was furious with Erik, I was infinitely more hurt and humiliated. It felt safer being angry rather than sitting in the he-didn't-pick-you zone. I knew to my soul that when I went there, *that* would truly break me apart.

We pulled up near the netball court and Theodore decided to stay in the car because he'd have a line of sight directly to me and it was bloody freezing. I got out, grabbed my bag, and as I headed toward the court, Fleur rushed at me, looking tweaked.

"What's wrong?" I asked her as she looked at me, then to the car where I knew Theodore would be watching, then around at our team in the distance.

"Well, it's not that something is wrong. It's that more information has come to light," she whispered.

"More information?" I asked, not sure what she meant. Clearly it was important because she was leaning in as though trying to protect us from prying eyes.

"Yes, more information. About the woman Erik is with," she continued in a hushed tone, looking around again to see who was watching. She didn't need to look far. Everyone was watching. Including Daphne with a smug smile on her face.

"Who is she?" I asked.

"Her name is Freya and she's his *sister*," she whispered.

"What?" I felt my mouth drop open. That was not what I had expected to hear.

"Shhh, don't react. It isn't common knowledge," she hissed, giving me big eyes.

"He has a sister?" I whispered back, still surprised.

"Yes, but he didn't know. Apparently she has been trying to contact him," she said.

"Shit," I said, wondering how he must be coping with this. While he hadn't spoken much about his mother, it was clear he held some animosity toward her. But this being sprung on him, and in a small town where everyone knew everyone's business, must've been terrible.

"It's a shock all right. Next to no one knows, but it will come out soon," she said, gnawing her lip.

"How did you find out?" I asked.

"Ben's sister bumped into me in the supermarket, and knowing I am close with Erik and you, she mentioned it. I'm not sure how she found out, but she said to keep it quiet. But..." Fleur trailed off, biting her lip unsure how to continue.

"What is it?" I asked, worried about what else was going to come out of her mouth.

"Well, Daphne is gloating that she knew the two of you wouldn't work. She thinks the new woman is a girlfriend but she said she *knew* it was coming. I don't know what that means but I don't like it," Fleur said, shaking her head, and I breathed a sigh of relief. Daphne didn't bother me. Not really.

"Her bullshit is to be expected and I actually don't care; she's a fool if she thinks she has a shot," I said, looking around to find the man in question, but I couldn't lay eyes on him. Maybe it was for the best. I'd planned to confront him about the other woman tonight like a mature individual, you know, have a conversation where I tried not to rip his head off. Fleur's news however changed all that, and now I was worried about how he was coping.

Netball practice was as I thought it would be and Daphne was a raging bitch, offering her condolences and telling me she understood how I felt. I did my best to ignore her, but when she told me she'd *wanted* to give me the heads-up but didn't know how to break the news, I'd told her to save her drama for her llama.

Afterwards, I decided not to go to dinner at the club; while I didn't actually care what Daphne was conjuring up, I was exhausted, heartsore, and now worried about the man who broke my heart. Besides, Theodore had waited long enough in the car. I wanted to go home and find a way to reach out to Erik and see if he was okay. Maybe that made me a masochist, but I did love him and I cared what happened to him. I figured that if he had his little sister with him, he likely wasn't at dinner. Perhaps I could pop by and check in privately.

"You still have it," Theodore said as soon as I got in the car, giving me a grin.

"Thanks," I muttered, feeling distracted and edgy. He sighed, knowing my mind was churning.

"Spit it out. What did Fleur have to say to you that was so important she pounced on you?" he asked as we peeled out of the car park.

"Not much, just that the woman staying with Erik is his long-lost little sister," I said.

"Come again?" he asked.

"It seems Erik's estranged mother had a child after she left his dad, and this girl, Freya, has sought him out," I explained, still not believing it.

"Why didn't she call or email?" he asked.

"I think she tried. Erik had mentioned some woman calling him, wanting to meet him in person to explain who she was. He'd rejected the calls, not liking being contacted out of the blue. I guess she got fed up."

"When did this happen?"

"Well, I doubt he knew about it at dinner on Saturday. My guess is Sunday morning."

"Well, that is something. Imagine having a sibling turn up." He huffed a laugh and I smiled at him.

"It is something. It's more of a *something* if you didn't know they existed. Now, despite his shit timing and not returning my wayward affections, I still feel for him," I said, and Theodore looked pensive.

"That's understandable. But you're right, he's still a shit," he said, and when I didn't answer, he looked at me. "You want to know he's okay, don't you?"

"The whole town will be watching him, judging him," I explained, knowing Theodore wouldn't be okay with me facing someone who hurt me.

"Annie, he broke up with you during a party at your friend's place." Theodore was exasperated, but when I looked at him, he sighed. "Fine, call him."

"I'm going to see him. This is not a phone conversation."

"Annie," he warned.

"Theodore," I whined like I did when I was sixteen. He blew out a big breath and I grinned at him.

"Can we have dinner first?" he asked.

"Only if you cook."

"Fine."

***

This was shaping up to be one of the worst weeks of my life. Don't get me wrong, it was great getting to know my sister. But since Saturday, I'd broken up with Annie and it still felt like part of me was missing. It was that I craved her, so much it was a physical pain in my chest. I'd grown used to sharing my day with her, sharing my bed, and I'd started planning for a future with her, a future that felt good and right.

Then there was Freya. She was cool and I was getting used to the idea of having a little sister. But I did not like having it shoved in my face. I understood how she came to be here, and like my proposal with Annie, I was kicking myself for not dealing with it earlier. The scary part was having to deal with a new family member and the past I'd avoided including my mother's accusations that my father was to blame.

The added kicker was dealing with this in a small town and knowing Daphne was involved. Interestingly, if you can call an infected splinter interesting, Freya had not told Daphne she was my sister. She had said it was a private matter, and Daphne had been more than happy to provide my details at a time when she *thought* Annie and I were together. It was plain old fucked up.

Since parting ways with Annie and me getting rip-roaring drunk for the first time in a decade, Freya had been staying with me, which was less than ideal. I was a dude, and I was not used to young girls I didn't know inhabiting my underwhelming, small space. I'd given her my bed while I took the couch despite her insistence that she would be better on the couch because she was smaller. That may've been so, but it didn't feel right to have her on the ratty old thing. She was a guest and my sister; she should have the most comfortable bed. I was exhausted from lack of sleep and feeling raw and defensive.

Aside from Ben and his family, I'd not told anyone of Freya's arrival, not because I was ashamed, but I wanted to get my head straight before I became the topic of conversation for the town again.

All in all, my head was more than fucked up and I was both torn and angry. I was torn; Freya was challenging my beliefs about my mother, and I was angry because Annie wasn't here when I needed her. I'd stuck by her when she needed help but now? She was nowhere to be seen. The harder things got, the more I believed that if she had actually given a shit and not been so self-absorbed, she might have seen that we had a future, instead of leading me around by my dick. But like my mother, she was doing her own thing, and now she had her brother back, what good was I to her?

Since Saturday night, my days consisted of texting my sister to make sure she was okay and had food to eat while I worked, then showing her around the place at night. She said she was okay on her own, but I could tell she was processing a lot too, and I didn't like to leave her alone. I'd raced home after training on Tuesday in part to eat with her, but also to avoid Annie. I'd seen her car at a distance, and her brother was there, no doubt ready to beat my arse. He wouldn't win, but I didn't want to break his nose or anything. He wasn't a douche bag and I was starting to understand brotherly instincts.

I'd showered at home while we waited for pizza to be delivered before watching *The Bachelor*, one of the most ridiculous shows I'd seen, but we both ended up watching it with a morbid fascination. It was like picking a scab at a slow pace: irritating, painful, and addictive. When I heard the knock sound at the door, I was surprised. I never had visitors and the pizza order had been complete. When I opened it and saw Annie looking at me with big eyes and a tight mouth my gut clenched and my head went fuzzy. It took me a moment to resist the urge to kiss her. But I remembered she did not want that from me. She was probably here because she'd heard I'd had a woman with me and was going to pull a Daphne and make sure I wasn't with anyone else either. That sounded about right for my life at the moment.

"Hey," she said, and the sound of her voice tore me in two. Part of me had missed it, but the other part wanted to lash out.

"What can I do for you?" I asked, fury at where things had gone between us bubbling under the surface.

"I came to see if you are okay," she said, brows raised, like it was obvious. I stepped out, leaving the door slightly ajar. Freya didn't need to hear this. Now we were illuminated by the fluorescent lights under the porch, and despite the harsh light, she looked like my beautiful, clever, sassy pixie. I clenched my fists to stop myself from reaching for her, reminding myself that she didn't choose me, or us. It was like dipping my heart in ice.

"Because you were worried about me? Or because you heard I was shacked up with another girl?" I bit out, wanting this to be over.

"Well, both. I am worried because I did hear…" she started, but I cut her off.

"I'm sure you heard, I'm sure everyone did. I can't believe you came here thinking I would do that to anyone, let alone you. I actually gave a shit about you, you know that?"

"Actually *gave* a shit? What are you talking about?"

"I cared about you." I jabbed a finger in her direction, like it was her fault I felt that way.

"Erik, I…" She seemed confused, which pissed me off more. What was there to be confused about?

"I made sure you were okay after your brother called. I tried to shield you from Daphne. I spent time with you, letting you process and get over the accident. I took you to my cabin, my space, and I've never done that before with anyone. So yeah, I *gave* a shit," I said, and she looked affronted. About what, I had no idea.

"I don't understand," she said, stepping closer, but I straightened, letting her know her touch wasn't welcome.

"I'm not sure why. I was there for you, and this is how you repay me." I laughed, surprising myself at how much of an arsehole I was being. A whisper in the back of my mind reminded me of my father, but I couldn't stem the tide.

"Repay you? Are you fucking serious?" She was getting pissy now but I was in too deep. That's when I noticed her brother, who must have been waiting in her car. Great, now we had even more of an audience. This, like Freya's arrival, was sure to be all over town tomorrow. More criticism about my personal life, made worse that people would be talking about my parents again. Her brother's presence was the final straw. I. Was. Done.

"Yeah, I'm fucking serious. And now you have your big brother to look after you. Who needs me, right?" I roared.

"You are a fucking lunatic. If you actually *gave a shit*, then why did you cut and run, leaving me in the middle of a party with all my friends? In fact, why did you come at all?" Her voice was getting thick with emotion, and part of me knew I should pull back. But I couldn't stop the hurt

"Cut and run? Are *you* fucking serious?" I huffed is bitter disbelief.

"Yeah, I fucking am," she hissed, hands on hips, not shying away.

"I left because I couldn't pretend anymore."

"Pretend?" she asked, her fury now touched with humiliation.

"Yeah. We had an understanding, remember? You brought it up often enough," I reminded her. Had she forgotten? And she was calling me a fucking lunatic.

"Well, it was your proposal, you prick. It's what *you* wanted." I fisted my hands in my hair, seeing she wasn't getting me.

"Wanted. Past tense," I said slowly, like she was an idiot.

"Past tense?" she asked as if I were speaking Swedish.

"Yeah, past tense. I wanted more than a shag and it was obvious. But shame on me, I should have known you wouldn't consider it. Fucking typical," I said, letting it all hang out now. Annie looked ready to detonate. She could have at it, I was about to go inside.

"And you *used* to care for me, but now you think I'm a piece of dirt? Sounds like genuine affection. You must really have meant it."

"Don't talk about genuine. You said you came here to see if I was all right, but really, you came here because you thought I'd shagged someone else. Am I right? That's how bitches think," I said, sounding more like my father than ever, and I sucked in a breath, not wanting to hear his tragic, pathetic disdain in my mouth anymore. I was so consumed with the effort not to say anything more that I didn't see Theodore's right hook.

"Ted." I heard Annie shriek but I didn't see anything. My eyes were doing roundabouts in their sockets.

"What is going on?" I heard Freya say as she came to the open door where I stood trying to get my shit together.

"Your brother is being an arsehole," Theodore said. Did he say brother?

"Freya, I'm sorry, I was checking on Erik after everything," Annie explained, and I could hear her voice tremble.

"Maybe you shouldn't have," Freya said quietly as I tried to focus.

"You're probably right," Annie replied, sounding defeated, then the door closed and Freya led me to the couch so I could sit down. Now my head, heart, and jaw fucking hurt, and I was wondering what I had done.

Chapter 22

"Annie," Leslie said sharply, snapping me out of my misery. I looked at her to see her frowning, and I tried to smile, but it was all wrong. We were having coffee before work the day after Erik shattered my heart, again, and Theodore had gone to help Fleur with some sort of leaking pipe emergency at her house. I should tell them both to be careful. I could see how they looked at each other, and if circumstances were different, they would probably be great together. But when it wasn't right and you *couldn't* make it right, the results were disastrous.

"I feel like I've been punched in the gut," I said, unable to fake being okay. "I could accept that he wasn't into me, that we were pretending to be in a relationship and it was too much for him. That? That I could take. I didn't like it, but I could reconcile with it. Then last night he accused me of using him and being a bitch who played games. I'm a lot of things, like a coward with no impulse control, but I am not a user or a player," I said, feeling sick that he could think that of me. He was out of line, and I'd been torturing myself replaying his barbed insults.

"You are not any of those things, love. You know it," she said, giving my hand a squeeze.

"But he *thought* I was. The man I love thought those things. About me. Here I'd been thinking he was the one and that maybe I should check on him to make sure he was okay. Well, I guess you can add a bloody fool to the list of my personal attributes," I muttered, finishing my coffee. It had been twelve hours since Erik had laid his true feelings out, since my brother had punched him, and his sister had given me a sad look that said Erik had not been okay and I'd made it worse.

"He shouldn't have said those things, and not in that way. I'm surprised to be honest. I did not see that coming," Leslie said as we stood to leave. I shared her surprise. Erik was normally chilled; it had caught me off guard.

I said good-bye to Leslie before heading inside to find Geronimo at the reception desk, standing in for Fleur. I struggled not to feel irrationally violent toward the whelp, and by the pathetic look on his face, I think he was starting to rethink his role in my heartbreak. He was an idiot for sure, but I was shocked that he would actively take pleasure in hurting someone, even me. He stood to speak to me, a look of wary apology on his face, but I held up a hand and kept walking. Given I was miserable, I decided he could feel the same for a few more hours.

"Annie," he called as he followed me to my office.

"Not now, I muttered without stopping.

"I need to let you know—"

"Not now," I cut him off as I raised my voice, not ready to let the poor bastard off the hook.

"It was Daphne," he said and I stopped dead.

"What?" I whispered as I turned around to face him.

"She told me," he said, looking like he was going to be sick.

"Told you what?" I snapped.

"About Erik and the woman," he said, and I blinked slowly, not sure where this was going.

"Yeah? Why would she do that?"

"Because she knew I would tell you," he admitted.

"And why would she know that you would tell me? We are not friends. We work together," I reminded him, and his shoulders sagged.

"I was out for dinner and she talked to me. Normally, she wouldn't be seen with me outside of the clinic, but this time she sat down with a glass of wine and talked to me. I mentioned Fleur, and must have let my feelings show. She told me that Fleur and you were close, and that you had told Fleur not to give me the time of day."

"I see," I said. In this case, Daphne could have been right. "Then what? She gave you the script?"

"No, we had a lot to drink and she told me how I should bring you down a few pegs and she knew how to do it," he said.

"You told me because you wanted to get back at me for what Daphne said I did?" I asked, feeling sorry for him. He had fallen prey to Daphne.

"Yes. You and Erik. I get that he is a local hero, but he plays football. That's it." I took in the little man in front of me. This was a personal point for him. No doubt loved Fleur and she was tight with Erik. Maybe love did make you crazy. I wanted to correct him, that Erik was more than that, but I wasn't sure there was a point. What I did know was that Daphne had set this up, and the fact she had been involved made my blood boil.

"Daphne is a bitch. You should steer clear," I told him, and he nodded, looking like he had more to say.

"Don't tell me there is more. I don't think my blood pressure can take it," I warned..

"She said she'd given the girl his number and address. She thought Erik had a secret baby with her and had been shirking his responsibilities," he said dejectedly.

"And you believed her?" I almost shrieked. Erik's actions aside, this was not on.

"Yes?" He looked outright sick at his error in judgment. I glared at him, but the longer I looked, the more wrecked he appeared. Lesson learned for him, I supposed.

"I have an hour before my next appointment. You'll need to hold the fort," I snapped before striding out the door, leaving Geronimo behind.

I knew Daphne worked at the council in some capacity, and she was going to get a visit. Erik and I may have broken up, and he may have been a dick, but my heartache was partly on her, and she needed to be set straight.

I called Molly, asking her to meet me there. She was confused, but when I told her why I was going, she could see the benefit of being there, likely so I didn't rip Daphne's hair out at the roots and strangle her with it. Theodore had already intervened once, and if he was helping Fleur with an emergency, I couldn't drag him away.

"Are you sure this is a good idea?" Molly asked as we met in the car park as it started to rain.

"I'm sure it's a terrible idea," I said as I pulled her toward the entrance.

"And wasn't Erik a complete dick to you yesterday?" she asked as though I were off the planet. She was correct on both counts.

"Yes, but he probably wouldn't have been as much of a dick if she hadn't done what she did and messed with his head," I said, my foolish heart hoping this was the case.

"And you want to set her straight for being mean to the man who broke your heart?" Molly asked as we made it to the front door, her warm eyes concerned as she assessed me.

"Well, yes. It's the principle of the thing," I said.

"Then you should have Hannah here. She is better in a *defence of principles* smack-down," she said, and I laughed. Hannah was far more combative, but I needed a hand jumping on my high horse and not someone to throw the first punch.

"I need you to be there for me," I said, gentling my tone, and I think she understood I needed to do this, despite how much it hurt, and I wanted Molly there in case I wasn't okay afterward.

"I can do that. Let's go be principled," she said softly, and I gave her a fist bump, which she returned as she rolled her eyes. We walked to reception and I asked to speak to Daphne. The girl gave me a surprised look followed by a small, almost conspiratorial smile, then called Daphne and told her that she had a visitor at reception. Molly and I took a seat in the waiting area, and before long Daphne arrived, looking around to see who was waiting for her.

"Annie is over there," the receptionist said, and I looked at her, surprised she knew my name.

"Annie?" Daphne asked the room, confused until she laid eyes on me.

"Hi, Daphne," I said as I stood and walked up to her. She was quite a bit taller than me, but the look on my face made her shrink back. Molly trailed me, giving me a few feet of space.

"What can I do for you?" she asked, going for insincere politeness.

"Well, I need you to explain a few things to me."

"I'm not sure what you mean," she said, looking around.

"Well, let's start with Geronimo."

"Geronimo?"

"Yes, Geronimo. You had a drink with him the other night. Left quite the impression," I said, and I could hear the receptionist cough to cover a laugh.

"Oh, we aren't involved like that," she explained, throwing a glare over her shoulder.

"I realise that. Unlike you, I don't assume everyone is shagging everyone else. However, he did tell me that the two of you had an interesting conversation," I said, and her eyes snapped to mine.

"Interesting?"

"Yes. Fascinating even," I added, looking at Molly, who nodded like she was confirming my deft use of the English language. Daphne smiled again, unsure.

"Fascinating?" she asked when I didn't add anything.

"Well, I found it fascinating. I wonder why you told him Erik had shacked up with someone."

"Well…"

"If you wanted to be with him so badly, why start a rumour that he is with another woman? Let alone one he'd gotten pregnant?" I asked her, emphasising how perplexed I was by her actions. She started to narrow her eyes as she realised why I was there.

"I am sorry if it led to your breakup, but I thought you should know and this woman deserved the truth," she said, going for empathy. It was pathetic and Molly sighed loudly.

"I doubt you were sorry. If you were, you might have told me yourself, as a fellow woman and teammate," I returned coldly, and she took a step back.

"I thought you were closer to Geronimo," she lied.

"I'm not close with him at all. That is no secret. Now it's my turn to be sorry."

"You're sorry?" she asked warily. Now she could see the trap coming.

"Yes, sorry to disappoint you. If you had engineered this whole debacle to break us up, you were too late."

"Too late?"

"Yes, too late. Erik and I had already parted ways," I said, glad my voice didn't betray how crushed I still was.

"I see." She had the gall to look disappointed at the lost opportunity. I heard Molly let out a low growl beside me, confirming she was keen for me to put Daphne in her place.

"I think you only see part of the picture," I explained since she seemed a bit slow on the uptake.

"Part?" she asked, proving me right.

"If you are telling people Erik is shacked up with the girl at his apartment, one who had his child, you might want to reconsider how well you know him."

"I *do* know him," she hissed.

"Then you would know he isn't into that sort of thing. Not only is it illegal, but Erik is anything but creepy."

"Into what sort of thing?" she huffed, not enjoying my smugness.

"Incest and paedophilia," I deadpanned.

"Incest? Paedophilia?" she asked, absolutely bamboozled.

"Yes, incest. You know, incest where you have sexual relations with a family member and paedophilia is where—" I started to explain before she cut me off.

"Yes, I know what those words mean. What does it have to do with Erik?" she snapped, not appreciating my sarcasm.

"Well the woman you think he shacked up with is his little sister."

"Sister?" She seemed half excited, half confused at the prospect.

"Correct, and before you get excited that he is in fact back on the market, you should remember that he will find out the source of the rumours," I drew out the word "source", taking no small amount of satisfaction as the colour drained from her face.

Molly grabbed her handbag and moved toward the door, ready to leave, but I kept my gaze on Daphne. It appeared she didn't know who Freya really was. In a town this size, it was only a matter of time, and at least I'd have the satisfaction of setting her straight.

"Well, I best get back to work. See you at the game, Daphne," I said before turning and walking out. I didn't feel any better about my split with Erik, or our argument last night, but at least when it came to Daphne, that shit was sorted.

***

It was Wednesday night and work had been cold, wet, and miserable and I was still kicking my damned self for being an arsehole. All I'd said to Annie had been true at the time. That *was* how I'd felt, but the way I'd gone about it had been fucked up. Worse was that as soon as I'd said them to her, I regretted it. I'd let everything get on top of me, hurting her in the process. Her astonishment that I'd wanted more still bothered me, as did her knowledge that Freya was my sister. It bothered me because I'd misjudged her and I didn't want to be the bastard who got it wrong, but I was starting to think that was the case.

I called Ben on my way back home from work, knowing his sisters would be across my fight with Annie last night. One worked in the pub and the other was a receptionist at the council, so they knew everything. The old guys who lived beside me hit the pub every day; there was no way they *wouldn't* let it slip to anyone who was within earshot, especially the part about me getting clocked on the chin. News like that would spread like wildfire.

"Erik," he answered on the first ring, probably expecting my call.

"Hey, man. What's going on?" I asked.

"What's news with you?" he asked seriously.

"I don't know where to even fucking start," I said.

"How about you start with Geronimo, Annie, and the showdown she had with Daphne?" he asked.

"What?"

"Isn't that why you are calling me?" Ben sounded as confused as I did.

"No, I had other shit to tell you. But you go first," I said, wanting to know about what was up with Daphne and Annie.

"Hang on, I think maybe you should go first," Ben said.

"I don't know how you don't already know this, but Annie came around last night to see if I was okay. I was a prick and out of line. To be fair, I'd had a shit day, including Freya telling me that my dad had threatened my mum."

"She said that?" Ben asked quietly.

"Yep. And I don't want to believe her, but I don't know anything anymore. I didn't know I had a sister until Sunday morning." I sighed, pulling over, preparing for a Ben psychology session.

"That's fair. Your dad was a drunk and a dick, but abusive?" Ben asked.

"Anything is possible. It's not something you want to hear about your parents though. I need to break it down in my head, but I'm not sure if I can."

"Maybe you should talk to your mum?" Ben asked.

"I don't know if I can do that either." I had been mulling the idea over since Freya arrived, wanting to have questions answered but not ready to reopen the door.

"You don't have to do anything now. You have other shit to deal with."

"I know. I can't stop thinking about Annie. Last night I accused her of using me, playing games, taking advantage of me, and that she only came around because she thought I was shacked up with someone else."

"Fuck," he muttered.

"That's not all," I grumbled.

"Please don't tell me you told her you hate England and that they cheat in cricket," he teased, and I laughed. Then I told him all the gory details, embarrassed by my actions.

"How did it end?" Ben asked without giving away what he thought.

"Well, when I called her a bitch who played games, her brother introduced me to his right hook," I muttered, rubbing my bruised jaw.

"What?" Ben let out a bark of laughter, catching me off guard.

"You heard me, dickhead. Her brother punched me and I didn't see it coming. It was after I hit the deck that I heard them talk to Freya. They knew she was my sister."

"Faaaark."

"I am a fucking idiot."

"Agreed, but you broke up with the love of your life, then your sister arrived shaking your foundations. No one would react well, especially you, who buries shit like that."

"Buries shit? Thanks, Oprah."

"You're welcome. But don't get excited, I'm not giving away cars or a Kitchen Aid mixer."

"What? Tell me about the Daphne, Geronimo, Annie showdown. It must have happened today if it has overshadowed my punch on last night."

"Well, I don't think it will make your head any clearer."

"Fuck."

Ben gave me a blow-by-blow of his sister's eyewitness account of what happened at the reception between Annie and Daphne. After my head exploded, again, I'd arrived home to Freya an hour later than I'd told her. I hadn't taken her that many places, not wanting to deal with the gossip, but that was another dick move. She'd been brave and I was being a coward, and the reality was it didn't matter. Everyone would know soon so who cared?

"Hey," Freya said, giving me a worried look when I walked in with burgers and sticky chicken from Tomahawk.

"Hey. I'm sorry I'm late," I greeted, letting her know I was fine, and she seemed to relax a little.

"It's okay," she said, standing to get plates.

"No, it's not. Sit down, I'll get us sorted. Want a beer?"

"Sure." She smiled and I grinned. Teenage drinking was universal. We sat down and I handed out food before I started to make things right.

"I need to apologise," I said, but she looked confused. "I haven't told people you're my sister. I suppose I didn't want people to bring up the past. When Mum left, and Dad went downhill, people had talked a lot and it had scarred me. I've not said anything and people think that you are…."

"So, they think I'm your girlfriend?" she asked, completely disgusted.

"I'm sure some people do."

"But I'm sixteen and you're old," she said, and I laughed.

"No shit," I said, feeling it.

"Okay, people think you are a dirty old man. Now what? Should we wear matching brother/sister t-shirts?" she asked, and I grinned.

"No, but I'm going to take some time off, show you around, and introduce you to people," I said, but her smile faltered. "What is it?"

"Well, you don't think much of Mother. What if people only see me as the daughter of the woman who abandoned you?" She was worried, and it was probably part of the reason Mum didn't want her to come.

"People have all sorts of views about why Mum left. I ignored all of them, and only heard what Dad had to say. But people here, other than being into gossip, are good people. They won't be like that with you. It's not like you had any say in the matter either. I wouldn't worry."

"Okay. What changed your mind? Was it Annie's visit?"

"Partly," I admitted, noting she was honest, brave, *and* perceptive.

"She seemed very upset. I didn't hear all of your conversation, but she knew I was your sister."

"I know. I was out of line last night. I'd let everything get to me and she wore the brunt of it."

"But you two aren't together?" Freya looked at me expectantly, waiting to really hear what had happened between us.

"No, we broke up the night before you arrived."

"Oh. I'm so sorry, Erik. Mother was right, I should have spoken to you first," she said, looking crushed that she had put me in that position.

"No, don't be sorry. What you did was brave, and to be honest, I was into my own shit and I would never have spoken to you. You needed to come," I said, giving her hand a squeeze, letting her know I meant it.

"Thanks," she said, blushing a little. "So, now what will happen with Annie?"

"I don't know. I care about her, and was convinced she didn't share the same depth of feeling. Now, I'm not sure."

"No? You must have had reason to think that," she said, and she was right. I did have reason to think that Annie didn't want me. She had been holding back but let me get further ahead. But then, I'd also told her about my views on relationships. She wasn't only to blame.

"Yeah I did. But I might've missed some signs. I've avoided relationships given what happened between Mum and Dad. I was pretty adamant about it," I admitted.

"When you're ready, I'd like to tell you what Mum told me. It might change things for you," she said, and I nodded.

"I'm taking tomorrow off, let's do it then. But now, we need to find out who gets to go on the group date," I said, finishing my beer.

"Good idea." She beamed. Then we sat on the couch while my eyes were assaulted, and I started to see things differently.

Chapter 23

With only two days left with Theo, I wanted to make sure we enjoyed that time, but I was tired, depressed, and confused because of Erik. After setting Daphne straight I'd worked all afternoon with my mind constantly running. It was like a scary, weird merry-go-round with unnerving carnival music and painted horses that looked at you like they knew my darkest secrets.

Aside from his worrying preoccupation with Fleur, I wondered if there was something else going on with Ted. He'd come back from helping Fleur distracted and said he was catching up with an old buddy in Albury that night, but would be back first thing Thursday morning so we could spend the day together before heading to Melbourne for his flight home on Friday. I didn't feel I could pry; he probably needed a break from the Annie drama. I sure did.

When he headed off, I'd caught up with Molly, Hannah, Leslie, and Carol for dinner. We had wine, Bangladeshi curry, and enough chocolate banana tart to sink a ship at Hannah's house because Howard was in Melbourne for work. I'd invited Fleur, but she said she had plans and that she would love to come next time. She probably needed a break from my drama too.

The girls all demanded an update and after a quick recount of my showdown with Daphne, they needed to know where my head was at. They knew I wasn't okay, and they weren't going to let it drop, so I told them that I felt for him. I also told them about his opinion of me. Right or wrong, he had thought that about me and made it clear that his feelings for me were in the past. That was the most painful part: if I hadn't been a coward and said something, everything would be different and we would be together.

Hannah looked like she wanted to challenge me but bit her tongue as I had done with her. She no doubt wanted to question my decision after her own experience, but it wasn't the same. I'd be fighting a one-sided battle. Erik had his own demons to battle, and if he wanted me, he knew where I lived *and* where I kept the spare key.

Thankfully my explanations had assuaged their concerns, leaving them satisfied I wasn't withdrawing. The rest of the evening was a perfect distraction. We talked about the new Community Services Hub in Bright. Leslie and Carol had finally convinced Hannah to leave her job and work with them. It would be a great place to work, but the community at large had no idea was about to hit them.

On the way home, Theodore texted to let me know he would be home by nine the following morning and that he hoped I was okay. I smiled while my eyes filled with tears. I would miss my big brother when he left. So, when I walked into my empty house, I felt a strange sort of happy-sadness. I had great friends and a brother who was back in my life. But my brother was leaving and things had just ended with Erik when I was ready to take a chance. He had broken up with me, then made sure that whatever connected us was broken.

The next morning, true to his word, Theodore came through the door at nine. He looked happy-sad too, and when I asked him if he was okay, he said he was sad to leave me behind but glad we had each other again. At this, I burst into tears and gave my big brother a hug, glad for his steadiness when I felt like I was about to break apart. As he packed his bag, he told me that he'd arranged to meet Paddy, who had been travelling, at the gate. I was relieved; I was not in the mood to see him so soon. As we prepared to leave, we chatted about when I would see him next. I told him I wasn't going to go home for Christmas, and he said he would come back soon, but I knew he had a life, friends, and a job he had to return to.

We left Wandiligong by midmorning. On the way out, I called Fleur to check in, but she said no one had mistakenly turned up for an appointment with me. With everything in hand, we drove out of the valley in the winter sunshine to see snow on Mount Buffalo, the Ovens River running high, and the fields so green it was like we were in Ireland.

"It is beautiful here," Theodore said absently as we headed toward the King Valley. We were planning on taking the long way to Melbourne, via Mansfield, so Theodore could live his Man from Snowy River dreams.

"Sure is, and property is cheaper than London. You should consider it," I said, grinning, and he gave me a sad smile.

"I have considered it," he said.

"And?" I asked excitedly.

"I'm not sure it's right for me, at the moment anyway. I have a good job, and getting a visa here isn't that easy," he said, watching the countryside roll by, and his distant, forlorn tone caught my attention.

"What's really on your mind?" I asked, needing to know what I could do for my brother who had helped me so much.

"Nothing, just thinking about you, and our parents, Paddy, all those people who are important to us," he said almost cryptically. I was going to push him but he beat me to it by asking me a question that threw me off the scent.

"What about you? Have you given forgiving Erik any more thought?" he asked me pleasantly, knowing full well the question was a weighty one.

"More thought? I hadn't given it any thought." Well, that was a lie. But I hadn't admitted it to myself yet.

"Annie, I know you and I trust you. I don't know him very well, and since I arrived things have been a little…intense. However, I could tell when we spoke before I got here that you were happy. Now, his breakup method was less than ideal, but I could see when he looked at you on Saturday night, he thought you hung the bloody moon. I think it must've killed him to step away," Theodore said.

"Ted, stop," I whispered, my hands tightening on the wheel.

"I will, in a minute. Just hear me out. He was a major dick to you. No doubt about it, but if I have learned anything from my accident and my relationship with Paddy, and now yours with me, sometimes forgiveness is what lets you live, and makes you stronger. You don't need to decide anything yet, but be open to the concept. I love you, and I want you to be happy no matter what. If Erik makes you happy, then so be it."

Bloody hell. I loved my brother, but he was killing me. If he could forgive, then the least I could do was consider it.

"But even if I could forgive him, it doesn't mean we will be together. You heard him, he's moved on," I said, exposing the real root of my anxiety. What if I was too late?

"No one ever really moves on, not if your feelings are genuine. Of course, it might not work out, but perhaps it is worth the risk?" he said gently, and I sniffed, desperate to hold back the tears that were welling in my eyes.

"Since when did you become such a sage?" I teased.

"I've always been this bloody brilliant. You know it."

"I do." I grinned at him, telling the absolute truth.

***

I'd taken Thursday and Friday off work to show Freya around and we'd started by heading out for breakfast then doing the Canyon Walk in Bright. It was winter so it was fucking freezing but then again Freya came from Sweden, she could cope. The Ovens River was running high, icy mountain water roaring through the sheer rock walls as we walked. As we explored, I told her about the history of the place.

"How do you know so much?" she asked as we walked over the wet rock steps, feeling the temperature drop as we got closer to the water.

"My father's family have been up here since the main road through was being built. They were pioneers of sorts," I said, feeling proud, but also unsure about where the topic might lead us. We hadn't talked about my father or what our mother had said about him yet. I wasn't ready to hear it, but I knew I couldn't move on without knowing more. As though sensing the direction of my thoughts, Freya broke the silence.

"She loved him, you know."

"Who?" I asked, not sure I caught her meaning.

"Mother. She said she fell in love with your father straight away, and that in the beginning they were good together. She loved it here and had been prepared to call it home," she said, and I tried hard not to go straight to the negative: if she loved it so much, why did she leave? But I'd resolved to be more open and not fly off the handle again after hurting Annie.

"She had a funny way of showing it," I said quietly.

"I know. I didn't even know about you until I overheard my grandmother talking to her one night after I'd gone to bed. I'd asked her about it the next day, but she didn't tell me anything; she'd just sobbed for a week. I was only ten and didn't fully understand, but given how upset she was, I didn't raise it again. Then a few years ago I was helping Mother clean out our storage room and I noticed a box that she kept on looking at but seemed afraid to touch. When she went to get lunch, I opened it and found pictures of a little boy with blond hair, carrying firewood outside of the cabin you took me to. I went through it all to find wedding photos, your baby photos, a lock of hair, handprints on a postcard, pictures of my mother patting a kangaroo, and a photo of you and her making cookies. She looked so youthful and happy. Happier than I have ever seen her," she said, ending on a sigh.

"That can't have been easy. Did you ask her about it?"

"Not straight away. I decided to wait for the right time to ask but it never came. Then at school last year we read a book where the main character had a child go missing and that even years later, the mother had never recovered. I wondered if my mother was going to end up like that woman, a shell because she effectively had a child still missing. I didn't want that for her, so I asked her about it. She told me to leave her alone, but I didn't. I kept telling her that I knew I had a brother, and it wasn't fair to keep you from me. She got very angry, then a few days later she came to me in my room with the box of your pictures and told me."

"What did she say?" The words came out before I could stop them, and I sounded afraid. My heart was pounding in my chest, and I could feel my skin tingle. Did I want to know? Of course. Did I want to hear it? Not a fucking chance.

"Let's sit," she said as we neared a park bench by the river. We sat in the sun, listening to the river as she prepared. Eventually, she spoke.

"Mother said she was living here, teaching skiing in the winter and working in the bar in summer. She was only twenty and loved Australia. Then she met your father, and he had swept her off her feet. He had come in to see her every night she worked in the pub to keep her company. Within twelve months she was pregnant, and said it was unplanned but that she was excited. So they got married at the courthouse in Wangaratta and had a party in the pub a few months before you were born," she said, looking at me. I smiled and nodded. I knew this part. Everyone did.

"The way people here remember it, my father landed the most beautiful girl in the valley. I think people were genuinely surprised because my dad was very average-looking. Is she still as beautiful as she was then?" I asked, having flashes of memories pass before me. My mum had been very beautiful, like a blonde-haired, blue-eyed princess.

"Yes, she is." Freya smiled and I nodded, my lips turning up of their own volition.

"We were both lucky enough to get her colourings, but I am short and plump like my father," she said, clearly irritated.

"That's not true. I've been worried about introducing you to my teammates on Saturday. They will be all over you like a rash," I said.

"A rash?" she asked, confused, and I chuckled.

"It's a turn of phrase. It means they will be very interested in you," I reassured her.

"Are any of them cute?" she asked, grinning, and I started to feel sick.

"No, they are all hideous, rude, disgusting men with warts and diseases, everywhere. Don't even look at them," I said sternly, and she laughed. It was nice to have some levity, but I knew we were both stalling.

"Can you tell me the rest?" I asked her, and she drew a deep breath.

"Mother told me she loved being a mother and enjoyed it here, until her husband became distant, only paying you attention. Your father became grumpier and grumpier with her, and more and more focused on you. She said he would hardly speak to her when he would come home after work, only to you. When you went to bed, he would go out to the pub and leave her home alone. This went on a while, and she felt abandoned. She was in a foreign country without any family, raising a child at a young age, and her husband barely spoke to her," Freya told me and I wracked my brains, trying to remember this. I didn't have many memories that were really vivid, but I did know my dad was a regular at the pub. That never changed.

"As you got older, she said it got worse. When he was home, you both would disappear for hours at a time, and sometimes she wouldn't know where you were. When she asked your father about it, he got angry, accusing her of suggesting he couldn't be with his own son. So, she stopped asking. It got worse when he started to come home drunker and drunker from the pub and he started to yell at her. She said she tried to keep him happy, but it didn't work. She said she did her best to keep him quiet because you would be asleep, but one night you woke up and came into the bedroom when he was yelling at her, telling her she needed to know her place."

"I vaguely remember that. It was Christmas Eve and I was staying awake for Santa. Mum had made special Swedish food on Christmas Eve, but Dad had barely been there, saying it was un-Australian," I said, only now seeing significance of his words. I remembered that he left again. I'd been upset, so Mum and I had played games late and I'd fallen asleep on the couch with her.

"She told me that too," Freya said, and I gave her a sad smile. Clearly I'd kept only the good part of the memory—the part about my mother.

"This was right before she left," I said.

"That's right. He'd come home very drunk every night after that and on New Year's Eve, he hadn't come home by the usual time and she was worried that he might be driving drunk. So, she called her only friend in town, someone who had a daughter the same age as you. Fleur?"

"That's right," I said, remembering Fleur's mum had been close with my mother.

"Mother asked her to watch you so she could find your father. She went into the pub where she used to work looking for him. When she arrived, everyone cheered and greeted her. She said she hadn't realised how much she missed the company. Your father was there, and when everyone accused him of hiding his beautiful wife, he'd gotten angry. She didn't understand at the time, but when they got home and he hit her, telling her she needed to stay hidden and stop drawing attention, Mother said she figured it was either because he was jealous or didn't want to share her."

"Shit." I sighed, feeling a heavy weight settle on my chest. Part of the relentless gripe Dad had vocalised after she'd left was about beautiful women being disrespectful, playing games, and not being honest. My father had sounded bitter and bitten anyone's head off who even mentioned her. So people stopped, and she ceased to exist. Looking back, it was like he'd coveted her, wanted to possess her, but hated himself for it too.

"It gets worse," Freya whispered, and I ran my hands through my hair. I knew my father was irritable and a drunk, but I was having a hard time coming at him being violent.

"Keep going," I heard myself say.

"The next morning, when he saw what he had done, Mother said he sobered up. She thought he had scared himself and was afraid that he could do that. So, he stopped going to the pub. Mother had thought he was realising what he had but that wasn't the case. He was sober, but meaner and crueller, and more focused on you. If she made a mistake, he would yell at her. If she didn't do as he wanted, he would threaten her. She was depressed and started to call home more often, speaking to her mother and friends in Sweden. They all said she should come home and bring you with her."

"Why didn't she?" I asked, my heart rate picking up.

"She tried. She had your bags packed and was getting ready to sneak out one day when a neighbour dropped in, for something normal. But he had seen the bags. Mother had lied but this neighbour must have told your father."

"Who was it? The neighbour?" Why could I not remember this? Dad had been home more that summer, but I don't remember her packing bags.

"Someone called Badger?" she said, and I froze. Badger was our neighbour and he worked with my dad at the mill. He also drank a lot and now lived three units down from me. Freya looked at me expectantly.

"I know Badger. He was exactly like my dad," I told her.

"He hasn't mentioned it?"

"Nope. But he is a grumpy old prick who doesn't think much of women."

"I see. It might be why he called your father. He ended up coming home before Mother could leave, and he said if she took you, he would track her down and kill you both. But if she stayed, he would tell the police she was unfit to be a mother. Mother believed him," Freya said, and I sucked in a breath. Dad did know the local officer; they were friends growing up and it was why he was able to get away being drunk all the time. He *had* told everyone she was an unfit mother. The words had come from his mouth often and I had listened to it. Believed it.

"Fuck," I whispered, feeling sick to my stomach.

"So she left, thinking it was the only way she would be able to live. She knew he would never hurt you, that he loved you too much. So she made a choice. She regretted it but had nowhere else to go."

I was silent for a long time. I needed to process this. Process it then find a way to move forward because this had the potential to ruin me. It was hard to look past all the domestic violence statistics in the media and the training we had received at the football club that had specifically talked about isolation and verbal abuse.

After she left, he'd drunk heavily and looked at me with sadness, irritation, and possessiveness. The older I'd grown, the more time I'd spent at Ben's house with his family. Anything to avoid being home, and he had got drunker and meaner. But was that really my dad? A man who would threaten his own wife? I could never find out the facts, but the longer I sat, the more I knew it was the truth. And it made me sick.

"You can call her and ask her about this, you know." Freya turned her sad eyes to me, sad eyes that were so much like mine and Mum's.

"I don't think I am ready for that," I answered honestly.

"Do you believe her?" she asked, looking worried. "There are two sides to every story, this is just Mother's. But I feel like she has never recovered, and that you are a missing piece to her. Perhaps you are the same?" Freya whispered nervously.

"The same?" I asked.

"Maybe you are missing a piece too. Didn't you break it off with Annie to avoid her leaving you?" she asked, and I slow blinked at her. *What?*

"That is different," I said.

"Maybe, but you are a sad person now. And I think it has something to do with her and with Mum. I don't know what really happened with Annie, I wasn't here. But when she came around this week before her brother hit you, she looked at you like she loved you. She also defended you to that woman I spoke to, Daphne. She didn't say bad things about you, she put Daphne in her place." I nodded but my head was full with all she'd laid on me. I couldn't take more.

"I don't know. I cared about Annie more than I thought I could," I admitted.

"Perhaps it is something to think about," she said, shrugging her shoulders and giving me a wan smile, "Well, something else at least."

I huffed a laugh because I longed to speak to Annie about it. I wanted to confide in her, and have her listen to me and offer me comfort and oblivion. I knew she would do it, be the safe harbour my sister couldn't.

"Let's walk," I said, standing, needing to clear my head and get on with the processing. So we walked back to town, and I drove her to the top of Mount Buffalo to the old chalet, then to Ringer Reef Winery for lunch. I let her drink all she wanted—she was clearly mature enough—but I had one glass. I already felt like I was in daze. We headed home after that, and while she had a booze-induced nap, I called on Badger. Badger confirmed that he'd seen her trying to leave and my stomach had plummeted. Next, I called Ben, and bargained my way to a dinner for the two of us with their family. Ben's mother would be able to help fill in some blanks too.

We turned up to their rambling house, and Ben and his family welcomed us both with open arms. As usual, the food was amazing and we sat at their well-worn kitchen table as I'd done for years, needing the comfort my second home provided. Freya had loved it, and Ben and his amazing mother and sisters had welcomed her like she was blood. Ben's sisters were regaling her with embarrassing storying of my younger years while Ben, his mother, and I headed into the lounge and I told them what Freya had told me. I'd looked to Mrs MacBride, wanting to know what she thought. The sad look on her face told me all I needed to know.

"Erik, I am so sorry. I should have done something, said something. I didn't think it was my place, and to accuse someone like that..." she said, getting upset, her face stricken with grief and guilt. I pulled her into a hug, not wanting to hurt her like this. The whole thing was a mess and yet again, I wanted Annie here with me.

"Don't say that. You were there for me in every way it counted, the only real family I've ever known. I think Mum would have known that too," I told her, and she gripped me tight for a long time.

On our drive home Freya looked at me speculatively, but I didn't know if she was interested in what Ben's mum had confirmed or if his sisters had put mad ideas in her head.

"What are you going to do?" she asked eventually, her tone grave. There wasn't much to do; I needed to accept it. But first, I wanted to talk to Fleur's mum. I felt I owed it to my father to really find out.

"I don't think there is much to do. I need to accept it, and it will take time because Dad was all I had for a long time," I said.

"I wasn't meaning that," she said, giving me a strange look.

"What did you mean then?"

"What are you going to do about Annie? Mother isn't going anywhere. You don't have to do anything if you don't want to either. It doesn't change who you are. You should take time to think about it. But after what the girls said about Annie *causing a ruckus* yesterday, they think it's clear that she loves you. In fact, it is more interesting to people in town than the fact I am your sister. Which I am glad to hear. That way, the boys on your team may not keep away because no one cares we are related. Ben's sisters are coming to the game to introduce me, given the *cat is out of the bag*," she said, giving me punch in the arm, grinning.

"Like hell," I said, immediately disliking the idea.

"Relax, big brother, if I can hijack my mother's credit card and find you half a hemisphere away, I can manage a few Australian boys," she teased.

"I'm sure you can, but don't make me have to beat their arses, yeah?"

"I make no promises." She grinned and I found myself astonished yet again. She was right. I didn't need all the answers now. I needed Annie.

I went to bed that night unable to sleep, caught between replaying my mother's side of events and trying to piece it together with my own memories. I longed to have Annie beside me. I knew that she would understand the mess in my head and my need for physical connection. By five a.m. I decided that I needed to grovel and beg for her forgiveness first, so I had her at my back, so I could find a way to put my life back together. I'd won her over once. I would just have to do it again. Feeling more settled than I had since we split up, I fell asleep.

I felt groggy and exhausted as I made coffee and worked out a plan for how to get Annie back. I needed to talk to Fleur first, to gauge where Annie was at so I didn't barrel in and fuck it up any more. I knew Fleur would be up getting Tate ready for school, so I left Freya a note and headed to Fleur's to catch her before she headed to work. When I pulled up, I noticed her car was gone. It was before eight so that was unusual, but I headed up the steps to knock on the door to check.

"Hey, Erik," Tate said as he opened the door dressed in his school uniform. I could hear the TV blaring in the background and the kid had cereal on his face.

"Tate, my man, is your mum home?"

"No, she had to go into the clinic early," he said.

"Why is that?" They didn't open until nine.

"Because Annie is gone and she needs to sort stuff," he said like it was all the same to him. My stomach plummeted.

"Gone?"

"Yeah. With her brother. I think the flight is tonight."

"Gone. Tonight?"

"Yeah, that's what Mum said. I don't know what is going on, but Mum was crying about it," he said and I nodded numbly. Was Annie going back to the UK? Surely not?

"Gone," I said, starting to feel sick. If Fleur was upset, then maybe.

"Yep," he said, looking at me strangely.

"Yep." I knew I was parroting, but I couldn't get my head around what he was saying. Annie was gone. I was too late. Any thoughts of my mother fled as I came to realise that my anger, my inability to deal, had meant I had lost the one thing in my life I'd really wanted.

"Erik, are you okay?"

"No, man, I'm not," I said before turning away and running to my car. My head was a mess, a cocktail of exhaustion, anxiety, confusion, and regret. I knew I should slow down and take a minute, but I was done with that. I needed to get to the airport and tell her how I felt before she left. So I called Freya, then Ben, then drove to Melbourne.

Chapter 24

Melbourne was cold and wet, and while I found myself apologising to Theodore for the poor weather, he reminded me where we were from.

"You really must be assimilating," he teased.

"There are worse places to be," I sassed, and he nodded.

"I don't feel that bad about leaving you here. I wish you would come home, but I get why you won't," he said with a sad smile. We were walking out of our hotel in search of breakfast. People rushed around the city, getting their coffee and going to work. It felt decadent to be wandering around with Theodore.

As we left the city, that gloomy heaviness that came with good-byes settled in my chest. Soon enough Theodore would be gone and I would be driving home to my empty house. I had my friends, the clinic, and the hills to comfort me, but I had to seriously consider what it was going to be like without Erik. Forgiving him was one thing, but getting back together was another, and nothing was for certain.

"Are you thinking about Erik?" Theodore asked as we pulled into the airport car park.

"You can tell?"

"Yep, you have that forlorn yet wistful look," he said as he got his bags out.

"I can forgive him, but it doesn't mean things will go back to how they were. He might not be in that place anymore," I said as we walked toward the terminal.

"It's like anything. You need to put your best foot forward and if it doesn't work, it doesn't," he said with a wisdom and sadness that made me stare at him for a long time.

"Are you sure there isn't something going on with you?" I asked.

"No, nothing else going on with me," he said, but I wasn't convinced. I wanted to push him to talk to me, but given we only had minutes left in each other's company, I didn't.

"You tell me if there is, big brother," I said as I looped an arm through his as we went to check in. It was well after four and the line was long. Theodore wasn't going to miss his flight, but he didn't have time to kill either.

"Hey, Annie, I'll be back," he said, pulling me into a tight hug and letting me cry a little before he pulled away slightly. "We'll see each other soon," he said, and I nodded as I unceremoniously sniffed. He laughed at this, and his smile made me give one in return.

"You better go," I told him. He didn't answer, just stood there looking to the side of where we stood, a strange look on his face.

"You're right, I better go," he muttered, returning his gaze to me. Before I could look to see what had taken his attention, he kissed me on the cheek, hugged me again, and said, "I love you, Annie. Be kind to yourself and call me if you need anything."

I looked up at him, tears forming again, but now he was giving me a knowing smile. It was an odd kind of look, given the context.

"I love you too. Fly safe," I said.

"Of course." He chuckled. I was about to ask him what on earth was so funny when he spoke again. "I think you left something on the seats over there," then he moved away and went through security, grinning. I spun around to see what on earth he was talking about, then I froze.

There was Erik, slumped in a chair, looking uncomfortable and asleep.

"Bye, Annie," Theodore called out, and I looked at him on the other of the Perspex, smirking. He gave me a wink, waggled his brows, and turned and walked away. I stared after him in disbelief before walking to the love of my life, sleeping like a degenerate backpacker in the airport.

***

My neck hurt like a bitch and I couldn't feel my arse. Fighting the urge to stay asleep despite how uncomfortable I was, I forced my eyes open. I had to blink. The lights were so bright, and the background noise was overwhelming at first. It only took a moment before I had my wits about me again, and the world came back into focus. I was in the airport, hanging out beside the only international security gate, and Annie was in front of me, fighting a smile.

"Hey," I said, my voice croaking from sleep.

"Ah, hey," she said, chuckling a little, but I didn't find anything funny.

I sat up properly and scrubbed my face, knowing that this was going to be one of the most important conversations in my life and I needed to pull it together. But in doing so, I knocked over the cold coffee on the seat beside me, and Annie, who was on her haunches, fell back onto her behind as I scrambled to keep the spill on the seat.

"Fuck, sorry," I said, pulling her up, but she was too busy laughing to care. I tried to find something to wipe up the coffee, but Annie was onto it, pulling tissues out of her handbag and mopping it up.

"You're a mess," she said, giving me a smile. I tried to smile but the truth of her words hit me. I was a damned mess.

"I know," I muttered.

Once she was finished she took the rubbish to the bin. I shook my head, desperately needing to corral my thoughts. By the time she returned I was only marginally more focused, the mental and physical fatigue of the last week still making my brain fuzzy.

"So, do you come here often?" she asked, giving me a grin. I didn't understand her reaction so I sat and stared at her.

"Erik, it was a joke," she said as her brows drew together. Even confused, I still thought she was the most beautiful woman I'd ever laid eyes on. Her big amethyst eyes were glittering as she looked at me, bewitching me. I wanted to touch the soft, pale skin of her cheek and put my lips on hers, but I needed to make things right first.

"I know it was," I said softly, and she smiled, then moved to sit beside me. I twisted on the bench so our knees were touching. This was my moment to make a grand gesture and win the girl. Instead, I was squashed into a plastic seat with hundreds of people milling about. I wanted to take her somewhere to talk, but the need to say my piece and stop her getting on that damned plane was too strong.

"Erik, what are you doing here?" she asked.

"I don't want you to leave," I said, not knowing how else to say it.

"What?"

"I don't want you to leave. I don't want to lose you," I repeated, needing her to know how I felt. "I'm so sorry I was a dick to you. You came to see if I was okay, and I was a complete arsehole. I said things that weren't exactly true. But that doesn't matter, I shouldn't have spoken to you like that. I'm sorry, I wasn't okay, and I lashed out at you. It was a shitty thing to do and I'm sorry."

"I know you are but I'm..."

"I wasn't coping. I'm not coping. It's not an excuse for being rude, but I was at my breaking point and when you turned up, it gave me something to focus on, to get angry about instead of what I was really feeling," I said, leaning toward her.

"And what was that?" she asked quietly.

"That my sister arriving and why my mum really left challenged everything I have ever believed. But in that moment, when I saw you then and even now, what I really feel is sadness that I don't have you. I can't escape the horrible, painful feeling that we have lost what we had. I don't know how to put it into words any better. It was easier being angry than it was to feel the grief," I admitted.

"Erik," she said, reaching out to grab my hand. I gripped hers tightly.

"Will you forgive me?" I asked, needing to hear her say it.

"I already have," she said, but it didn't register. I needed to let more of my feelings out. Ben would bloody love it.

"Seeing Freya, and hearing what she had to say, it changed things, threw me off kilter and I'm so sorry but..." I started to explain again but she interrupted me.

"Erik, I've already forgiven you," she said, and I blinked slowly, her words sinking in.

"You've already forgiven me?" I asked, unsure if I could believe it.

"That's right. I'm also not leaving," she said, and now it was my turn to be confused.

"You're not?"

"No, I'm here to see Theodore off," she said, giving me a soft smile.

"Right. So, you're not leaving," I said, not knowing what to think.

"I'm not leaving." She said it fighting a smile, and I began to realise how I might look.

"Perhaps I overreacted a little when Tate said you were gone," I said, running a hand through my hair.

"Maybe a little, but I appreciate the gesture." She looked at me with eyes full of concern. I reached for her to reassure her, but she put her hands up to stop me and froze.

"I see," I heard myself saying, "You're staying but you don't want to—"

"No, I didn't say that," she interrupted, and I held my breath. "But I need to be sure that *you* want this, want us," she continued.

"Annie, I'm here because I was afraid you were leaving. The thought of you not being around made me crazy," I told her, needing her to know how important she was.

"I'm getting that now. But when we ended it, we both let it happen. I did because I thought you didn't want that from me, that you weren't in it like I was."

"Annie…"

"Erik, we started out together on a premise of not continuing, but I fell hard. Every time I thought you were too, you would say something or do something that made me think differently. It's not all on you, I know that I am also at fault here. I wasn't brave enough to take a risk and tell you that I wanted more. The fact is we both let it end. I did because I was scared. But I don't know why you let it happen," she said, gripping my hand again, and I let go of the breath I didn't know I was holding.

"Well, I guess we are both cowards then." I shook my head. "I'd tried to convince myself that relationships were something to be avoided, that they never worked and left you angry and miserable. But you made me want to be with you always. I guess I didn't know why I should put myself out there if you weren't on the same page. I knew you wanted more, but I thought you were fighting it. I didn't want to put myself on the line when you weren't willing to be open to the possibility. I didn't get why you were fighting it," I told her, and her eyes filled with tears.

"I'm sorry. I didn't want to lose someone again. It had almost broken me last time, and I knew that if we went any further, I wouldn't recover." A big fat tear rolled down her cheek and when I moved to capture it with my thumb, this time she let me touch her.

"I love you," I told her, and those words on my lips felt sweet and true.

"I love you too," she sobbed before throwing her arms around my neck and crying into my shirt.

"We are two of the biggest cowards I know," I said, and she laughed into my neck before taking a deep breath and leaning back to look at me.

"I'm feeling a bit brave now," she whispered. I grinned before I pressed my lips to hers, her face in my hands, the salty and sweet taste of her invading my senses.

"Me too," I whispered against her lips. She smiled and kissed me hard on the mouth.

"How brave are you feeling?"

"Brave enough to show you how much I've missed you in the middle of the airport," I replied, and she laughed. "I'm sure the security guards have had an eye on me already."

She peppered my face with kisses while her hands slid into my hair. "Let's get out of here."

"That's a great idea."

ABOUT THE AUTHOR

As a girl growing up in Australia, Laura was lost in the world of *Anne of Green Gables* and *Little Women*. During high school, volleyball dominated her life. There had to be something positive about being 6'1" with red hair. Representing Australia from a young age she eventually took a scholarship at the University of Iowa. Living in America and being a full time athlete in a college town was an eye-opening experience and lots of fun (from what she can remember). #gohawkeyes

Returning from the States, her career took a different turn as she started working at the Red Cross and completed her Masters of Law in Human Rights. As one of the few non-lawyers in the class, her essays were far more floral than the rest, something that caused the discerning professors to shake their heads. Through working and studying, she realised there are other ways to win hearts and minds.

While she's spent the last 14 years as an advocate against poverty and homelessness, the desire to change the world through storytelling has only got stronger. She now lives in the Alpine Valley of North East Victoria, Australia with her husband, daughter, son, two dogs and seven chooks. When she's not doing the whole mum thing, working at a homelessness agency, renovating her farmhouse, or trying to do laundry bleary-eyed at midnight, she is writing.

Say G'day to Laura:
website: www.lsimpsonauthor.com
facebook: facebook.com/l.simpson.romance
twitter: @ladyporepunkah
instagram: @lsimpsonauthor
linkedin: linkedin.com/in/laura-simpson-47278971

OTHER BOOKS BY L. SIMPSON

Love Sabre
Beyond Today

www.BOROUGHSPUBLISHINGGROUP.com

www.ingramcontent.com/pod-product-compliance
Lightning Source LLC
Chambersburg PA
CBHW031325170626
46807CB00002B/575